Those

People

Russell C. Arslan

Books previously published

by Russell C. Arslan

Highest Stakes, "All In"

Matt Papaz's life begins to change one morning when two Homeland Security Agents came to his gates asking about an Armenian organization. Over the years he sent money to an Apostolic Church in Harpoots, Turkey called the Armenian Benevolent Union Church, but Homeland Security told him it was never a church. It's an Islamic Mosque and he is a person of interest because he has been supporting a terrorist network for twenty years. Despite the fact that he has no knowledge of the reality or the truth, he must avoid possible charges of espionage and terrorism.

Edited by Mary Ann Peck
Cover design by Mary Ann Peck

Library of Congress Control Number: 2010907735
ISBN: Paperback   978-0-9857695-0-5
           Ebook   978-0-9857695-3-6

For further information contact:

russellcarslan@mail.com

DISCLAIMER

Some people, places, events, and scientific theories are real but have been changed for fictionalization and entertainment purposes. *Those People* has been written as a docu-drama. All political situations represented in this book are fictional and do not embody real political figures' actions or thoughts. Artistic license has been taken with political leader's names and how they would articulate their positions or political actions. All embellishments have been used as literary entertainment and enrichment. Visit for more information about the author and his other books

russellcarslan.com

THOSE PEOPLE

RUSSELL C. ARSLAN

One

East Africa had changed nothing in decades. David Russell, traveling in Kenya with his two grown, adopted sons, was there to share his earlier life experiences. He had left Los Angeles hoping this rite of passage trip would broaden understanding of their world and widen their views putting them on a track to becoming the men he had envisioned. At the advanced age of 72, he had taken it upon himself to bring Hunter and Ashley to Africa, the land of his youth.

As his father before him, David, self made financial consultant, was with his sons, passing on wisdom and his hard earned goodwill. He hoped Hunter and Ashley would mature by example, not by mistakes, as he had done. In this place of his youth, David knew today's mistakes were costlier and potentially life threatening. Today's world is so complex and sophisticated that a youthful error could change one's life and cause irreparable damage even a well-heeled father could not straighten out.

Mr. David, as he was called at the Mt. Kenya Safari Club in Nairobi, was driving with his sons from the Kenyatta International Airport to that once prestigious hotel. The extensive blight caused by decades of stagnation was oppressive. There had been no perceivable changes in the city for the last 40 years. Nairobi of his youth still insulted his senses, but here was where he wanted to be, and what he wanted his boys to experience. The rancid stench of poverty and deprivation still lingered in this old mega-city. They drove from the airport to the hotel in a rented land rover, skirting the Huruma slum where tribal territorialism still existed. The dominant Kikuyu tribe had segregated the smaller Lois and Kalenjins tribes into squatters' quarters of unimaginable conditions.

His boys could not fathom what they saw before them. It was so grotesque and heavyhearted that it could not be assimilated. Hunter and Ashley were filled with the anxiety and confusion, so manifest for privileged children. They were what you would call little rich kids, viewing the slums with hands pressed upon the window glass, looking at the deprivation and not enjoying their ride. They did not know why they were in Kenya but could not turn away. This was Africa. This was to be a land of lessons and a land of pain. Africa was subliminally unacceptable to the two boys. They felt it in their stomachs and felt something in their hearts. But they were with their father; this was his trip, not a trip the boys had envisioned. Just a few minutes after clearing customs and driving through this horrible city, the boys felt betrayed. This trip was supposed to be fun; its appearance was obviously otherwise.

The boys' disdain and lack of empathy for what they were seeing bothered David. It was appalling. It took just a few minutes for the boys to display signs of superiority, not sympathy, for the plight of the sub Saharan African people. Was it because his children were rich, or was it that the people were black? It really bothered him. These were his boys. Were they bigots, were they out of touch? They were here with him, he would find out.

They kept looking out the side view windows and saying, *"those people."*

He tried to hide his feelings, but his emotions were evident. Ashley, the younger of the two boys, at 23, could not absorb poverty of this level without pointing to personal responsibility. The blame of the human condition was entirely that of the individual. It made no difference the extent of their poverty; hundreds of thousands of these people and it made no difference. Starvation, anger, violence, the lack of dignity, all their shortcomings, it was the individual; it was their fault. Ashley's puritanical Eurocentric view of humanity was chilling to his father. A mere boy of 23 and he was so callous about the human condition. How could this be his son?

Hunter, the eldest at 26, was more cerebral about his intellectual feelings for others. Imperialism was the cause of poverty, and misdistribution of wealth was the cause of impoverishment and suffering.

"Ashley," Hunter blurted out in his boring intellectual monolog, "it's incomprehensible what European imperialism and hegemony has done to these people. The marketplace has failed and its expression is a huge slum of hunger, and pain of unimaginable size."

Ashley was gazing out the Land Rover's front window trying to block Hunter's constant intellectual blah blah blah. His pseudo-whatever was trying at best. Why couldn't his brother have spoken like a normal person his age when he felt threatened was what Ashley was thinking.

"Man he sounds so screwed up," muttered Ashley to himself.

Finally, almost in pain from the sights that lay before him, Ashley soberly looked up from the window and said, "*those people* are almost inhuman. There is nothing behind their eyes. They look like another species. Look at them," as he pointed to a young woman, maybe thirteen years old, with a child in front of the Land Rover near a heap of garbage. "She's got two kids next to her. Do you think they're hers? They have flies all over them. They don't look anything like us, they don't look human. Where are we? Are we at some kind of freak show? How could Dad have done this to us?"

By this time David was wishing for quiet. What kind of kids had he raised? The banter and shallow, material expression and uncompromising arrogance tolerated at home in West Los Angeles was now deafening to David's ears. David muttered to himself, "How can they be mine?"

"Listen guys, for the first time in your lives I want you to listen to me. I don't want you to talk or give me those expressions of pain. East Africa was my life, this is who I am. I suppressed my will and a lot of my feelings for many years to better your mother's and your lives. Now I want to share my past with you. I want to help you create a new view towards the future. You can be better than any expectations you have for yourselves," he paused disdainfully, "if you have any at this time in your lives."

He was angry, almost verbally heavy-handed. "Instead of me always being socially correct, never expressing my opinion, always being the perfect father and husband, I am now bringing you to a new world. I was a very different person when I was just about your age. It was a different world, different rules, and different values. I want to pass on my knowledge and convictions. I want you to see things are not small and parochial nor are they easy. I want your world to be large and experienced so you can make better judgments and have better lives. God damn it guys, you're too young to have the opinions and positions you sometimes express. You're so arrogant."

The traffic light changed and as they started to move, the girl with the children threw her crying baby into the street, hitting the car behind them.

Ashley had been watching and yelled, "Hay, Jesus H. Christ! Dad, we have to stop."

Hunter yelled, "No, go, go. She just ran into the street and jumped up and down on her child."

David was continuing to drive and didn't see the incident. "I really love you guys, but I want you to see life more clearly, and here you are going to see things you've never seen before. I hate to say it, but you will have to become men if we are to survive this trip."

Hunter and Ashley looked at each other, for the first time in their lives they were at a loss for words.

"Dad you really didn't see what happened." Ashley persisted.

"Do what I tell you to do and when I tell you to do it; your lives and mine may depend upon it."

Ashley yelled, "Dad, did you see that? She just killed her baby. Is that what you want us to see, is that what you think will make us into men?"

David said, "What are you talking about?"

Raising their eyebrows, Hunter and Ashley again looked at each other knowing that their dad was what he said he was, a master of another world. It was overwhelming, but they believed their father. His intensity and demeanor was certainly new and a little frightening to the boys.

Ashley imagined a chameleon. Flashing before Hunter were visions of Dr. Livingston roaming through darkest Africa. Upon reflection they had surmised the idea of another life for their father but it had never surfaced. Things did not always make sense about their parent's past. Being adopted makes objectivity a hard life's view.

Hunter's intellectualism had left him. He felt the excitement and the fright of a new adventure, looked at his younger brother and said, "Well, little brother, I guess Dad thinks he is a white buana or something. I just hope it's true or we're in for deep shit, tough times ahead."

They both knew their dad was successful and a little eccentric, but solid as a rock. He had made inferences about his previous life but never talked about it. They knew this was truly a new world and would change theirs. They were approaching the Mount Kenya Safari Club, now an aging relic of the past in a land unchanged. The boys estranged from the suburban opulence of West Los Angeles realized these were two different worlds, two different peoples.

The kids knew they were in for something big. Out there was a compelling future no matter how scared they were. They felt a transformation in their father, he even looked different. David possessed a calm strength they had never seen before. He was in command over their new world. His past could be frightening, they would know soon enough. They didn't want to contemplate the future. The unknown was mind numbing.

Two

While exiting the Land Rover and having their bags taken to reception, Hunter expressed his relief at having finally made it to the hotel. He didn't know what was more frightening, his new father or the adventure lying ahead.

"Man, what a day and a half getting here. Can't wait to take a shower and have a good meal. Ashley, you really think we're going to leave tomorrow? Dad said something about getting permission to go to Masa Mara. Does he think we're going to go camping or something? I heard they have tents already set up, some kind high-end camping. I don't know what's going on anymore, Dad seems so different. He's in a new element. I've never heard him say let me teach you something by example, that stuff this morning about shut up and listen to what I say, do what I tell you to do. I've never seen this side of him. Man, sometimes he's real honest in a way that makes me feel uncomfortable, but, shit, never like this. I hope we're not in over our heads."

Ashley said, "I need a drink, how about you? You know you're fucking right, I feel really weird being here."

"I'll call room service for some food," as he opened the refrigerator Hunter sees inside, "Hay Ash, the fridge is full, how about a beer?"

"Man, look at that, I'll take a local brew. Let's try that. You get it while I make the call to room service."

Ashley's drinking was unfamiliar to Hunter. It was only one of the many things he would learn about his younger brother.

Down in the lounge, Martin Olingo, a very old but distinguished looking gentleman with deep-seated eyes, flashed a smile as David entered the hotel reception area and said, "Asante, old friend."

"Many years have gone by but it seems like yesterday. David, our correspondence has held time frozen. I know it was impossible for you to come to Kenya these many years, but my heart feels you have never left."

He gazed at David's face. "It is good you are here, my old friend. I will have the hotel present their best for you and your sons." As he put his hand out to Hunter and Ashley, "My name is Martin Olingo. You are my family now, for you are in my country. Mr. David is a brother of my youth."

Hunter and Ashley just looked at each other. They saw changes coming fast. They were not first and foremost in this land on the Horn of Africa. Their lives seemed to be on unsure ground, and an inkling of the future had raised its head.

"David, much has been altered here in Kenya, but in name only. The hotel, once William Holden's treasure, has had many owners but still the same staff. We're old but firm. The ways and wishes of Kenyatta and the Mau Mau have given way to Moi and Kibaki. Thirty years of corruption and greed, more of the same tribal hatred, but the wounds are deeper and darker. There has been change, but so much is the same. There are others out there who are not like us. Their anger, their violence, is not seeded in honor. They are different and they frighten me, David, my brother. Your help over the years has sheltered many of us from the harsh burdens of life. We see so much and have no power over it, even with your generous assistance."

The boys just looked at each other. They were bystanders in a conversation of the past and seemingly not participants in the future events of this new world.

"Let your dad take you kids to some adventurous place for the rite of passage quote unquote," their mom had said. This phrase haunted the two boys. The expectation of being with their perfect but mundane father now somehow seemed turned on its head.

"It's very clear who the leader is now," thought Ashley, "and it ain't us." The boys were to learn things about their father that would be hard to comprehend and could take a lifetime to accept.

"David, I have many subjects to cover, but first let's hear about you. I feel I know your boys from our communications over these many years." With a tear in his eyes, Martin gave David a hug.

Ashley, looking directly at Hunter, whispered, "I've never heard of this guy or this place, all I remember was seeing Dad's animal pictures in eastern Africa and the silverback guerrillas in Rwanda. Let's excuse ourselves and let Dad have time with his brother. Oh shit, I can't believe I said that. I can't believe we're here. I can't believe we've lived with these lies. This may be too much for me to fucking absorb! I just don't want to think about it. Let's go up to our rooms. Shit I can't believe any of this."

Three

After Ashley and Hunter went up to their rooms, they decided a visited to the gym would help counteract their jet lag, might be better than a drink. The hotel was old but still showed its once elegant and star driven past.

The aristocracy of Europe, William Holden's Hollywood crowd, the game hunters of pretensions and obnoxious adventures and game photographers, were once its honored guests. Tonight the Russell family would be especially indulged.

After working out in a small well-equipped hotel gym, Hunter suggested they get some food in the formal dining area of the hotel.

"Let's kick back and absorb our new righteous dad and make what we can of all this. Ash, I'm not worried, but it all seems a little strange. He really seems to have control over all this stuff. He wouldn't put us in danger, I know it. But, how could Dad have hidden all this?"

"Mom's gotta know," said Ashley.

"Yeah, he's like some secret agent. You know, the company, the C.I.A. What else has he done? I don't want to think about this any more. I'm afraid he's going to tell us he's a killer or some unbelievable shit.

Let's clean up, get something to eat, and see what tomorrow brings," Hunter exposited.

Just at that moment David called up to the room and invited the boys to dinner with some of his old new friends and informed them they would stay in Nairobi for a couple of days to renew old acquaintances and get provisions. They were to be ready in an hour.

When the boys arrived in the dinning room, David was holding court with numerous guests. His ease in discussing Kenyan economic issues was a new revelation and another remarkable, unraveling of the past. The Russell Group, their father's major investment vehicle, had control over vast holdings of Kenyan securities since the early days of independence. David's involvement in internal Kenyan financial matters was obvious. Is this where their father had made his fortune at such a young age?

The dinner was cut short. However, they broke up after a mere three hours, short by Kenyan social etiquette. Even in their quiet spectator roles, the boys were so engrossed in the dinner conversation; they thought it had passed in an instant. Most meetings of this importance and re-acquaintance were long and followed traditional customs.

After dinner a messenger signaled to Martin outside of the dinning room. When he came back to the table, he handed a number to David who excused himself immediately, asked the boys to wait here and went to his room where he made one phone call. He called William Mkabi who lived in the Kibera slum. William, who later in his life had carried portfolio in Kenyan national government, was once a fierce freedom fighter for the Mau Mau. He was old, but a man of extraordinary wisdom and knowledge. It seemed strange that all David's contemporaries were chronologically older than him. He never looked on yesterday as being younger or lesser but looked at these men as his equals. They had similar feelings for him. As a youth, he was quick of judgment based on great preparation, and his reading of events was insightfully accurate. He was not viewed as a boy but as a peer of unusual instincts and actions. He had been a leader of men in the Revolution of Kenya. William was aware of David's arrival as if drums had spoken his name.

William had lived for this day. He was old, but not frail even though he suffered from the dregs of consumption. He was just happy David came to see him before his death. He felt as a terminally ill person who had waited to see a loved one before his passing journey. William still had years in him, even though he was weathered, but was ecstatic to see David now. They had not spoken for almost 30 years, but their communication by letters was William's lifeline to David. David was considered not only William's son but a member of the Kalenjin tribe.

Before placing the phone call, David was cautioned not to speak openly about important matters as the call could be tapped. An emotional William answered with open heart.

"My son, my son, come at once to Kibera. Martin will bring you. Martin speaks of your boys, bring them here tonight, they must be engaged in our hopes and our dreams. They are younger, are they not than the daring David when he was brought into the cause, he who became a master of men. David, my son, you've finally come home, I will see you shortly. We have many subjects to discuss. I look forward to our time passage together."

Martin, David, and the boys were escorted out of the hotel by guards, as was the case in all upscale hotels in Nairobi. The boys were stunned to see David get into the driver's seat of the old Land Rover and head towards the worst slum in Nairobi, a place where anti-white, anti-Kikuku, and anti-government sentiments were the fare of the day.

The boy's trepidations were apparent. They did not understand the vastness of poverty in the slum. Europeans were in grave danger if not escorted by William's cohorts, one of the many tribal leaders' armies that resided in the Kibera slum. The boys gazed out the old innocuous Land Rover's darkened windows waiting for light to shine into this vast pit of inhumanity. Glimpses of impoverishment and unimaginable depths of despair flooded their eyes. They were speechless, but at the same time, an unquestioned calm prevailed.

It was Martin's and David's eagerness to see William and their perceived control of the environment that settled Hunter and Ashley. Their stomachs stopped churning, their palms became dry, and their necks became supple once more. Their anxiety evolved into calm, and a sense of adventure prevailed. Dismay abated. Who was William? How did he play a role in all this? The anticipation of answers to these and so many other questions riveted the boys.

However, the pervading question was how did their father and mother hide all this? How did he become the man they knew and how did he cover up his past so completely? The answer would eventually emerge, but its depth and complexity would be enormous. Their focus on William and their father curtained the dangers of the Kibera slum.

Four

Driving through the Kibera area of Nairobi was not physically eventful, as was most often the case. Carjacking and kidnapping were always problematical, but not this night. There was an oppressive stench of pollution hovering over the depressed area. In spite of all this, a sense of calm prevailed.

The kinetic nature of the nocturnal brethren meandering about was a distinctly separate issue. The stillness of the night juxtaposed the tensions of the explosive human energy on the streets. The constantly moving mass of humanity had no structured purpose. People were on the move everywhere, an amalgam of human activity with no pattern or plan. Just a stressful tension of activity and changing dimensions waiting for the unseen circumstances of chaos. These frenzied people seemed different. They had a distinct gate, a distinct gaze, and a distinct, almost random, aggression. Hyperkinetic marching existed for no known reason.

Martin tried to express his observations to David. "There is anger out there, something I cannot express, something we have felt recently and not before. I feel out of place. I feel out of touch. Am I soft? Am I eccentric because of time and age, or are there new things uncommon to my nature? There's no sense of honor or human feeling in *those people*," as he pointed to the masses on the streets of Kibera. "Some of them are the lowest animals, but even animals don't kill their own. They are truly different. The Kikukus ravaged and subjugated all other tribes through land redistribution and corruption that forced people from the countryside to the city, but no matter what their condition, our proud Lous and Kalenjins remained strong and fostered protection for one another. We are not cannibals. We never violated each other. We are a proud people of tribal laws and customs of the ancient ways and practices. I will always understand our people and their plight. This is different! I have no common bond with these new people you now see on the streets, I have no feel for them."

Martin continued, "Am I too old, or do my senses deceive me? They're so young and so angry and they have no purpose. They kill, they rape, they maim, and they steal, but only against the weak, never the strong. They have no code, but it is more. It is as if they cannot help themselves. They have no discipline; they are people with no souls, wrapped in anger. David, there is nothing behind their eyes. I don't know if they are human. I think they are a problem that we may not be able to put our arms around and solve. There is no solution to their anger. They are truly different than us."

This was the second time David had heard this in less than 24 hours.

Five

Twenty-five minutes of navigating the narrow, pitted gravel streets of the west side of Nairobi brought the Land Rover and its passengers to a small wood carving manufacturing plant. The streets were teeming with wandering people. The oppressive heat and humidity drove them outside the sheet-metal shanties. The jammed together homes built from scavenged materials made intolerable conditions in the sweltering heat.

Ashley could not believe the number of laborers carving wooden figurines at 12:30 a.m., while *those people* milled aimlessly in the streets right before their eyes. He directed questions to Martin. "How much money do they make a day? I can't believe their conditions."

He watched a man urinating in front of the large room filled with scores of workers. "Where and what do they eat? How long are their days? Do they always leave their work areas to just piss in front of everyone?"

The workers' simple carving tools harkened back a hundred years or more, chisels and mallets, no computerized lathes to replicate the wooden animals. Subsistence labor in horrid conditions was what Hunter surmised. They were no better off than the oppressed masses Karl Marx had written about in his 1848 Communist Manifesto. He held the same curiosities as Ashley. He was impressed by his younger brother's straight forward inquiries. Men were sitting on the ground with pieces of wood held in place by their feet as they sat cross-legged, carving and honing. They stooped in a sitting position as they shaped the black and caramel ebony into craft items for the tourist trade. Why are they here so late? Why would Dad bring us to such an exploitive place? How could Dad meet a man in a place like this?

Martin looked at Ashley and said "The men who are working here live in conditions better than anyone's living on the streets. They are workers, not beggars. These men have jobs. They take care of their families as they can. Life is hard, and they are noble because they provide for others even if it is meager. They work 16 to 17 hours a day with shade over their heads and water at their disposal. They are treated well. For every man working, five men seek his job."

"Ashley, life is hard; it has been this way always. Before people were forced into the cities, it was hard on the savanna. We are goat herders, we are farmers, and it's always been difficult. We migrated to the changing seasons to find sustainable grazing for our animals. We farmed the land of our ancestors and it was not always fertile. We had to learn how to survive. Living in the city and working with tools of industry is not nature for us. We have no schooling, no capital as you call it, but we have an inner strength to live day to day with hopes of a better life. We know nothing else. It is our way."

It was as if Ashley had opened the floodgates of conversation with Martin even if it seemed one-sided.

"Ashley, we will continue our discussion later. We're approaching William's quarters. Thank you for being concerned about my people."

Ashley whispered to Hunter, "Boy did that set him off. I didn't think he would ever talk to us. It wasn't like talking about the Lakers. Did you see the resolve and passion in his eye? If this is noble and good, I don't want to think about the others. Can you imagine anything worse?"

Six

The Russell's and Martin cadre was whisked through the wood carving factory in a militaristic, efficient fashion. This parade of visitors had been performed many times before. Hunter looked at the four to five thousand square feet area where as many as 100 carvers were working, and noticed the dim lights hanging from the ceiling.

"Ash, look," he said, "there are just electrical wires with light bulbs attached at the ends. Half of them are burned out. Look at the holes in the ceiling; you can almost see the sky."

Ashley responded, "What a shit hole."

The walls consisted of termite laden plywood with gaping seams and nails protruding in places.

"What happens when it rains? This place is a disaster waiting to happen."

There was a stench of urine and defecation; there were no bathrooms, only a ditch outside for workers to relieve themselves. This must be like the stuff in English literature, Hunter thought. A *Tale of Two Cities* and *Les Miserable* came to mind. You hear about this stuff and it never really makes sense. Shit, now it does. Martin says these men are lucky. They have jobs, and they live with honor. What world does he come from? What kind of place is this? The visitors reached the limit of the factory floor and two men were stationed with automatic weapons in front of a small, reddish wooden door. The dingy factory with dirt floors and dark gray black corrugated metals interspersed on aging plywood and ceiling beams seemed like an anti-chamber leading to a symbolic door. It was ominous.

"Was the devil in there?" thought Ashley. "Who is this William guy?" It was almost like a macabre horror scene.

As they waited, Ashley and Hunter noticed the workers and the guards were different from the many wanderers on the street. There was something behind their eyes; they were just men working extremely long hours. They were just normal people, but of unimaginable circumstances. The environment was very odd, but it started to make sense to them. The boys were not as worried as they were upon entering the factory. Ashley and Hunter were no longer paying attention to the factory or its workers. Their thoughts turned to William. The anticipation of him behind the door was emotionally exhausting. They knew they were safe because they were with David and Martin, but time elongated into a standstill as they waited for the red door to open. It was surreal. That door and this man, William, were the only thoughts of the two boys. The armed guards opened the door and a man presented himself. He had strength and presence, not frailty, as the boys had anticipated.

If William, the man standing at the door before them, was old and in failing health, he must have been like a Greek god when he was younger. He was aged, but his size and posture were that of a warrior. His gray hair posed a marked contrast to his dark Ebony skin. He looked formidable. There were no outward traces of his advanced consumption. He had a great physical advantage, even at his age. The boys were mesmerized. They waited with bated breath for him to speak.

"Asante, David. You must be Hunter and Ashley? Please come into my study".

The room behind the red door was filled with books and a cluttered desk. This scene seemed out of place in the old, dilapidated building. The rugs were Persian, placed upon a teak floor. The book shelves were filled with leather bound books, the walls were stucco. It was an oxymoron, this office in the midst of a 19th-century factory.

"David, how are you, my son? It has been almost a lifetime since I gazed upon your face. Your boys look like the young David, softer of face but leaner. Come sit down."

The guards moved papers and writings to clear off some chairs for David, Martin, and the boys to sit.

"David, we must talk, but I must engage your sons first. I want to see how you have performed as a father. Martin confided in me I feel that I know the boys. I seek their council, for it's their new world that perplexes me. David, we will have time to confer and speak of yesterday, but now may I discuss some things with your sons?"

"Yes, of course," David replied.

David felt honored. William was politely making the boys feel comfortable. It was William's way of earning loyalty from new acquaintances. David was well aware of William's methods. He had displayed the same politeness upon his first reception with David many years ago. David had learned everyone wanted recognition and William was master of making people feel important, while being engaged by someone of stature. He creates loyalty while analyzing other's resolve and integrity. He uses the ruse of asking for an opinion and while examining one's soul effectively he was reading a person's intentions. A person's soul was more important than the person's knowledge. Knowledge could easily be transferred to someone but integrity and loyalty, the basic goodness of a man, was innate. No physical or emotional costume could hide one's soul.

William's life and power were based upon relationships and loyalty was its benchmark. He was a reader of a person's mind and that reading determined all of his many relationships. As a chieftain, a tribal leader, a man of power in the European environment, his relationships determined his fate. His power and control came from the synergism of the many couplings that he had created over his lifetime. William was indeed a powerful person. He had cultivated life-long relationships based on reciprocal loyalties with people from every socio-economic stratum.

Seven

"Hunter, Ashley speaks to me of your beliefs. We in East Africa are subjugated to the aftermath of English imperialism and a lingering personal lack of achievement. We are not of European tradition and, therefore, have not the will to grow and prosper as other peoples do."

Hunter was immediately taken aback for he thought William was going to be congenial and say, "Hi, how are you? Having a good time?" Or maybe he would say something of a personal nature. Being the older of the two brothers, he felt trapped. He did not want his younger brother or himself to be subjected to this. He felt that he had to answer. His less cerebral brother Ashley was still with a quiet fear of saying something wrong. This would change, for in Africa things evolve quickly. It was a political question directed at Hunter, but it felt like undo pressure for him to retort. He was angered by being put into a box; he suddenly knew why rats strike at someone's jugular when cornered. Trying not to be intimidated, he said something startling.

"May I be candid?" he said, trying to be mature and holding his own. "I have been here for less than a day, no sleep, no way of knowing how difficult it would be. I'm frightened, and I don't know a darn thing about you. Why should I? I don't know how to act, my father seems different, and you asked me how I feel about some inane political question. This shouldn't be an inquisition. I'm just a kid, but I wouldn't put you in this position of being uncomfortable. You are so serious. It is very threatening. I know I'm supposed to be respectful, but I'm tired and I'm afraid and I feel that you are too aggressive."

He could not believe what he just said. It was as if it just slipped out of his mouth. He internalized the reward of standing up to the bully. Nothing more to be said, but confident that he had stood his ground was a strange feeling, indeed. It was good, he thought, that he stood his ground. William did not change his expression and looked at Ashley.

"What of you, my son?"

Ashley tried to be light and bring relief into the room.

"Don't ask me, I don't talk to you till I see my lawyer."

Hunter smirked with acknowledgement, but the room was quiet. The awkwardness was oppressive. William's demeanor immediately changed. He felt he had stepped beyond his bounds and must change the tact of the conversation. He did not want to offend. David knew that the new direction of the conversation would follow "bad cop, good cop," as it were.

"Hunter, Ashley, I am sorry for my abrupt seriousness, though we do have great problems to address as Kenyans. May I start anew? I am truly embarrassed for my lack of manners. Boys, welcome to my home."

He put out his hand and smiled with warmth that filled the room. A personal transformation had taken place that is common to all great leaders.

"I want you to try our traditional red banana beer," William offered. "It would be my honor to toast my new guests."

The mentioning of the beer occasioned a response from his faithful guards to immediately present the boys with a drink. Hunter and Ashley felt the social awkwardness ease into a simple conversation more to their liking. William's niceties and cultural jokes calmed the boys, and he was no longer perceived as menacing. Their apprehensions upon meeting him moved to a genuine feeling of affection. He seemed like an old uncle. It was strange, but after a while, they felt as if they had known him their entire lives. Even the office that seemed so out of place in this antiquated and dirty factory now seemed natural to them. The thought of danger and strange people receded, and the warmth of family prevailed. William had the gift of making both Ashley and Hunter feel he was speaking directly to each of them. He could hold court with hundreds of people and while talking to them in aggregate, he made you feel special, for he seemed to speak to you alone. You connected to him in a very personal way. You were the only one with William no matter what the size of the crowd he engaged.

Time passed quickly. William offered the boys a respite of adult company by suggesting one of his guards take them to the restaurant Carnivore for dinner. It was 1:30 a.m. but dinner was customarily late in Kenya. With the departure of the boys, accompanied by guards, William and David could at last engage in conversation. Impersonal letters, e-mails, and the occasional phone calls were no match for personal interaction. They loved each other, but in East Africa male affection could only be displayed in deference and respect. Their bond was ever lasting and crystal clear.

"David, before we are at last in conversation, I suggest you call Diana, the mother of your children and the woman of your life. She must know of your arrival and the disposition of your sons."

He handed David a cell phone. Some things in East Africa had changed, but technology had not made William a lesser man. He loved this man dearly.

Eight

David placed the call on William's Blackberry.

"Diana, we just arrived a couple of hours ago. I've got a lot to tell you."

Diana interrupted, "How are Ashley and Hunter? I figured that by now, they are discovering situations are not exactly to their liking. Have they met Martin and William? Do they feel deceived about my suggestion they go on this trip with you? They're my babies. How are they? Don't startle them with the David I know and love. I sheltered them from your candor. You know how much I love you, but don't be brutally honest. You let me bring them up. I wasn't as serious with them as you were; remember all my 'lighten up' talks? This trip mustn't be too difficult for them. You promised."

David listened intently to Diana's maternal instincts. That's why he loved her so much. He wasn't brutal to his sons, but he was always honest to a fault. He was not there with them as much as he should have been when they were growing up. He had a lot of guilt about that, and it manifested itself in seriousness with the boys. She brought them up. She was a great mother.

"Diana, everything is okay. A little tension for the boys, but that's all right. It's extremely different for them, but they're okay, they seemed taken aback by the poverty and hardships they saw on the drive from the airport to the hotel. Kibera is difficult for them. Ashley even said something about people here being "animal-like." It really bothered me; he was either scared or he's a lot more insensitive than I will ever know. I think Hunter probably feels the same way but didn't say much. About Hunter, you would be proud of him. When he met William, William came off real strong, and Hunter stood up to him. I have never seen Hunter like that, formidable is an understatement. I'll tell you all about it in detail when we get home. For now, trust me, it was just unbelievable. I have to tell you a little. We were at the factory and Hunter was out of his element. Hunter, Ashley, Martin, and I, and a couple of William's guards were with William. Hunter felt verbally cornered by William, and his response was totally unexpected. He even lashed out at him. Everything is cool now. The boys like William and Martin a lot."

"David, can I talk to the kids?"

"They went with one of William's guards to… do you remember the old Carnivore restaurant? It's still here. They went there at about 1:30 this morning."

"Isn't that a tourist place?"

"I know, but William sent them. It should be quite an experience. It might be like the old Thompson Farm, when we thought *those people* were really Massi, you know, just like Disneyland. As long as the kids are safe and feel it's an adventure, it'll be okay."

Diana said, "Oh, my love you're showing them everything, aren't you?"

"Diana, just one more thing, when we got here, Ashley had an observation. He said the people were inhuman, nothing behind their eyes. That ticked me off. I mentioned it. Then later, Martin said almost the exact same thing. Martin said there are some people here who frighten him. He didn't understand anything about them. He said they were violent for no reason. They had no code of honor; you remember Martin and how we felt about honor, tradition, and kinship. It's not like that movie Invasion of the Body Snatchers and the pods and all that stuff."

David continued, "But Diana, there is something uncommon. On the way from the airport, we stopped at a light. I was driving and only saw a commotion in the rearview mirror. A young girl was sitting with three other children and a crying baby. She suddenly threw the baby into the side of the car behind us. She and the other children tore the dead baby apart and some others threw the body into a burning barrel."

"It seems a little riskier than I thought it would be here in Kibera. I can't put my finger on it. On the drive to William's house, and in front of the factory, it was different. I know it's been thirty years, but I felt danger and did not know from where it originated. Not from the militia and the opposing warlords, but maybe from the people in the streets. There are wandering hordes of people whom Martin described the same way Ashley did. Don't make too much of it. It's my gut telling me something; but I always pass everything by you. I don't want you to be impulsive and fly over here. You know how dangerous that would be for you. I'm sure it's just protective paranoia. It seems strange, though I want you to know the kids are safe no matter what I say. I'm being a little overprotective. I'm just tired. The stuff that Ashley and Martin said shook me up a little. Diana, its okay, just different than I figured it would be."

"I trust your instincts. William would never let harm come to the children. If you sense something, then it is bigger than you know. Be careful, and tell our old friends I send my love and appreciation for what I know they will be doing for the boys. I love you very much. Call tomorrow. I know you want to talk to William. Oh, David, you are probably not in danger, just something a little different, you are just in survival mode, talk to William about it. If I thought something was wrong, I would say so. I love it that you still share important feelings with me and that you trust my judgments. I am sure it's all right, but don't forget to look over your shoulder. Love you, darling."

Before she said goodbye, she asked to talk to William for a moment. They chatted for a while, pleasantries between old friends. Diana said, "I love you William, now you can have my husband all to yourself."

Nine

"William, my old friend," David said, "We must discuss matters of money. I may sound formal but it is important that I am clear, and no questions linger as to what must be done."

David opened his notes and began, "Since the revolution, my oversight of your financial resources has been very successful; over 17% annualized rate of appreciation. Our original investment of $11 million derived from expropriating funds the exchequer's office adjusted for my 2% management fee and taxes is now worth more than $900,000.000. Our crimes against the British have paid off handsomely. We were vilified and briefly jailed, because of the retail end, the illegal ivory the animal trade, even the horrible kidnapping for ransom in the early years, but in the long run we have done well. I mean really well. We were criminals and look at us now, there are no two more up standing people in our own countries than I and you. I have sent monies to you as if they were an annuity from our legal investments. We have accumulated as much principle and working capital as possible to increase your yearly allocations. You're now receiving more than $1 million a month. The dispersements are sent to four personal accounts, the primary being the Midland Bank in Mombassa. They are sent in Euros because we hedge in the foreign exchange market. Your money was held in the street name of Russell and Associates, a hedge fund. Our tax rate is 15%, lower than the US personal or corporate taxes. Taxes on hedge funds are classified as capital gains; therefore at a rate of 15%, not the rate of 38%, which is the common case. As you know, taxes are the reasons for all your assets being held in my fund's name. Because of the sub-prime loan crisis in the United States and its auxiliary effects on the European Union, government regulation looms its head. It will bring openness; we call this transparency. When this happens, you will be seen as a greater enemy to the powers that be, our many extralegal activities we were involved in — yours and mine and past business relationships will be viewed as hostile terrorist acts. With the bombings of the US Embassy in Nairobi and the problems in Mombassa, you may be considered a potential enemy of Kenya. Your support for independence from the Kikuku makes you a person to be watched carefully. If we don't make the necessary title changes immediately, you could be viewed as an international terrorist, not the nationalist you are today. It has been very difficult, but not impossible or illegal to convey your monies up to this point. When the United States government starts regulating hedge funds and investment banks more carefully, it will open scrutiny upon you. Under our Patriot Act you will be defined as a terrorist and could be pursued as such. It is important that we act before there is new regulation. We must separate ourselves from impending oversight. For that purpose, I am suggesting the following: I will sell the funds, and the proceeds will be allocated to a

European foundation administered by Credit Suisse. It will be humanitarian in nature, a Kenyan wild life organization. I have asked John Leakey to be a participant. It will give you more legitimacy. It is a foundation set up for you. It has the advantage of open- ended withdrawals, money rotating on a 30 day basis. All assets are re-purchasable and backed by AAA rated bond funds that specialize in RPs. You will have total anonymity at the same time. There are a few questions I have for you. Who will be your heir, and what control will he have over matters that affect your monthly annuity and principle enhancement or depletion? When will he be given authority to act with you or on your behalf and under what circumstances? We must prevent future problems and always provide direction for your money. It must be bullet proof. I have laid out such a plan and know it will be to your liking. I will no longer be able to act in the capacity as overseer of your money. Tomorrow regulating circumstances will have eyes that can compromise you and the Kalenjin people. We must act now. This will ensure the future."

"It has been difficult for me, my old friend, not to have been able to visit you all these years for fear of jeopardizing you. Mine and Diana's involvement in the Hutchinson Ranch raids in the Revolution were truly a mistake, a mistake that caused many deaths and Diana's conviction of murder in absencia. She is a fugitive and can never set foot on Kenyan soil. Many years have passed but my presence here would have stained your life's work. My history in the Revolution and flirting with the law on the investment side could have hurt you. Therefore, I have not come back to Kenya until this day. I have missed you, my brother. From this day forward we will no longer have financial ties. My presence in Kenya can now be a regular occurrence. It has been a long time; too many years have passed without seeing you. I am rich because of our financial involvement, and you have almost one billion dollars. Have we done enough? Could we have done more to help our people? Much seems the same here in Kenya. Can we do more? You have given so much of yourself, my brother. William, when did you leave the great house in Norfork to live here with your people? We must talk of matters personal."

David and William talked until the arrival of the boys. It was five a.m. before they said good night. It truly was a good night. It had taken almost thirty years for this night to happen.

Ten

The next three days were a whirlwind of activity. David and William met with Kalenjins elders to discuss strategies for the upcoming general election. Kenya was ruled by Kikukuian cronyism and corruption. Paradoxically, they had free elections with international monitors and oversight. It was viewed by many Western countries as the most democratic East African nation, even though Amnesty International sighted it for numerous human rights violations. Entrenched political ties going back to British colonialism gave the Kikukus an almost insurmountable political advantage. The same party controlled the parliament for more than 30 years, a de facto one party system. Callous disregard for the human suffering of 80% of the population and the blatant opulence of the oligarchy were glaring results of Kikukuian rule.

David and William felt conditions were right for changes in parliament. Corruption and greed in combination with inept government plagued Kenya. A stagnant economy with 40% unemployment, inflation of 30%, and food shortages caused by exportation of Kenyan food stuffs were solvable issues which could sway even a fixed election for parliamentary seats. The

Kalenjins and the Lois peoples were in a political parity position with the Kikukus, if they held tribal hatreds in abeyance. This election could put them into a coalition government with meaningful power sharing. David and William attended to every detail in planning a political strategy for shared governance. In Africa, historically bad begets bad, but in this case, bad conditions of unimaginable pain could conceivably lead to unprecedented political change. Any weakness in Kikukuian rule must be pursued. A splinter of light could lead to a burst of sun.

Hunter and Ashley were busy with Martin in the final details of their impending safari. The decisions about wildlife reserves and hotels were cemented. Samburu, Amboseli, Governor's Camp, and finally, the historic train to Mombassa, were agreed upon. Provisions were purchased, vehicles rented, and porters and guides for trekking in the bush were secured. All major decisions were made by the boys. They planned every detail of the impending trip. The planning discourse down to intricate detail was gratifying. It was a long day, but everything was arranged and they were ready for adventure.

Later that night, Hunter and Ashley were brought to a dinner meeting with William and David that surprised them; they were to participate with others as if they were equals. The currency of David and William opened many doors. They were now viewed as members of the Kalenjin entourage and were shown respect. They were asked many questions of a very general nature. The boys were being felt out, as was the case by the elders to all outsiders. Hunter and Ashley knew listening more and speaking less was a powerful tool. He who speaks little has a powerful voice. Once an utterance passes one's lips, it cannot go back. Both boys were measured in their responses. To their dismay, neither David nor William set parameters for their participation. The boys showed a maturity well beyond their years. They received the dignity and respect afforded all delegates at the gathering. This independence seemed to help liberate them into adulthood.

During the day they planned for an adventure and at night they were part of the political process affecting millions of Kenyan people. They embraced this new responsibility. Not all young men had such power bestowed upon them. It was clearly a testing ground for their manhood. It seemed as though David ceded power to Ashley and Hunter, and they ran with it. Nothing was spoken, but a clear admittance to the club of authority and privilege was awaiting the boys.

They were going to contribute, but at what price? How much of a sacrifice would it be worth? Whatever it took, they wanted to participate. They were allowed to play the game of men; they had the future of people's lives in their hand. It was as if their upbringing had prepared them for this day. They felt nothing special about how they had been raised, but they were up to the task. Was it by their parents' example of dealing with complex and sophisticated matters? How did they have the ability to contribute at this level? Ashley and Hunter would revisit this many times in the coming weeks. The greater the responsibility, the more they were up to the task. The boys felt comfortable in the proximity of power.

After dinner, David, Hunter, and Ashley were attending a political gathering of the Kalenjins and the Lois. European participation was 5% at best, but the

Russell family was viewed with honor for its many years of allegiance to the cause. The meeting of the Democratic People's Party was held in the main conference room of the Hilton Hotel across from the central business district. This commercial district was also the seat of the Kenyan Federal Government complex; the area housed the parliament building, the national court house, and the ministry of defense. The site of the old US Embassy destroyed by terrorists in 1998 was contiguous to the hotel and its environs.

William, speaking to the delegation, revealed his visions for sharing power with the Kikukus. He began, "My fellow Kenyans…today we have the ability to throw off our oppressive chains. We have learned retribution is beneath us. We must change the old ways of holding other tribes and peoples hostage. Corruption and greed must be rooted out of all civil service jobs. The tolerance of random violence and aggression will forever more cease. No excuses for civil disobedience. The Kikuku, the Kalenjins, and the Lois will all be judged similarly. No entitlement for men or women based on tribe or station. No tolerance for those who do not subscribe to the common good of the people. Properties, both personal and institutional, will be equally accessible to all. No restrictions to freedom or liberty as were the old ways of the Kikuku. We will move to normalcy through truth and conciliation."

The applause was thunderous.

Ashley and Hunter asked David if they could walk back to the Mt. Kenya Safari club with a bodyguard Martin had instructed to watch over them when the convention was adjourned.

They walked the mile of blighted city streets back to the hotel. The vision of William and his Democratic prognostications did not correspond to the reality the boys were seeing as they walked watching masses of *those people* milling on the streets. The conference participants were so different from what the boys were seeing on this street. Thoughts of *those people* dampened the joy of William's speech. Were *those people* a greater threat to society or even humankind than the boys could foresee, or were they overreacting?

The fear and intimidation of walking back to the hotel in the midst of *those people* was truly chilling. As it always happens, when you think it, it plays itself out in the worst way. Jewish people call this a cunnahara. The boy's were confronted by their greatest fears on that lonely street. They were challenged by *those people*. On the way back to the hotel they faced the anger and violent nature within ten minutes after leaving the conference.

It was as if the fear of something cosmically caused it to take place. Just outside of the convention center the boys heard a slow resonate chanting coming from street thug gang. The street was flush with security so Ashley and Hunter paid little attention as it applied to their safety. The thirty or so young people who were congregating on the sidewalk as they passed didn't seem out of place, but they took due note of how disgusting their appearance was.

Hunter said, "Ash I can smell them from our side of the street they must be covered in shit. Man it's a good thing there is all this security from the conference."

Ashley just grunted in response. He was too busy following the action across the street.

Before they traveled a few blocks, the security details were gone and the boy's adversaries were still positioned directly across from them. For every step they took *those people* took a parallel step.

As they passed an alley with burning tires in trash barrels, abruptly, without hesitation Ashley and Hunter took flight back to the hotel. There was collective consciousness of eminent danger. In pursuit of the two young Europeans *those people* threw stones as if they were missiles, uttered unintelligent sounds and some postured with knives and sticks.

As they reached the hotel there was a horrendous scream. When they turned to look back the guard grabbed their arms and practically dragged them into the hotel lobby.

Hunter later said, "They would have killed us just because we were white."

Ashley said, "You're wrong. Shit, they would have just killed us. Color didn't mean a fucking thing to them. They are animals. We're lucky to be in the fucking hotel."

"Ash, we can't tell dad."

"Yeah, he wanted us to stay till the end of the conference and he said it would be dangerous."

"They wanted to really hurt us."

Ashley said, "Man. There was nothing behind their eyes."

Entering their rooms, their moods changed from somber to diligent; they had to prepare for tomorrow's journey. No mention of drinks this night. They were expectant of an adventure and a confessional from their father. Would David speak of his past? Why did he and their mother deceive them their whole lives? Was their past the reason they lived such perfect lives? The

Russell's were flawless and pure in their dealings with other people including their sons. Too perfect, it was hard for the boys to live up to their parents images. Was this a product of what happened in Kenya? They were perfect parents, maybe too perfect. Would they have to demand the truth owed them since their adoption?

The thought of having to bring up the subject of their parents' past and confront their father was overwhelming. Neither Hunter nor Ashley slept that night. At 8:00 a.m., they would be off to the Samburu River where porters and guides awaited them. More importantly, the truth awaited them.

Eleven

Hunter knocked on Ashley's door. "Ash, I want to make sure you're ready for tomorrow."

"Shit, Hunter, I know. You don't have to say it. If we are on time, we are late. I know what you're going to say. You are just as compulsive as Mom, don't worry I will be on time. Shut the f'in door and let me go to sleep"

Hunter, leaning on Ashley's doorway, said, "We should be in the lobby at 7:30 to make sure we have leverage over Dad so he feels some pressure to talk. Maybe he'll speak to us about the past. Don't say anything first. He'd expect that. Our silence should make him uneasy. It's got to be bothering him that we have said nothing so far. I'm going back to my room to watch CNN. See you early tomorrow morning. 7:30, right? No narcoleptic stuff from you. We've got to get up really early. Be sure to get a wake-up call."

"Freaky, Hunter, you plan everything. It will probably be redundant for me to have a wake-up call. What time did you request for me?"

Hunter just threw up his hands and walked away mumbling.

David was in the throes of readying for tomorrow's excursion. He was almost anthropomorphic. He was robot like in his preparation for the journey; his mind was on the conversation he must have with the boys. He felt contrite; the boys had complicated things by not being confrontational. David's guilt was Roman Catholic in proportion. When called upon, he had made speeches all his adult life to investment groups, academics, political strategy groups of national importance, but he could not script out this conversation with his own children. He knew he would not sleep for he had a pseudo-sleeping disorder. Fast working, highly efficient minds did not sleep at night; this night would be extraordinarily long. David would gather himself early and wait for the boys in the lobby.

At 7:15, Hunter and Ashley arrived in the lobby, almost 20 minutes after David and Martin. David was waiting for his sons with a thermos of coffee in hand. He almost laughed at the boys' psychological ploy of early arrival for advantage. He was very proud of his boys. They had placed importance on their "little discussion with their father" in a circuitous way. The guise of early participation in the adventure, shown by being in the lobby early, was effective. The boys faked being effusive. They were ready to go with no outward signs of wanting to air out their concerns with their father. Their self-control gave them a tactical advantage. The silence was heavy. David felt the weight of guilt heavy on his heart.

He said, "We are early, how about some breakfast?"

The boys did not want to eat. They had their bags taken outside and loaded into the waiting vehicles.

Almost instantaneously, David felt a need to clear the air. They were his children, no need for gamesmanship. He was impetuous for the first time in many years. The adage of "don't speak early, and speak from a position of power by making the other person feel uncomfortable" did not hold for his children. He loved them. He felt he had wronged them, no matter what the reasoning. He would shoulder the blame for both himself and Diana.

Before they left the valet parking in front of the hotel, he said, "I must clear the air. I've got to talk to both of you. Martin is part of this, so please don't be offended by his presence."

Martin felt strange but honored, as if he were a member of the family, part of a discussion bigger than him.

"I am going to make a long story short. I know you will have a lot of questions, and rightly so, but please let me say my piece and then we will talk. Now, please. I hope you understand I've got to discuss this my way. You might not feel your mom and I were justified, but we reasoned we had to hide our past completely from the two of you until now. We lied to you by omission and sometimes just blatantly. We saw no other alternative."

David discussed how he and their mother were students at the London School of Economics and met at a meeting of students who were interested in venturing into colonial Kenya for a summer curriculum on foreign investment. They felt it would be highly social, nonacademic, a sort of respite from school. Once in Nairobi, they met William and Martin and were persuaded that imperialism was evil and became sympathetic to Kenyan independence. Diana and

David lent support to the Mau Mau serge to unseat the British. They perceived themselves as freedom fighters, not terrorists. Diana and David played a logistical and tactical role in the Mau Mau insurgency.

David did not want to go into much detail for specificity would cloud his and Diana's youthful intentions. He described the Hutchinson raid as that of an insurgent task force trying to free captured Mau Mau. The farm house they attacked, burned down, with many injured and dead, but the mission was a success. This haunted the two of them for the rest of their lives. He discussed their capture and incarceration. He discussed Diana's extradition and her conviction of murder in absencia. The boys were silent. Finally he alluded to the actions of the expropriation of $11 million from the colonial treasury office before the collapse of British rule.

David continued, "Now for the hard part. I have never talked about personal stuff with you guys. I haven't been there for you two. I never let family interfere with business. You always came out on the short end. You have a nice life, a great mom, and an absentee dad. I never gave you myself! Your mom was always there but not me. I am not much of a dad. I should have been with you and I wasn't. I want to change all that. I hope it's not too late. People look at me and say what a lucky guy and from the outside I am but I need you to fill my life. That's why we are here. I need a second chance to make it right. I have pushed the envelope all my life in business at your expense. I buy people and things just for show. I have a flawless image to hide some of the terrible things I have done. Look at what your mom and I did when we were young, almost your exact ages. I have what I have at someone's expense has always been the rule. I have never been good at kids and now you are men and I want a chance to make it right. My success at your expense has been the biggest mistake of my life. I wasn't there for you. Can you forgive me?"

The speech of a lifetime was concise and forthright. It lasted for an eternity in David's heavy heart, but in reality it was said in mere moments.

Upon conclusion, he looked to Martin and said, "Did I omit anything?" Waiting for the silence to pass was excruciating.

Ashley looked at Hunter only as a 23-year-old could and said "Shit, I thought it would be something important. I didn't sleep and missed breakfast for that?"

He cleared the air just as he had done with William. Everyone laughed.

David looked at his son and said, "Boy, do you have a gift."

Hunter held out his hand to his father sitting in the front seat and said "Ashley said it all, but if we ever need to talk about this again, can we? I know what you did was for us; it was the best for us. I am not angry. I don't feel betrayed. Someday I want to hear the whole story, from beginning to end, to tell my kids, if I ever have any."

They had eight hours of bumpy and dusty roads ahead of them, but the air in the land rover had cleared and was as rarified as that of any sacred place in the world.

Twelve

The drive to the Samburu River was uneventful, but eerily strange. Guard posts were stationed every 100 km on the main road to the reserve. The road, like all highways in Kenya, was made of composite rock which washed away during the summer or rainy season. It was now winter, a cooler and drier season. The summer rains were torrential raining as much as 50 inches a season making roads impassable and the life line to commerce and tourism shut down for weeks at a time. The summer was always a time of rain, insects, and hardships. The dregs of winter were dust and potholes of unimaginable size. Windows had to be closed for the purpose of keeping the red iron-laden dust at bay. Martin and David wore scarves over their mouths; Hunter, in short order, followed suit. Ashley, the manly but foolish twenty-three-year-old, did not.

The guard posts, acting as military posts, were interspersed on the main transportation arteries of Kenya. They checked all vehicles repeatedly during the journeys, tracking and searching for illegal contraband and weapons. Poachers and highwaymen were notorious for their brazen robberies and hijackings on these isolated roads. During the two to three hour intervals, the time it took to pass from one post to another, vehicles could be intermittently tracked on an unsophisticated traffic grid, much like the air traffic controllers' grids used for civil aviation. Constant surveillance was imperative because of the dangers awaiting unescorted vehicles. Law enforcement was nonexistent outside the cities and villages. The army was responsible for security in the rural areas and countryside. The nature of military's Draconian policing policies made illegal activities predictable; brutal violence was an unintended consequence of the military's harsh punishment for any kind of lawlessness. Harsh penalties caused crimes to be darker and more serious.

All crimes faced the same unequivocal punishment: death. All crimes committed by the perpetrators were viewed as egregious and thus precipitated killing victims. Since the punishment was the same, leaving the victims alive after executing a lesser crime was considered unintelligent. Why leave evidence? Robbery led to murder. Travelers had to be on guard all the time. Nocturnal travel was solely at one's own peril.

The road from Nairobi to Samburu traveled through many small towns and villages. The boys were intrigued by the Mobile and British Petroleum gas stations. Ashley asked Hunter, "What's next, a Starbucks?"

American and European signage seemed out of place. This was a vestige of colonial rule, thought Hunter. The ever expanding agribusiness in Kenya with its large farms of up to 20,000 acres, coupled with very modern European farm equipment, was not anticipated. It looked like Middle America, except all the laborers were black.

The sight of Mt. Kenya, one of two great East African volcanoes, was breathtaking. A persistent haze was ever present. Dust and wood burning was a decade-long practice of harnessing energy for one's home, and the particulates from small handicraft industry in quasi regional economic production zones stole from the openness of this large, interrupted, undeveloped chunk of Kenya. The boys thought the haze looked like June gloom in Southern California. Coastal clouds covered much of the topography in California until the temperatures increased in the summer and ushered in clear skies. But here in Kenya, the haze was pollution and dust that hovered over nature's beauty. It looked drab and not visually entertaining. Hunter and Ashley became mindful of many things.

The sights of rural Kenya were not of a threatening nature but different than they had envisioned. The people seemed more natural here, they were not moving at a frenetic pace as was the case in Nairobi. Though the haze was omnipresent, it was not oppressive. The ride in the countryside was soothing but not stimulating. It was not adventurous. The boys had expected more. Kenya was clearly a land of many faces. It was as if the boys were birds of prey. Nothing passed by their eyes.

Time passed by quickly. They were expectant. They assimilated everything that lay before them. The party reached their predetermined rendezvous with the guides and porters just a little after 3:30 p.m. Ashley felt cheated because the trip went so effortlessly. Hunter was surprised that the guides were so proficient in English and were so considerate of all of his needs. He had not yet fully grasped the power of money and privilege. The future would teach it, he would learn. The sun was high in the sky and temperature was in the mid thirties centigrade. The river seemed inviting.

Ashley asked Martin in front of one the guides if he could venture into the water to cool off from the dusty ride. His eyes and nose were filled with red dust. "Martin, can I jump in for a few seconds to cool down and get the dust off of me. Is it okay?"

Before he could take a single step, Martin grabbed his shoulder and firmly saddled his progress.

The guide then said, "The Samburu River is known for its crocodiles. They are sometimes seven to eight meters long. They are the most dangerous predators in Kenya. Do not get close to the river's edge for a crock can leap to one and a half times its body length to grab food. It will bring you down deep into the water to drown you and later devour you. Stay here and cool off. Our guides will bring you water. Never think you are alone. In the bush the animals are always near. It takes trained eyes and ears and yes, sometimes a nose to be safe. We will tell you how to function in the savanna and on the river. You will be fine, but you must follow orders at all times."

Ashley said to himself, how did Martin know? He is an old man. I am really out of my element. He questioned if the guide was talking down to him or was he that out of touch with his environment. Are *those people* like those crocs?

David interrupted and said, "Sometimes it will seem counter intuitive, but these men are trained and will protect you and the animals."

Ashley looked at his dad and said, "Don't we come first?"

The look on his David's face made Ashley believe the animals were valuable, maybe too valuable. Licensed guards in Kenya had years of training and were certified. They were protection against nature and all its elements, may it be fauna or flora, or in the worst of circumstances, other humans. The Russell party was well protected and safe. They would rest from the long ride and gather themselves for the two hour trek to their first camp site.

Thirteen

"Hunter, this doesn't seem much different than the Santa Monica Mountains near Pepperdine. No ocean, but it looks the same," observed Ashley. Pepperdine University was located in fabled Malibu, California.

The sun was set high in the sky at 4 p.m. when the party headed towards the fixed camp. Ashley again noticed something extraordinary.

"Dad, remember when you got us a special tour at the San Diego Zoo and we went to some of the areas designated for grazing animals?"

David replied, "Sure, why?"

"Well, looking at this small herd of impala they look different."

He was viewing a grouping of maybe 200 impala and their companion baboons. They were no more than 100 meters from the herd and the impalas were not skittish. Their markings were exactly the same, their hair glistening like silk; they were all perfect, nothing like the zoo animals. They were remarkable. They were exactly the same, exact replications of each other.

"The San Diego zoo animals look like crap compared to these, guys." The guide Nelson was amused. He looked at Ashley with Hunter at his side, as the party walked two abreast into the bush. Looking directly at the boys and not breaking rank, he said. "Here all animals are exactly the same, they are exact reproductions. It has always been this way, for every pattern of life is the same. If there are any distinctions, they will die. The old, the young, the weak, and the stupid are eaten. So, any prey that is different, in any way, may it be large or small, will stick out and be sought by the predators and killed. Everything here in the bush is part of a food chain. These animals are killed by big cats or hyena, if they're different. They're pried from the herd and hunted and killed if they are different. It seems savage to you, but it is the way of nature. Some die of old age and are eaten by scavengers or termites. Nothing is free from the jaws of other animals. Tradition has been the same here in the bush since the beginning of time. All animals are similar, they blend into the landscape, they run as if they are the wind, their movements and lines and colors cover their identities, they cloak their scent by rolling in excrement. These are the ways of survival, but in the end, all are still eaten. Sometimes fast, sometimes a long life, but they all die and are food for other animals."

Hunter flashed to the people in the Kibera slum, and said to himself, "*those people* were different. Are humans different than these animals? Is something else going on? Do we blend in? How long does it take for us to change?"

As the party walked into the bush, the grass was no more than one foot high. The alluvial plains of Samburu opened up into a landscape bigger than the eyes could envision. The savanna's size and the party's relative smallness were not lost on the boys. They felt almost insignificant; the scope of the world around them was enormous. Within an hour's trek, the landscape started to change; the lower brown grass hovering close to the earth was now coupled with green shrubs. As the landscape diversified, so did the food or fuel for the animals, hence new species appeared. Zebras, wildebeest, and different types of deer such as springbok, eland, dic dic, and even the blue balled monkeys as the tree line heightened.

As the different animal's numbers increased, seeing their relative calm in close proximity to each other was amazing. It was still hot in the day and the predators were resting in cool rock formations or in shaded areas under trees. Their work would not start until the angle of the sun gave them an advantage and they were fully rested. The prey would be calm until the sun closed upon the horizon. Later in the afternoon the party's anticipation of reaching camp was matched by the prey's anticipation of the predator. The dance from diurnal to nocturnal and costumes of the prey and predator have been the same for millennia on the savanna. Replicated day after day, similar events and environment existed for thousands of years. Only incremental changes in nature over time could trigger evolutionary differences in the animals. This process would take many more thousands of years for newly evolved species appearing on the face of the earth. At any one moment in time things seemed stagnant. Evolution was a slow process. Hunter wondered about nature's process for change and *those people.*

Their arrival to the fixed camp showed three by six meter tents with wooden floors and bucket showers affixed to ropes hanging from a tree. They welcomed this bit of luxury. A perpetual fire of slow burning iron wood was central to the camp. This is where the guides prepared food. David, Martin, and the boys had pangs of hunger from the day's ride and trek to the camp. They ate heartily and slept under the night sky. The stars shone so brightly one felt like reaching up and touching the Milky Way. It was magical to the boys. They had never seen anything like it. Sleep was deep and wonderful. Camp would be home for three days. The party ventured out early mornings and late afternoons to view the animals. They stayed in three different reserves in three different terrains and saw the diversity that only Kenya possessed.

Fourteen

The first morning came early. Hunter awoke when the first light of day flashed upon his face; this was his usual way. He always slept close to the nearest window. Last night he positioned himself next to the tent's opening, as it had no windows. Light was his friend, his morning companion.

He said, "Hey, Ash get out of bed, it's time to get up. Let's go up to the main camp fire and see if anyone is there."

Ashley pulled the covers over his head. The tent was self-contained and spacious beyond belief. Hunter stood tall; his head did not reach the high point of the permanent canvas structure. He unzipped the tent and stepped out to discover elephant dung just outside the reach of his left foot. It was not there the previous night. He thought Ashley was restless throughout the night which accounted for the slight movement of his cot. This was not the case, as a clear path from the reeds leading to the river below suggested that elephants had walked past their tent. On their way to the river, one had brushed the side of the tent as it was seeking a path to the fresh flowing water. Hunter was taken aback. He was frightened. He was truly alarmed.

He could not believe an elephant had come so close. He immediately woke up Ashley and showed him the dung. The two went up to the center camp fire, 70 to 80 meters away. It was located on an embankment overlooking the river.

As they walked, they vowed not to separate and always watch each other's backs. David, Martin, and the guide at the camp fire listened to their story. It landed on deaf ears, when they were informed, their imagined close encounter with death was not unusual. Animals always ventured into camp. This is where they lived.

After a warm breakfast and coffee, made by the porters over an iron wood fire, they were off to follow the elephants. Hunter thought maybe they would see the ones who had trespassed upon them while they were sleeping. Walking into open fields of brown grass looking for the occasional Acacia tree, the main food of elephants, it was apparent that trekking was work. It was hot and dirty and the elephants were always one step in front of them.

"Nelson," Hunter said softly, "Why can't we find them?"

Nelson whispered, "They are always on the move. They think we are predators, we stand tall and they think we are hunting them. They feel like prey, and they are very aware." Nelson continued, "We will catch them, but we must be careful not to threaten them. They will charge if threatened."

At intervals on a path he forged, Nelson stopped and picked up grass or dirt and threw it into the air to detect its direction. He had to know if they were upwind or downwind from the great beast. After one hour of fast-paced walking, the group came upon a family of three adult female elephants, seven adolescents, and four babies. They were throwing dirt and mud at each other with their great trunks. The two babies of no more than one year were pulling at a large stick. The boys were mesmerized as the babies took turns holding the large end of the stick that gave them leverage in this tug of war game. They were no more than 30 meters behind a large embankment shrouded with trees viewing the action of these animals. Hunter was taking pictures with a Canon EOS Mark Three with 24-105 professional lenses. They stayed for almost one hour until the wind started to change, a harbinger of danger.

On the way back to the camp there was silence but glee in the air. This was better than anything the boys had expected. The next two days passed with outings in the morning and late afternoon. There were sightings of a leopard in a tree with its precious treasure of an impala draped over a limb. The boys witnessed the dance of vultures and brown back jackals over fallen prey. The secretary birds and the horned billed wobblers seeking snakes were viewed with amazement. Hunter and Ashley were gazing upon nature and could not get enough. To David and Martin it was still exciting and exhilarating, but its romance and luster was seeing the boy's enjoyment. In the coming days they visited Amboseli under the great Kilimanjaro volcano and then Governors Camp where lions were numerous.

It was mating season, male lions battled persistently until one became dominant over the pride. Near Governors Camp, they came upon a clearing where female lions and their cubs were resting.

Ashley wondered where the great male was. "How much bigger are the males, Nelson? Can there be two males in one pride? Do the males hunt? I heard they don't."

Nelson discussed the lions from the males' supremacy battles to females hunting in teams. He said, "The females will wait for their male to arrive. We aren't in danger in the heat of the day. These majestic animals only hunt in the comfort of afternoon's cooler temperatures."

An hour had past and Hunter with his ever present camera had taken 200 or more pictures. A male of at least 450 pounds of muscle, entered the pride settled atop a clearing nestled next to a small pond. His physical proportions were staggering. He was quantumly larger than any female. They deferred to him in a matter of almost neglect. His presence was felt but not openly acknowledged. He lay with his enormous front paws crossed and seemed permanently sedentary. In an instant he leaped into the air and with a roar, gathered a male club within its powerful jaws, and killed it. This ritual would play itself out over many days until all the newborn offspring of lesser dominant males were dead. The party was witness to one of many brutal killings. Ashley was stunned to see the male devour the cub.

He shouted at Nelson, "You have a gun -- shoot him."

Nelson had a single shot 50 millimeter rifle.

Ashley yelled, "Kill him, kill him, stop him, Nelson! Don't let him kill the cub! Don't let him!"

Martin grabbed Ashley and held his hand over his mouth to silence him.

Very coldly Nelson looked at Ashley and said, "It is nature's way. New dominant males must kill the little ones, for they have the genes of the weaker fallen males, and the cubs must die. This is how the species stays strong; the weak traits cannot be passed on. To survive, the lion must pass on only the strengths of the dominant lion. To interfere would go against the most important law of nature: survival. No man can interrupt nature's ways. We must remain motionless as nature does its work. You must understand, we don't meddle in nature for we don't know of its great plans."

The boys, especially Ashley, could no longer bear to stay amidst this cruelty and asked if they could leave. David motioned to Nelson that they were ready to go. Not much was said in the camp that night of the cruelty that was witnessed.

Hunter said, "I've learned more about evolution than about the animals."

He said, "Isn't it strange that we have been here in Kenya with the animals longer than Darwin was in the Galapagos? He was there only two weeks and we have been here longer. Man, I feel like I've learned more than he did."

But the main conversation of the night focused on something that Ashley said. He mentioned *those people* with nothing behind their eyes. Martin chimed in with his misgivings about *those people*. David listened intently following Diana's adage, "If you can feel it, it is larger than you think. Follow your intuition." He would think about *those people* often and consider their importance. What were his thoughts of *those people*? He hadn't yet fully developed an understanding of them, so why was it such a nagging issue? The night pressed on and they discussed many matters of insignificance, but no one wanted to go to bed. The night was passing too quickly for the boys, David, and Martin. They feared it might never be replayed.

"Guys," David said, "We have to call it quits. Tomorrow we must to go back to Nairobi and get on the train to Mombassa. Oh, yeah, I have a great surprise for you. One day in Mombassa and then we fly to Cairo."

Hunter looked at David and asked, "Cairo?"

"Yeah, Cairo. Mom is going to meet us there," David said with a smile on his face, "yeah Egypt; it is a country she can visit."

The boys would get used to David's and Diana's past. Their history would be the directive for the family's future. The stars twinkled the completion of a wonderful trip. The boy's first adventure with their dad would be everlasting. Tomorrow Mombassa, the next day Cairo.

Fifteen

David said goodbye to his old friend Martin at the Kenyan Railway Service Station in the heart of Nairobi. "Words are always hard upon departing, my old friend and brother. It was important that the boys be in your company, for they will always be touched by your presence. They will transit to Nairobi to further our work on many future occasions. We are no longer in the money business, but we have much to do both socially and politically. They will see you before I can come back. I know you will take care of my boys."

Martin, for his part, could only say, "Asante," and give David a big hug. In his heart he had feelings to convey, but only a few words would come out; this was the Kenyan way.

The boys were sad to say goodbye. Their lives had been changed in Kenya, and Martin was an accompaniment to their transformation. He was family; they would return. "Asante, Hunter. Asante, Ashley. You are my responsibility now for you will always be in my heart. Time will pass slowly until you return."

David, Hunter, and Ashley boarded the blue and red train cars for the 13 hour trip to Mombassa. They would be in luxury, viewing the wildlife as they cruised through Kenya. Even though they were in sleepers aboard the first-class cars, the boys stayed awake looking for the legendary ghost of the black, maned lion that killed nine workers during construction of the 743 km railway. His presence haunted the car where they rode. They were riding in the original car retrofitted in the line's modernization in the late 1990's. The ghost lion was still felt, especially late in the afternoon or at night when it was on the prowl. It had maimed and killed a worker in this very car.

The trip was beautiful. At 2:30 p.m. they arrived in Mombassa, a city of two lives, one African and the other Arabic and Indian. Very few Europeans lived in Mombassa but their colonial power was omnipresent. The close quarters of Old Portuguese Town and Fort Jesus protected the old 16th-century city. A Hindu temple functioned as one that signified diversity and peoples of different cultures. African workers sitting on chairs, selling their handicraft wares on sidewalks next to artisans sewing clothing made by antiquated and vintage sewing machines, was totally different than being in Nairobi. The boys were more comfortable and could actually feel the pleasures of being tourists. They did not feel the presence of *those people*.

Hunter said, "Ashley, I read about a jewelry district in the old marketplace selling great stuff. I'll ask Dad if we can go there and bargain. Let's surprise Mom, let's get her something. Dad, do you mind if we go to the Bombolulu District and find something for Mom?"

David was impressed by the research the boys had done. He had only heard of the district in passing; not really a tourist trap.

He replied, "Sure let's go. We'll do whatever you boys want; this is your part of the trip. But bargaining is more difficult than you think. I'll keep out of it. It should be fun."

David knew the pain the boys would face dealing with the merchants. The jewelry hawkers did it for a living. They were in the marketplace sometimes sixteen hours a day, seven days a week, and the boys would be here once and never return. Money meant less to Hunter and Ashley than it did to the hawkers. A few schillings were enough to do verbal combat. In hard times, or times of high emotions or drink, bargaining could lead to physical confrontation or violence. The air in the marketplace was thick with intimidation. The boys were at a total disadvantage in negotiations. After a few failed attempts at negotiation, the boys were better with the acrimonious arbitrage that led to a deal. The neophytes held their own; as if anyone can match wits and energy with an Arab trader.

"Hunter, what do you think? Think we got a good deal?"

"Ashley, just don't ask the price if we see another necklace. We got this one for Mom, which is good enough for me. I don't want to know if we got a good deal. I just want to get out of here. That was too much work. He took ten years off my young life."

David did not say a word; he surmised that the necklace was probably produced in China. It didn't look like an Arabic masterpiece to him. After four hours of shopping and sightseeing, they made it to the Coral Beach Hotel 35 km from the city center and rested on the white sand beaches overlooking the Indian Ocean. They would leave from the Mori International Airport the next day to see Cairo, and of course,   Diana.

Sixteen

Flights from Mombassa to Cairo were segmented. The first leg was on Air Kenya, a small, crowded and smelly Boeing 727. The Russell party, as was the case with all passengers, was seated in coach. Domestic flights had neither business nor first-class seating. All three Russell's were oversized for the scrimpy seats. Leg room was nonexistent. The one hour and 20 minute flight back to Nairobi seemed like an eternity.

Ashley looked at David and said, "You know I don't complain much, but that flight was terrible. I am not as big as you and Hunter. I am only six one and you guys are six four, so I can't imagine what it was like for you."

The respite in the Nairobi airport and subsequent placement in the British Airways lounge was greatly appreciated. "Dad, even though we have to sit around here for three hours, after that flight, it's fine with me."

Sitting in the lounge, Hunter started to peruse a Fodor's travel book on Egypt that he picked up walking from the jet way to the lounge. It was interesting to him that all airports, no matter where they were or what their size, had some retail shopping.

"Hey Ash, when I got the book I forgot to ask if you wanted anything. I'll go back if you want. Is there anything you want?"

"No, it's all right. There are some magazines and newspapers here in the lounge, and the flight is only five hours. I have my iPod, so I'll use that, everything is okay."

Hunter had always dreamt of Egypt. Maybe it was the Indiana Jones character or the Nicolas Cage character in the National Treasure series, but he felt being a gentleman archaeologist would fit well into his self-image. He identified with Egyptology and he had read voraciously about Egypt.

He said, "Dad, I can't wait. I can't believe we're going to arrive in Cairo in six or seven hours."

David looked at Hunter smiled and said, "Yeah, Cairo is great but I'd rather see your mom. I've seen Egypt... You know I have traveled there on business. Like I said, I'd rather see your mom." He smiled.

Kind of romantic for an old guy, Hunter thought. He flashed back to trekking in Kenya and hoped he would age like his father, still physically imposing, still in great shape. Hunter smiled inwardly and said to himself, "And he still has all his hair."

Ashley said, "I love Mom too, but you're joking, aren't you Dad, about Mom over Cairo? It's going to be so cool there."

They smiled knowing they would be seeing Diana and Egypt very soon. The family would be together, and it would be wonderful. The sites, the pyramids, the Sphinx and the city were beckoning. All they had to do was endure the five-hour trip to Cairo. That would be easy. The Russell's as per usual were flying business class aboard the British Air BB 380. The luxurious accommodations made time pass quickly. They arrived refreshed and eager to get to the hotel and see the ancient city. Diana was waiting for them at the airport. She had porters attending their disembarking the plane. A little money and a few sky caps made all the difference in getting through baggage claims and customs in a smooth expeditious manner.

Walking off the plane, they saw an Egyptian man holding a sign with their name on it. He walked up to the party and said, "I'm Hosni. Your wife, Mrs. Diana, employed my services. Please give me your tickets and passports. I will go through customs with you but first, I must buy visa stamps."

David reached for money in his pocket even though they were American dollars. Hosni held up his hand to stop David and said, "Mrs. Diana gave me money; there's no need for you to give me anything."

He walked to the visa line and placed his large frame in front of 30 or 40 people who had been there for a protracted amount of time. No one uttered an audible word of displeasure for his size rendered him someone of importance. In a matter of two to three minutes he waved for the Russell party. They followed him through the side exit customs line and had a customs officer come from his work station to stamp their passports. The rest of the flight's passengers watched, knowing clearing customs would take them at least one more hour. By the time they passed through the airport exit doors, the bags were already taken from the carousel to a waiting SUV. Diana was standing next to the Toyota land cruiser, plane to SUV in less than 15 minutes.

"Hosni," Diana said, "Thank you," and handed him a bundle of Egyptian pounds. The currency was small and looked like Monopoly money. It had an exchange rate of approximately 6 Egyptian pounds to one US dollar. It looked like a lot of money to Ashley and Hunter. They conjectured that she must have paid a fortune for them to be picked up and taken through customs and circumventing security. If their mom could do it, why couldn't the other terrorists? David embraced Diana. It had been a long but a good three weeks. He was proud. The boys, had seen a many things, and were better for it. Ashley and Hunter were growing up before his eyes.

She looked at the boys and said, "You know I spoke with your dad and I owe you an explanation. It would be great if you were as easy on me as you were on him." Her guilt about her past was heavy upon her heart. Events in Kenya were her life's defining moments.

Ashley hugged his mom and said, "Did dad tell you what it cost him? We figure we can think of something you can give us. You know, how about a new car or something to ease our pain and suffering."

Hunter looked at his mother and said, "You owe Ash and me a lot, this is big time," and then they all laughed. They would talk later. She wanted to hear about *those people*.

The SUV entered the freeway from an airport exit artery after being cleared at the military guard post next to the terminal. Traveling for the first twenty minutes into Cairo on the uncrowded freeway seemed a lot like Los Angeles late at night: easy travel. When the freeway merged into Srharia Salah Salem, the notion of overwhelming traffic became a reality. Cars traversed from left to right with drivers' hands on horns and feet off the brakes. It was unimaginable. Hawkers were selling water, flowers and artifacts, everything a person could carry. They were running between cars with reckless abandon trying to sell their wares. Frequent stops and starts amidst a snail speed of three to five miles per hour was the fate of all motorists in city central. The SUV pressed towards the Cairo Marriott Hotel on the bank of the River Nile.

The boys were transfixed with sights on the road -- the many military complexes, the red granite Barons Palace, tall apartments, beige and brown finished complexes, the Heliopolis district where large silk flags draped retail shops, as people were seemingly walking from one shop to another. It was hectic and crowded.

"Hunter," Ashley said, as he pointed to the train station with queues forming for blocks, "I can't believe all the people waiting for trains."

They were driving on a thoroughfare maybe 30 to 50 feet above the surface streets. The train station was below, and thousands of people were milling around. They passed the Cairo Museum; the Nile River came into view. It was covered by cement walls making it look like a flood channel a half-mile wide. It didn't look like a river. On its banks were large hotels and in its waters were barges turned into restaurants.

Diana pointed across the river and said, "Well, gang, that's the hotel over there."

The pink colored Marriott Hotel was no more than three quarters of a mile away, but with Cairo traffic it would take 20 minutes or more. The heavily traveled frontage roads that followed the Nile brought the SUV to an alleyway leading up to the hotel. They drove up to a swinging gate with multiple guards carrying automatic weapons. Two guards flanked the vehicle while a third checked the undercarriage with a large mirror affixed to a pole. The driver's papers were checked; they were granted entrance to the hotel grounds.

"David, the security is impressive. I believe it's like this at all the major hotels."

She pointed to two Hilton Hotels and the Intercontinental Hotel to their right. It was at the Intercontinental that the Moslem Brotherhood had taken responsibility for the bombing that killed three tourists in 2000.

David stressed that Cairo could be a dangerous place. "You must be mindful of strange or out of place events," he said to the boys.

Diana said, "We will have bodyguards with us at all times. Your dad is right, Egypt is dangerous, but we will be safe. Still, you guys be aware of everything. If something feels funny, tell them immediately. Our bodyguards are actually our drivers."

Kamel and Tereak were sitting in the front seat and turned around and smiled.

She continued, "They speak good English, both have degrees in Egyptology at Cairo University, but more importantly they are both professional security agents."

Kamel looked at Ashley and Hunter and said, "You will be safe. We will not be a bother to you, but we will always be close by."

The Russell family exited the SUV and walked along the hotel foyer up to its large beveled glass, front doors. The doors opened to airport type metal detectors. The boys were taken aback by all the security. They went through the x-ray machines into the lobby. The hotel was magnificently appointed with large paintings, baroque interior and winding staircases.

This part of the hotel had previously been a palace Napoleon Bonaparte had built for his wife, Josefina, in 1803.

David was anxious to see his old friend and business partner, Sharif Abass. Sharif was waiting in the lobby reception area. David extended his hand, hugged Sharif, and gave him the customary cheek to cheek kiss.

"Sharif, you have done well, my old friend. The hotel looks magnificent. I know it is rated in the top 20 best in the world and deservedly so. It is magnificently beautiful."

The boys listened intently, for every day something new was divulged about their father. They would find the LLC who owned the hotel, being managed by the Marriott Corporation, was set up by their father. He had a percentage of the hotel as did Sharif.

Sharif looked at the Russell family and said, "This is Yusuf. He will be your concierge. The rooms are ready, of course. I will see you after you have refreshed and rested."

David told the boys, "Yusuf will take you to your suites. We will see you for breakfast around 10:00 A.M."

"David," Diana said, "let them have some fun; they're safe. Let's tell Yusuf to set up a club for them tonight. They can have Kamel and Tareak drive them to one of the clubs on the river."

David looked at Yusuf and got an answering nod before saying, "You can entertain yourselves tonight. Kamel and Tareak will guide you and will always be in the background wherever you want to go."

Their sons would have an enjoyable night.

Seventeen

Yusuf said to Hunter and Ashley, "When you are ready for the occasion, that is, going to a club, I will chaperone you." He made it clear that nightlife in Cairo was late. Clubs were not popular before 12 a.m.

"Mr. Russell if I might call you that," said Yusuf, "I will meet you and your brother in the lobby next to the small bar at your convenience. What time should I expect you?"

Hunter said he would coordinate with Ashley, but maybe 12:30 a.m. "Yusuf, can you suggest any restaurants in the hotel or close by? Also, what do we wear to the club?"

"Mr. Russell, you may wear anything you would like. Most people are coming from work or dinner before going to the club. They may wear suits, some may even wear jeans. Anything is fine, you will fit in. It is a very nice club, very exclusive. It's close to the hotel."

"Thank you, Yusuf. See you at 12:30. But you don't have to chaperone us, we will be okay."

"Mr. Russell, I will escort you and Mr. Ashley, but just to the club. Don't worry, I will not bother you. I will depart once you are seated and attended to. You will be with Kamel and Tareak; they will drive us and wait for you to leave the club."

"Yusuf, what if we want to stay out for a long time or go some other place? I would feel strange having them wait for us."

"Mr. Russell, I strongly suggest, for your first night in Cairo venture no further than the club. Kamel and Tareak will be with you but stationed outside for as long as you wish. They will accommodate you. Don't worry. They are lucky to work for the Russell family. As for dinner, I suggest eating here at the hotel, either on the patio or by the pool. They both have excellent messa, even good American food."

The boys cleaned up and ate at one of the many poolside restaurants in the warm Egyptian night. The garden and pool area of the hotel was beautiful. Their table was perfect for people watching. The sounds of popular Arabic music were light in the background; it was a mix of Arabic and rock. They sat at a table overlooking one of the many manicured gardens and had what was called an American hamburger. It was actually quite good.

"Hunter, let's go up and get ready, I can't imagine going to a club here in Cairo. I'm sure it will be like any club in West LA or Hollywood, we'll see."

Hunter thought for a moment and said, "How would you know, Ash?"

Ashley looked back and said, "John and Hawk and I go to clubs all the time. Listen, Dog, it's going to be great." His face had a grin of anticipation. "I kind of like ethnic women; don't imagine many blondes are going to be there tonight. Just trust me."

Hunter shook his head. "Ashley you're out of your mind, I guess there is a lot to learn about my little brother.

He shot back, "you got no idea." Ashley said, "Just follow me. I'm good at this stuff."

Ashley, younger of the two boys, was much more social than his older brother. His easy-going demeanor and feeling of entitlement, because of his parent's wealth, pushed him a little to the far side of young adulthood. He, as his friends often said, partied too much and unbeknownst to his older brother did recreational drugs and sometimes binge drank.

He came off as a perfect kid, maybe a little precocious to some people, but his rebellious nature tested the Russell family image of proper and genteel behavior. He was respectful and well spoken with adults, which masked his rebelliousness.

At 12:30, the two brothers were wearing jeans and shirts outside, not tucked in. They were ready to go. They took the elevator from the 12th floor to the lobby, where Yusuf waited for them. He handed each boy an American Express card which had their own name on it.

"Mr. Ashley this one is for you. Mr. Hunter this one is for you. Thank your parents."

Hunter was aware at home you could not get an American Express card, let alone a platinum one, until you were 25 years old. How had Mom and Dad pulled this off for Ashley?

Ashley said, "Hunter, if Mom and Dad trusted us, they would have given us a black American Express card."

Hunter had never heard of a black card, he didn't think he wanted to know. "Ashley, how do you come up with all the stuff? There is a side to you, I sure don't know anything about."

They proceeded to the SUV waiting in front of the hotel. It was parked on a long driveway leading to the street. Tareak was driving, and Kamel opened the doors.

He said, "We will be at the club shortly, it's only a few minutes from here. Later, if you want to walk back, you can do so. We will follow. It's up to you."

They parked in front of a dark blue barge. It had been used for tourism on the Nile. The old barge/ship had been retrofitted into a restaurant and club. The "Moonlight" was one of six barges permanently moored on the bank. A long gangplank led to the 300 foot nautical structure. It was a permanent fixture on the river and of contemporary architecture. They saw a line of people winding up the spiral staircase to a second level entrance.

Yusuf said, "Follow me."

At the ropes holding back the crowds at the front door, he pulled out some money and gave it to one of the bouncers. They were whisked inside.

Yusuf said over the extremely loud music, "I'm leaving now and when you leave the club, the body guard will be waiting. He will find you."

He was not wrong. Hunter looked down and saw Kamal standing near the entrance/exit of the club. A strategically placed table was reserved for the boys, and as they were seated, a waitress asked for a credit card. The night was beginning.

The noise was loud and the smoke so thick it insulted their senses. The gray haze smoke in the club was so heavy the brightly lit banks of the Nile view were muted. It was as if they were looking out a dirty car's front window.

The club was a solarium of sorts. All glass walls and a glass ceiling. It reverberated with sounds of American rock music. Wall-to-wall people made the decibel level similar to thunderous applause at a sporting event. It was almost deafening.

Hunter shouted to Ashley, "Can you believe this place? I can't imagine any place in L.A. being better than this."

Ashley yelled back, "It can't be if we don't meet up with some outrageous babes."

All the women were in designer clothes from the most prestigious houses in Europe, they were bejeweled. All the men had on the finest watches. A Paneri or a Rolex would be out of place; they would look common. The club was European with Semitic looking people. They could not have imagined a club of such opulence being in Cairo. Ashley was in his element. Hunter was uncomfortable.

Ashley said, "Hunter, stay here and guard the drinks; I'll get us some dates."

"Yeah, sure," Hunter shouted.

Ashley had already picked out two beautiful Egyptian women sitting at the bar. He walked up to them and introduced himself and asked, "Would you ladies share our table?"

"Hunter, this is the Imam and Sabah."

Hunter said, "Hello."

He felt a little uncouth because he had to yell over the noise of the club. He became stressfully warm in the proximity of such beautiful women. He could not tell their ages, but he thought they might be in college.

Imam said, "We always wanted to see who uses the owners table, but you are so young it must be your families." She laughed, "You must be absentee owners." The girls were American in all their mannerisms.

Ashley asked how they spoke English so well. Sabah told him they were sisters and both had attended the American University in Cairo, and because of educational reciprocity, after their first year, they both transferred to NYU. Imam was a graduate student in mechanical engineering and Sabah was a senior majoring in finance. They were one year apart in age and schooling. Their beauty had no separation, both sisters were lovely. It was hard to hold a conversation because of the loud music and the oppressive heat in the club. The dance floor was small, and the drinks were strong, so Hunter suggested the four should step outside and get some fresh air.

They gathered on a patio outside the glass walls constituting the club. It was still loud but they could converse more comfortably. Hunter paired with Imam, as they were both of a technical mindset. They were at ease with each other and did not have the club mentality. Imam told Hunter she was relieved when he suggested they come outside.

"I am here because of Sabah. She loves clubs and all the noise and music. But she is too much for me sometimes; she is pretty wild, especially at a club."

Hunter said, "Yeah, my brother says he loves being in clubs and I can't stand them really. I guess you and I feel the same way. It's a little too much in there. It is very unnatural for me, it's too loud and when I yell, it makes my voice scratchy. I don't drink that much. It's good that you feel the same way; now I don't feel so out of place."

Ashley and Sabah were back in the club, dancing on the floor that appeared to be 4 meters by 4 meters with 20 other couples. It was 3:30 a.m. Imam and Hunter were tired, not of each other, but of the club scene. They felt awkward wanting to leave, but they had had it. Imam went to Sabah and said she wanted to go. It was uncomfortable because the Sabahs and the Ashley's of the world never wanted to go. Ashley did not know the convention of saying goodnight to Sabah and longed to kiss her. He tried, to restrain himself but he could not. Standing outside the club next to their respective siblings he just grabbed her and kissed her deep and hard on the mouth. She was receptive in an unexpected positive way. Ashley and Sabah would meet the next day. Not knowing Ashley's mindset Hunter had already asked Imam if she would share his company again. She gladly said. They would be together again. Simultaneously, the brothers made dates for the next day without the thought of David and Diana. The boys walked the sisters downstairs to the sidewalk stretched before the barge and suggested they should take them home knowing that Kamel and Tareak were at their disposal. Imam thanked them, but her family's bodyguards were instructed to take the sisters home; no one else.

Sabah looked at Ashley and said, "Dad is very protective but when he meets you, he will like you. Tomorrow we will take a tour of Cairo."

"We look forward to seeing you again," said Hunter.

The boys escorted the girls to their car and helped them inside.

They looked for their car and saw it nearby. Ashley said, "What are we going to tell Mom and Dad at breakfast? I hope we eat late; it will give us more time to figure out what to say."

Eighteen

Sharif had made dinner reservations for David and Diana at the Fish Market restaurant, a boat docked in front of the Marriot Hotel while the boys were at the nightclub. The balmy night made the short walk pleasant, especially for David after his long trip. Sharif was astounded by the maturity of the two boys. They are not the little king's common in Egyptian families. He thought Diana did a magnificent job in sheltering them from the curse of a parent's money and influence.

They quickly approached the restaurant; it was a five minute walk from the hotel. The Fish Market was like the many fine eateries along the Nile. Its menu was extensive, with both Egyptian and European fare. Sharif had already ordered dinner when he took it upon himself to make the reservations.

"David," he said, smiling, "I took the liberty of ordering."

They both laughed because David did the same thing when Sharif came to Los Angeles, and they went to the trendy Westside restaurant, Koi. Sharif ordered mezzes, the traditional small portions of Egyptian dishes. They were brought to the table. Aish, a flat bread, hummus, chickpeas, emulsified Koshari, a dish of potatoes, rice, lentils, and tomatoes, stuffed grape leaves, babaghanoush, grilled eggplant with almond paste; it was endless. These appetizers were a pre-curser for grilled meats -- shish kebabs of lamb, beef, and chicken. And finally, desserts and fruits were served. Dinner took almost two hours to complete.

After eating a meal appropriate for royalty, they sat atop the restaurant with its magnificent view of the Nile. Being with a dear friend and business associates was, as Diana said, simply the best. The three old friends would have a single drink of Egyptian wine. Business was to be discussed even if they were on their first night of companionship in Cairo.

Diana was resourceful in David's business and political decisions. She was not involved in number-crunching or financials. Diana was a very conflicted person. Her impetuous decision making and lack of discipline in the early revolution years led up to her murder conviction in absentia. It caused her lasting guilt and emotional trauma and made social investments of the Russell's assets an imperative. It was a way of cleansing her soul. She helped direct projects of social and political significance from earnings of their numerous investments. She set up offshore account models to surreptitiously transfer their money into worthy causes. These models involved charitable contributions, foundations, fronts or dummy corporations, any means to funnel funds to fight the oppression of dictatorial rule in countries throughout the world. The tools of her trade were money laundering, lines of credit, safe havens allowing for liquidity, such as bearer bonds or transnational stocks. These models were used in Russell's complex investment strategy.

The problem to be discussed with Sharif was the same one they had faced with William in Kenya: transparency. It was to be imposed by U.S. government regulation on hedge funds because of the sub prime loan crisis, and it would open them to public scrutiny. They would be major targets under the Patriot Act and must divest now before they were in harm's way.

David said, "Sharif, I have laid out our intentions. I have dissolved our financial relationships and have provided a new structure of legal entities for which you will be solely responsible. Sharif Abbas and Associates, LLC will be your financial umbrella. It will consist of multilevel partnerships as well as some larger limited liability corporations to minimize your taxes. It would be in the form of a trust set up in the United States. No one will suspect onshore duplicity. The FBI and Treasury Department financial scrutiny and oversight are considered monumental stopgaps to financing illegal activities. To be based in the U.S. is logical and safer. In reality, there will be more danger in offshore accounts or even Swiss accounts. We will enter the front door, my old friend. The back door is a vestige of the past."

Sharif was in total concurrence. The plan seemed masterful. "David, I know you have passed these ideas by legal and accounting eyes. As always, I am confident in your judgment. But I have also made some changes. The monies we, may I say, you, have made that forged our financial strength, are being redirected. Our autonomy from the fund that supported arms sales with Agnon Kasogi and high stakes lending with the BCI Bank of Saudi Arabia have changed to oil, gold, silver, and real estate purchases in the United States because of the devaluation of the dollar. We are in many partnerships with Dubai that are totally legal and above board. Money is easy to make with the weak dollar. We have a 30% advantage, but we still use Diana's organizations to expedite our missions."

He turned to Diana. "Diana, do you see danger in this transparency and deregulation if we stand firm and make no changes? We feel safe in our legitimate business practices. We make our contributions to humanitarian organizations and foresee little change as far as oversight is concerned. Am I a fool? Are my ways old and ripe for exposure and eminent danger?"

Diana was thoughtful in response. She was impetuous in social terms, but when it came to business, she was measured and concise.

"Sharif, if I may speak off the top of my head..." This actually was not the case. "I'll do what I always do when our conversations are of such importance. I'll be frank; I think there must be some refinement of our business and charitable practices, but to have wholesale changes or move large sums of money would assuredly be noticed. The electronic surveillance of financial transactions would show too many anomalies if we switched our way. Moving cash is and will always be easy, but in the long run; it would be of little significance if we can't transfer large financial bundles of instruments to organizations of our choosing. We must make some systemic changes. In the new post Patriot Act world, we could potentially come into the light. It could be dangerous. I will think upon this. It could be a concern and we must attend to it."

David interjected, "we should speak further, and I want the boys to be privy to all discussions. Hunter has worked in Russell, LLC as a financial analyst and we feel it's time Ashley gets his hands into these family affairs."

"We have spent enough time on business. May I suggest we get some cigars and toast our good fortune?"

Diana expressed that she looked upon their friendship with pride and love. "We are truly fortunate." She held up her glass. "David, Sharif, it's time for that cigar and a drink."

David could not help himself. He motioned to the waiter and said, "She will have a cosmopolitan, Grey Goose, please not too dark. And we will have," pointing to himself and Sharif, "two McCallums, straight up."

Things never change. He had a need to be in control, and Sharif just shook his head at his old friend in a gesture of acceptance. Anything different would be disconcerting. He felt protected by David's control and strength and by Diana's vision and organization. Let the night begin.

Conversation would proceed from Hunter's surprise at his father's love of Egypt even though his father knew his son's favorite movies were *The Mummy* and *Return of the Mummy*.

Diana was amazed that such a brilliant person as David was child inept. The Indiana Jones character and the Agatha Christie book, *Death on the Nile* were so important to Hunter, but were lost on David.

They talked about Sharif's wife and three children, and how lucky he was, and that they should spend the day with them in Alexandria.

And, of course, they talked about politics. Sharif discussed the Moslem brotherhood and terrorism. He held very interesting and insightful views. As always, he was emotional and heartfelt. The Brotherhood was responsible for the assassination of Nassar and Sadat. They were the masterminds of the mass murders of German tourists at Queen Hachasoup's Temple in the Valley of the Dead.

"They hatched 9/11 upon you and horrible crimes against our people, but they are very much like us. They are driven by belief. So are we. I think it's much like the old Communists before, an intelligentsia of well-educated and semi-wealthy people led the blind masses. In this case, it is self-righteous Mullahs. They found a way to personalize their power and belongings and holdings. Through the Koran and Sharia Law, they have manipulated the non-integrated followers."

Diana asked, "What do you mean by 'non-integrated?'"

Sharif responded, "In the Arab world, there are many people who have nothing but Allah. They have no material belongings, they are not skilled, their lives are uncertain, and religion is their only possession. They are non-integrated. Islam has no centralization. The laws of each region or village are determined by religious men who have their own agenda. The Wahhabi teachings of fundamental Islam and its perversions present the world as Muslims versus the Crusaders. These people are xenophobic by design to give themselves more personal power. Some are sincere and strictly believe that their understanding of the Koran is honest and true. There are others with designs on power. Their followers have nothing to lose but much to gain doing God's work. They have a simple choice based on a non-integrated life, and they have personal integrity. The cause is important. Their zealotry is logical and sometimes predictable. Sacrifice to a higher calling, especially God's work, is intuitively appealing. We, on the other hand, are integrated. I myself am a businessman, a man with a cause, a player of reputation as a gambler, a father, a scholar. I could go on and on."

David looked at Sharif and smiled. "I thought that fanaticism was purely a form of religious indoctrination fostered by propaganda, but your idea of integration gives me a different understanding."

"David, I have thought about this and crystallized it down to non-integrated people. Not so much disenfranchisement, but they are people of limited experience and no worldly possessions. They are rational, and we might be the same, but for the grace of Allah. They are like us. We would be zealots if we were in their position. They must be terrorists if life is presented to them in Wahhabi terms. It is honorable. It is logical and gives people a chance to advance something bigger than themselves. There are people who have a cause, no matter how misguided they are. They are malleable from birth, and they have only religion. They are presented a path to heaven, and terrorists are created. They are responsible for what they do. They are reprehensible in our minds, but they believe they are performing the most noble of causes. It is clear that the lamb is taken to the slaughter and that these lambs praise their own death."

David brought up the observation of those other people that his sons and Martin had discussed, as if they were one and the same as the potential terrorist. Sharif had a similar recognition of *those people* but never put it into words or cognitive thoughts, just a gut feeling. He said that there were different people, different than people of causes, for they were detached from recognition of something bigger than themselves. They were like dogs looking into a mirror, no recognition of self. These people were a lesser people that Sharif feared personally because they made him feel uneasy. They were social animals, psychopaths. Law and order was important for protection from their aberrant behavior, but there was no understanding of why they were different.

The rest of the night turned to music and drink. They would venture back to the hotel around 4:00 a.m.

David said, "Diana, let's leave a message for the boys that we will have a late breakfast. Maybe we will let our family Egyptologist, Hunter, have a day. We will leave a message for Yusuf to set up something special. It would be nice if Ashley would tag along. We'll see them at breakfast and get it sorted out."

Nineteen

Diana called each of her sons at 9 a.m., leaving the same message. They were asked to meet in a retail mall coffee shop on the lobby floor at 10:30. The late evening dinner and drinks had put her and David off schedule; they needed to regroup. A leisurely small breakfast of tea and fruit would be sufficient. Hunter and Ashley, after showering to clean the stench of smoke from the nightclub off their bodies, were both on time to meet their parents. Six hours sleep was not enough, but they must put on a good face because grouchiness and ill-manners from sombolescence deficits were not tolerated in the Russell family.

"Hunter," Diana asked, "did you get my message about today? Yusuf can set up a day of sightseeing per your own itinerary. I know how much Egypt means to you. Ashley, if he wants, can go along with you if it's all right. Ash, you can be with us, but as of right now we are going to a meeting with Sharif to discuss business. Or you can go with your brother."

Hunter, with a sense of relief in his voice, said, "I didn't sleep much last night, trying to figure out a way of asking if we could be alone today. This is great."

David said, "There has to be more to it. What's up, guys? Why do you want the day off?"

Ashley blurted out, "We met some real nice girls last night, and we want to see them again. They're going to show us around Cairo."

David and Diana looked at each other. The boys had grown up. Hunter with a girl was a surprise, but this was par for Ashley.

David said, "Look guys, Cairo can be dangerous, so Kamel and Tareak will be with you. Who are these girls?"

"Dad, they're sisters. You won't believe this, but they both go to NYU. They are outrageous."

David said," I know you're not going to like this, but what is their last name, if you even know it?"

They said it was Al Nassar, Imam and Sabah Al Nassar.

"Well, I am going to call Sharif and have him ask around so we know what we're dealing with, just a precaution."

While the family was sitting in the coffee shop, Sharif responded to David's request.

"David, you won't believe this. The girls are part of the Al Nassar clan. It is not only okay, but the boys are lucky. I am told of their beauty and that they are well respected. The Al Nassars are one of Egypt's great families. We even do business with them. The boys will probably meet the father; he will scare the hell out of them. But he is honorable. Shall I tell him who the boys are, or should he find out for himself? I will call you later today."

David replied, "Don't say a word; the boys are on their own."

Sharif said, "David, by the way, he will be at our meeting tomorrow. He is one of our investors."

David passed along most of Sharif's observations. "Sharif said everything is copasetic." David looked up and said, "Those aren't his words, but everything is fine, just a couple of things. One, their family, should I say the Al Nassars, are powerful, and we do business with them. Two, do not discuss our business relations with him if you meet him, or with the girls. You don't really know what we do. As for tomorrow, we will meet with some business associates, and that means you will be with us. Tomorrow's a working day, so if you're lucky and want to see the girls again, it will not be tomorrow. You're booked the full day at least until 12 a.m. If you want to see them again, it will have to be a late night arrangement. We do not work the following day, so you can get up late." David looked at the boys and said, "Guys, have a great morning. I'm going back upstairs."

Diana mumbled to herself, "Just unbelievable, the kids are grown up."

A large black Mercedes 600 pulled up to the front of the hotel. The boys were waiting for Imam and Sabah, who were late. It did not seem like they would be the kind of people who were predictably unpunctual to have leverage over others, or discourteous because of privilege. The angst of youth was apparent.

Hunter asked Ashley, "You think they got tied up in the horrible traffic? Imam sounded so excited about today."

Hunter said, "Ashley, maybe it's their way in the Middle East."

The door of the impeccably clean Mercedes opened, and a tall, dark, mustached Arab man of about 50 years came out.

With one stride, he greeted Hunter and Ashley and said, "I am Omar Al Nassar. It is customary that you follow my requests as they apply to my daughters." He rattled off dos and don'ts, and chaperones, and a plethora of places that were off-limits.

He motioned to the car and waved to an attendant, and the doors were opened. Imam came out first, and then Sabah. It was apparent where the girls got their beauty. They looked like their father. The three Al Nassars were a sight to behold.

Ashley said "Hello, Sabah. Hello, Imam."

Then looked at their father and said, "Mr. Nassar, it is a privilege to escort your daughters as he extended his hand. We will be respectful to the Nassar family, and of course, Imam and Sabah, but may I make a suggestion? You spoke of the chaperone for their safety; I must insist that Kamel and Tareak be part of our party of bodyguards, as they will surely guarantee the safety that your daughters so richly deserve."

He leaned toward a quiet, now docile father, and kissed him on each cheek. "Thank you for the opportunity to be with your daughters. They, of course, will be in good hands. It is our honor to be in their company, and we will provide them comfort and safety."

There was an easy silence. The crowded street below the hotel driveway stood still as if time was frozen, as Omar Al Nassar kissed his daughters and entered the back seat of the Mercedes.

Hunter looked at Ashley and stammered, "You amaze me. You're just like your mom. I can't believe how you handled that."

The SUV with Kamel and Tareak pulled up, and the two pairs of romantic adventurers, plus chaperone, were off to see Cairo. The first stop was less than 2 miles away: the Cairo Museum. Tareak spirited the vehicle as directed by the chaperone into the back of the immense structure where 10 parking stalls were squeezed into an area of 100 square meters. It was historic for anyone to park on the actual grounds of the museum. Tareak, a professional driver for more than 20 years with a client list ranging from Bill Clinton, Mikhail Gorbachev, and Steven Spielberg, had never parked in the museum. The idea of the power of the Russell and the Al Nassar families was staggering.

The director's office door was ajar, and they were motioned to come in. The director of antiquities for the Gaza Plateau would escort the party through the museum's exhibitions and later to the Pyramids and the Sphinx. The day would culminate with a felucca ride up the Nile at sunset. The evidence of two blossoming romances was a picture of two handsome couples holding hands and laughing with light hearts, as only youth could display. Imam, the most stoic of the girls, told Hunter they must be back to the hotel by 10:00 p.m. as was customary in the Al Nassar household.

Sabah, directing her comments to both Hunter and Ashley, said, "If we were with our girlfriends or cousins, we could go to a club and stay out all night, but on a formal date, it's always 10 o'clock. We must go back; Father will have a car waiting for our arrival."

"This has been a wonderful night, has it not?" asked Imam, as she looked at Hunter.

Ashley said, "It would be nice to see you tomorrow, but we have an engagement with our father and mother and some of their business associates. It cannot be broken, but we can meet all day Wednesday and go to Saqqara and the stepped pyramids if you like."

It was Sabah's idea to travel to Saqqara. Ashley stole it and presented it as his own. He had his mother's way of social orchestration, be a leader, present a plan. Imam expressed her desire to take them to the Khan al Khalil bazaar and the mosque of Mohammed Ali and some of the Coptic district. They said goodnight. It was as if they were little puritanical Mennonites on a first date, but it was alright. It was so pure, and innocent. The girls were special and this was Egypt. All the two couples did was kiss good bye, but the rage of hormones was over powering.

The boys felt lucky, and indeed, they were. They felt like destiny was waiting. It was too perfect, but being Russells they were accustomed to everything just seeming to fall into their laps.

Twenty

Hunter and Ashley entered the hotel lobby with what can only be called a hitch in their step. David, Diana, Sharif, and some associates who were dressed in Arab garb were sitting in a small bar next to the steps leading to Josefina's palace. Diana noticed the boys and excused herself. She intercepted them near the medley of elevators going to the towers housing the hotel suites.

"You look like you're floating on air and at such an early hour," she said. "Come over and meet some of our friends. Sharif is here."

"Mom," Hunter said, "We had an unbelievable time." And he recanted the day almost activity by activity, conversation by conversation. He was ecstatic. Ashley could not get a word in edgewise.

Diana knew that the introduction to their friends and associates was useless and said, "Dad and I want you to go to the shopping mall at the hotel pool level to purchase some clothes. I take it back. Stay here for a moment, and we will go to the mall together."

She went to the assembly of men sitting in the Baroque bar and excused herself, saying she had to attend to the boys for the rest of the evening. She took Hunter and Ashley directly to the new haberdashery shop in the lobby's retail mall for business suits fittings and accoutrements for the next day. She was assured the clothing would be ready for their scheduled business appointments by 1:00pm the next afternoon. Retail shops at major hotels in the Middle Eastern countries stay open until early morning; the Marriott Hotel was no different. Conversation during tailoring their clothes was singularly a rehashing of the boys' day with Imam and Sabah.

Ashley said, "It was weird. Mom, I felt we were on a play date. It was so pure, like we were at Disneyland for high school graduation. Let me take that back, intermediate school. I don't know what I expected, maybe sex or something," he laughed, "but it was different, it was real cool."

Hunter said, "You know, it was the bomb. Mom, it was awkward, something different, and just really innocent." He started laughing, "Whenever I talk about stuff like this to you, I get uncomfortable, as if you are going to pick on me. I'm not shy. I am a regular guy, kind of a stud. This was different, what a day, what a place. It's almost like we're living in another time, it was so cool."

"Okay guys, I will see you tomorrow," their mom said. "By the way, I've seen you guys act like juveniles before, but right now it's as if you had your first sexual experiences. You are both so smitten. Are you sure you're telling me everything? Wait till I talk to your dad. Maybe you guys should both have joined some little Christian right wing political organization to practice abstinence." She always picked on the boys.

"Mom, you always rag on us, usually we never say anything to you."

Diana said, "It will make you tough. Don't be wimps. See you tomorrow."

"Ashley, I couldn't help myself, sorry I said anything about our dates. I should have known. She always rags on us. Can you imagine what she was like when she was younger?"

Ashley's demeanor changed instantly. He said, "In the three weeks we've been here, we are finding out so much stuff about Mom and Dad, incredible stuff, unimaginable stuff, and we haven't really had to ask any questions. You think Mom is more than an outspoken jokester?"

"What an understatement she must have been out of control," said Hunter.

"Shit, more likely she must have been an international fugitive comedian." Ashley kept shaking his head.

"I know how accomplished she is, but she is so out there socially. Let's go upstairs I want to recapture my day." Hunter replied.

"I'll deal with Mom later. This has been a great day."

At breakfast the boys strategize their participation in the next day's meetings, held in the Hilton Ramses Hotel conference room. The Russell's, Sharif, and invited investors were seated at a long mahogany table. Most of the parties had done business before. The Russell group had forged together deals with Sharif acting as a conduit. The promotional fee of 20%, plus equal participation in profits as to their principal investment, was the template for all deals. Omar Al Nassar was taken aback by the sight of the two boys.

Upon his introduction he was mindful of their acquaintance the day before and how the advantage of age and self-assurance was taken from him. He tried to be of the mindset that "this was business and that was social," but their meeting had been painfully revisited once he saw Ashley. Few people ever made him feel uncomfortable, especially on his own turf. He held his hand out to Ashley and reintroduced himself to both young men. He then shook Hunter's hand and sat down.

David took the floor. His power point presentation on the Russell's' impending separation and transparency was well received. He passed along a reservation.

"My friends," he said, "social unrest in Egypt has caused you to hedge your investments and take much of your portfolios out of country. Is it the corrupt ways of Mubarak? Is it his son's ascent to power and asking for greater shares of every deal and having no skin on the table? Is it the Muslim Brotherhood or Al Qaeda? There is something that portends disaster for you in your minds. We feel the fundamentals are excellent here in Egypt. If you start to reinvest in social capital, there will be a reversal of fortunes. In the short run, we can change the tide of totalitarianism and stem the threat of fundamentalism. Our plan is to give concessions that are marginally cheap and reap profits and political stability. Higher wages, housing, subsidizing food are all compatible with our investment goals, if we look at middle and long run placement of assets."

"We suggest socially oriented programs tantamount to green investment. They will create social stability. The oligarchy, the four major families that control assets here in Egypt, will be hard pressed to maintain power unless there is redistribution of land, access to education and access to money for the masses. Up to this point, case has not been very different from our proposal. It is obligatory that we do something new. If there are no major structural changes in Egypt, it will lead to great social unrest and the eventual overthrow of the Mubarak click. We can forestall insurrection; we can stop the sectarian advances of the Brotherhood, if we create a vehicle for domestic investment. I know this is counterintuitive because you are housing funds abroad. But we feel it is your country and it would be better if you stay."

Omar Al Nassar stood up after the presentation and said, "May I speak? Mr. Russell, you have made our monies work in ways beyond our wildest expectations. We have acquired great wealth, each one at this table. I think I speak for all of us. It is our money at stake. We all have plans to flee Egypt at a moment's notice. We have guards for our wives and children. I think we know Egypt better than you."

Ashley uncontrollably levitated to an upright position and said, "Mr. Al Nassar, I speak as a young member of the Russell group."

David felt a sense of release, his compulsive desire for control in all business matters abated, and he relinquished authority to his son by a movement of his head. "May we please let Ashley speak for the Russell group?"

"Gentlemen, you have been presented with the financials and a powerful case for reintroduction of investment in Egypt. May I put a different, more human face on it? When there is corruption and the amassing of money into a few hands, we do not see all the disparate impacts, but we do see some of them. The underclass live in smaller quarters, their food is less, their lives shorter. We all know this, but their loss is apparently someone's gain. These opportunities have been usurped by Hamas and Hezbollah and Al Qaeda and the Brotherhood. They are all recipients of advantage from this poor distribution of wealth. Their forays into kidnapping, killing, bribery, and things unspoken give them ill gotten profits that are socially invested. If food prices go up, they pass out food to the needy. In Palestine, they control schools and hospitals. They pay salaries so families can afford the necessities of life. They are a government within a government. In Egypt, when you at this very table export or inventory grains to manipulate prices, it affects many people adversely, the Brotherhood benefits. They will steal power from you. You do not let them form political parties. You feel your secular profit seeking ways in jeopardy, so you plan to evacuate when the time comes. This is the same as the futures market, except your bets are selling short in a potentially long market. You want to do the opposite of what you should do. To keep Egypt and other Middle Eastern states viable politically and financially, our business' social investment plans must be implemented. You are old and my brother, Hunter, and I are young, we see that your business strategies will limit our future and make you flee as the vanquished do. What will be left of your Egypt, Mr. Al Nassar? The future is to stay, not to run."

It was an Ashley neither his brother nor parents had seen before. A mere twenty three but willful and more importantly he was correct. Diana and David both had flashes of Kenya. Their sons as David put it later were Russells.

Omar Al Nassar was stunned. He was not accustomed to being talked to in a condescending way. He felt personally attacked.

Before he could react, Diana interjected, "Youth has a way of personalizing things that are not meant to be, Mr. Al Nassar. His exuberance is just that. We at the Russell group would never offend, but we feel the truth must be conveyed in clear, direct terms."

Ashley lowered his head slightly and offered his sincere apologies, "Please excuse my exorbitant insolence, Mr. Al Nassar?"

Diana, taking the floor once again, said, "Our model shows it is to your advantage to have direct investment here in Egypt. ROI's that exist can provide margins which allow implementation of social investment. The fire is hot, we must strike now. It is personal Mr. Al Nassar, for we at Russell are devoted to and love Egypt and its people."

It was evident mother and son were of one mind. Like mother, like son.

Leaving the conference room, David put his arm around Hunter's shoulder and said, "I think you know most of the financials came from your work. Next time, speak up; they were your numbers. It would be good for us if you could moderate the next power point presentation.' David smiled, "Anyway, it makes it much easier for me. I felt like I was stealing when I was presenting the spread sheets. Hunter, this is your stuff, and you did a great job. Your brother! Wow, does that kid have a mouth? He is just like his mom. Their words cut like a knife. Just ask me how good I feel? You guys are great, thanks."

Twenty-one

"Ashley, I don't know how Mom and Dad do it," said Hunter. "I am wiped out from all those meetings. It's too intense for me. I was so caught up in the numbers and financial stuff and all the presentations. It was just too much to focus on. My brain is fried."

"Hunter, I feel the same way. I got carried away. I really fucked up. Al Nassar must want to fucking kill me. I hope Mom cooled him down. But his face did not show it. Do you think he will tell Sabah not to see me again? God, I hope not, Boy, did I act like an asshole?"

"What about me?" Hunter said. "We are in this together. Listen, I'm going up to my room. I'm done for the night -- long day. We are supposed to meet Mom and Dad at 10:30, and hopefully the girls at 2 p.m. Talk to you later."

The boys went to their separate suites, and opening their doors, both found gifts sitting on the coffee table in their living rooms overlooking the Nile River. Both sisters in collaboration had sent letters of thanks for the wonderful day and expressed their appreciation with gifts of a key of life necklace and an eighteen karat gold chain. Calls from both boys were the immediate response, and conversations went on late into the night with the girls.

Hunter and Ashley approached their parents at the coffee shop both wearing gold chains with the keys of life dangling outside their t-shirts. Nothing was said, but Diana had that look. It was a lot of pressure when she said nothing. She had that Cheshire cat look on her face.

"Hey, Ash, get up and get me an International Herald Tribune paper. You can buy one at the tobacco shop down by the end of the mall." David said, handing him a 20 pound note.

Ashley purchased the paper. His world almost stood on end. Its headlines, with pictures, said, "Migrants burned alive in South Africa. At least 22 burned in 10 days of anger towards foreigners in crowded shanty towns. Thousands have fled." The byline: Diepsloot South Africa. The front page was a picture with one of *those people* hovering over the burning body of a Zimbabwean immigrant. It was chilling; those eyes with nothing behind them, his face deeply etched with hatred and anger towards humanity.

Ashley gave the paper to David, and he proceeded to read it aloud to the family.

"South Africa awoke on Monday to the shocking front page images of a man in flames, one of several to be burned alive. Onlookers in the Reiger Park Township east of Johannesburg, laughed as the man rocked in agony. Neck lacing them with spare tires pinning their arms, gasoline was poured on and then lit and left burning for hours."

Diana said, "The existence of *those people* must be deeper than we know. If we can see it, smell it, or feel it, even in a subliminal way, it must be pervasive. Our social sense mutes our ability to comprehend things outside our comfort level. If things don't fit, like *those people*, we delude ourselves into thinking they are less threatening than they are. Or we demonize them like wild animals, thinking we are better than them, thinking we don't have to understand them, and thinking that we can simply kill them. *Those people* must exist, and indeed they are different. This could really be a problem…bigger than we know. The question is what do we do?"

"Dad, what do you think?" asked Hunter. "They are really unnerving."

David thought for a minute and responded, "Listen, I have an idea, though this is not in my purview. Maybe Mom will be more well versed in this, but let me speak for a moment. I know she can help us with this but let me set it up… We always hire consultants to give us a pulse on political conditions as a precursor to investing in foreign countries -- a social, political, and environmental briefing. I want the two of you to take the lead in researching *those people*, if you want, and what impact they have on social conditions and the dangers they pose to our investments. I think it will lead to bigger things, but it is just my intuition. Diana, what do you think?"

"Listen guys, in general it sounds good to me. Maybe this will be a way for all of us to work together. We are much older than you realize, your dad and I," looking at David. "This may be our last chance for all of us to do something important as a family. This is more important than school, Ashley. Hunter will tell you, working with us is just a kind of education. This will be very special for your dad and me. We will set this up and have some oversight so you can't fail, but this will be all yours. I will say it again, I think this is more important than school. This will be a great learning experience. Leave everything up to us. You will do the research, Ashley, all that time on the internet has to pay off, somehow." She grinned.

"You will grow into this and grow into it quickly. It will be great for all of us to be together. One more thing, it won't steal your youth." she laughed. "You still will have plenty of time to be with Imam and Sabah."

It was as if they were in a fact-finding meeting where ideas were introduced and explored.

Diana said, "Maybe we should have the boys set up an in-house team of researchers under their direct supervision and go from there. Hunter, this will be research-oriented, not so much of a financial approach -- pure methodology. I want the two of you to work as co-leaders."

"Ashley, you set up the parameters for a social research product. Hunter, you set it up for a socio-economic model. Ashley, how important is it to you? I know you're only 23, but how important?"

"If you don't want to do this, and you are feeling I am pushing too fast say something. I know I'm a hard charger. I really want this for our family, but if you guys are not up to it that's fine. Never let me take you places you don't want to go. Always 'man-up' to it even when you're not comfortable."

"Mom! You got us here, didn't you? We're here aren't we," Ashley responded, "Mom, It's very important. I really do think something is wrong. It is important enough, I would put my heart and soul into it. I am young, but I would give anything to do this."

Diana thought for a moment. "Okay, you will take next semester off and direct all your energies to this project. One proviso, you must take some classes, not a full schedule. We will coordinate with the Marshall School of Business at S.C. to expedite your withdrawal for one semester. We are major contributors. We can get it done. There's something else: you know Dad and I want the two of you to take over the Russell group. That's why we've come on this trip. We also felt you should find out about our past, which creates our present motivations. Let that be for one second."

"We were going to set up an office in New York later this year. We will do it now. The Russell group will use it as an office for your work. Ashley, we will set it up so you can go to NYU extension at night. Hunter, Wall Street and its analysts will be in closer proximity. We want you to hire the best people for our project. Money will not be an object."

David said, "Your mom and I have been thinking about you guys taking more responsibility in the company for a long time."

Diana said, "When opportunity knocks, you know. We won't let you fail on the project, but we'll call it off if we have to, if we feel we cannot succeed."

David continued, "Diana, does this have anything to do with Imam and Sabah? A little premature, isn't it? Are you doing what I think you're doing? They really don't even know the girls yet -- Once a matchmaker, always a matchmaker."

"David, you know business and pleasure; you can't have one without the other," Diana winked at her husband.

The brainstorming lasted for well over an hour. The boys found Diana's impetuosity and her years of guarding social activities was spot on. Maybe *those people* project was too fast. Maybe the boys' relationships with Imam and Sabah was crazy as Ashley called it, and maybe the boys were too immature for directing this project, but what did any of them have to loose? They had money and time and even though David and Diana were older, they did not see a downside.

As Diana put it, "Well guys, we have nothing to loose and everything to gain." She was comfortable living her life with premonitions. She felt good, really good, about this one.

"Okay, guys, I am going to change the subject." David looked at Ashley and said, "I want you to call Al Nassar and apologize. Someday you might need him. He is potentially a good resource for the Russell group, and Sharif said he is a good man. I want you to apologize for the way you treated him at the meeting."

Hunter smiled and said, "I think he needs to express something for the incident in front of the hotel, too."

Diana said, "I don't want to hear what else the mouth said, just settle this thing. Settle this for us and maybe for you and the lovely Sabah." She punctuated her words with that grin. "See you guys later."

It was now almost 11:30. Ashley went directly up to his room and placed a call to Al Nassar at his office. Knowing the importance of the conversation to his father made it an even greater burden.

"Mr. Al Nassar, please."

The secretary who received the call spoke perfect English, and asked who was calling.

After an extended period of time, a voice on the other end said, "This is Omar Al Nassar. How can I be of service to you, Mr. Russell? I am speaking to David

Russell, am I not?" This was his way of putting pressure on Ashley. Make the young man uncomfortable, as he had done to Omar, to create leverage in a conversation.

"Mr. Al Nassar, this is Ashley. I am calling to apologize for my curt and disrespectful manners on both of our acquaintances. May I apologize?"

Al Nassar knew it would be devastating to Ashley, if he would not hear him out. He waited for a long moment and said, "Be precise and of few words in your explanation for treating me with a lack of respect and with disdain."

Ashley was slow with his words, trying to say exactly what he had practiced over and over in his head. "Mr. Al Nassar, I was taken aback and threatened by your stature. I did not know what to expect upon our meeting and I was caught off guard. I also had no understanding of the importance of Sabah to me until that instant. I think I was showing off, as well as reacting to you as a threat. As for the business meeting, I overreached and personalized something that was very important to me. I became unprofessional. I did not speak with a clear head. My emotions were not personal toward you. I know that sounds like an excuse, but what I said was with passion and came from my heart. One last thing... if you don't want me to see Sabah, I will understand. Please don't punish Hunter and Imam for my indiscretions. They are not at fault."

He was trying to sound as grown up and contrite as possible. It seemed like an hour passed before Omar spoke.

"My daughters will be at the hotel at the designated time without chaperone. But as we say in Egypt, once is once. It shall not happen again. I am accustomed to respect-- not for my name, but for my actions, and you did not stop to evaluate me as a man. We shall not discuss this again. The hole is deep enough. If I let you speak more, you can only deepen the hole you have found for yourself."

He said nothing more. Ashley again awaited a long pause for further conversation; he only heard hang up on the other end of the line. He had relearned something. A few words say a lot. There is a commonality about power and control. Less is more.

Twenty–two

The black Mercedes with the Al Nassar sisters approached the Marriott's vehicle checkpoint at 1:55 p.m. After an extensive search by the hotel security force the car parked in front of the hotel's main entrance. It was two o'clock, and the sisters were prompt. They were exactly on time. The boys were waiting outside in shorts and polo type T-shirts, each with a small athletic bag in hand. The girls leapt out of the car. Both back doors opened simultaneously.

Sabah ran up to Ashley and asked, "What did you say to our father? He said he trusted us with you, no chaperone; we can stay out past the traditional time of 10 p.m. We still have to be home early, 1:00 a.m. It's a matter of trust. But what did you say to him?"

Imam said their father seemed impressed. "This was not a usual reaction of his to any young man we have shared with our family. We have today all to ourselves and it's been planned out. Where are Kamel and Tareak?"

Hunter asked if shorts were okay or even proper for some of the places they were going. If they weren't, they had a change of clothes. He held up his Nike athletic bag. The girl said it was fine; they were both in True Religion Brand jeans and short sleeve tops. The boys felt like they were in Beverly Hills where the women dress much better than the men.

"We are going to Memphis and then Saqqara to see the stepped pyramids. Then we will come back to Cairo and go to Mohammed Ali's Palace and the Shaw of Iran's mausoleum, and then finally, to the marketplace," she said.

The drive to Memphis and Saqqara was visually surreal. Where the green belt of the Nile Delta's vegetation and the stands of the Sahara joined, there was a blatant disconnect. No tampering of one landscape to the other. Either all green or all beige. No places where the sand had smatterings of grass or low ground foliage. One or the other, no commonality; they were completely and absolutely different. Ashley had an uneasy feeling -- a physical paradox, nothing in between, a bifurcation. Was this the case of us versus *those people?*

Sabah noticed the change in Ashley's countenance and grabbed his hand and said, "Ashley is everything alright? You look so serious."

He said, "I'm fine. I don't want to disturb anyone or ruin our day. I may say something later. It's not about us, not about you. Something just came to mind."

Hunter said, "That is his way of wanting to talk about something different. When he wants to get heady, he insists it's nothing. Sabah, it will pass. Let's not get serious. It's just Ashley trying to be intellectual."

Imam said, "Okay, Ashley, talk about it, so we can enjoy each other and enjoy the day."

Ashley said he would only mention it in passing; he didn't want to cause a problem.

Hunter said, "Just get it out."

Ashley mentioned that distinct separation of vegetation and desert and how it correlated to *those people* versus normal humans. Sabah and Imam were quiet.

Imam said," There are many of *those people* in Egypt. They are violent and it's impossible to read their intentions. They languish in the deepest poverty, almost sequestered from the middle class and, of course, they are not from genteel society." She said," They are not beggars asking for Baksheesh or money, or radical Muslims with a deviant cause, but they are people living by the irrigation ditches or by factories that belch pollution in the air or foul the soil and they don't seem human."

"We call them the 'toxic people'," added Sabah. "There are many. My friend, Fatme said they multiply like rabbits. They look like us, but their eyes have no soul. They frighten us as well as the police; they must be watched carefully for they can be violent. When the Islamic fundamentalists protest, it seems these are the people who are uncontrollable and dangerous. It is as if they cannot stop their ways of aggression. They get so excited they lose their ability to function as humans. They become active at a pitch different than ours."

Sabah pointed to an irrigation channel in the lush delta region just before them. She said, "The water in the ditch or channel is so polluted and so vile the fish float to the top. People use the ditches to relieve themselves, it was downstream from industrial pollution, and large amounts of chemicals are thrown into the water. It is a pool of poison. In the heat of day *those people* wade in the water to cool themselves down. The boys could not believe she used the word 'those'."

Sabah pointed to the children playing in the water and sitting on the channel banks, they appeared to be small versions of *those people*. They were animatedly active, playing like normal children, but something was different. They were peripatetic. Their wandering about in the shallow water was unnatural. Viewing them from the SUV, in the canals' waters and on the roadside, it was clear they were different.

Leaving the agricultural belt and driving toward Saqqara, the landscape started to change. After a twenty minute drive, the desert pyramid of Saqqara popped up on the horizon. It looked like stacked boxes atop each other. From ascendancy to the floor, the box structures were ever larger; not a pyramid of unbroken diagonal sides, but steps. It was the first generation of pyramids on the plateau. They were called steps to the gods. More than a thousand were built in the Saqqara area.

It was interesting to see the progression from the smaller stepped structured to the great pyramids of Giza. The beautiful symmetry and the soft flowing lines of the Giza pyramids, compared to the disjointed, harsh steps to stair risers, steps of descending sizes, was apparent. Many changes had been made over the years. The burial chambers in the great pyramids were deep in the center of the giants, with small passages leading to large chambers. At Saqqara were deep holes under the pyramid itself. The pyramids of Giza were so much more advanced than the pyramids of Saqqara, but the stepped pyramids were still wonderful, the four walked in amazement on ancient desert paths and acted as young people do. The somberness of talking about *those people* had passed.

The drive back to Cairo to tour Mohammed Ali's palace and visit the Shaw of Iran's mausoleum flew by in an instant. The beautiful Turkish architecture of the Hottentot's built palace was evident. Arab design and workmanship was different from that of Egyptian antiquity. The boys became aware and understood that there were two distinct cultures.

One, the ancient peoples of great power and wisdom that were the pinnacle of knowledge and civility, were the majority of the population. They prospered, even though they were subjected to pharaohonic rule. They were Egyptian. And the other: the Arab people of today who had lost their way. People of newer generations by two thousand years, and did not have the stature of their ancient forefathers to live in a land where people's ancestors were brilliant, noble, and powerful and now to be a people on a lower path, where the majority of people are poor and deprived, must be psychologically disabling, the boy thought. It seemed like the rich never changed. Over time, they accumulated more wealth and material belongings. The ever-increasing numbers of the masses progressively suffered greater hardships. Ancient Egypt did not have the plight of poverty that this Arab nation now possessed. Ashley wondered what it would feel like to be a nation whose ancestors were superior to its present-day people. Could this be the same for us and for *those people*?

They filled the rest of the day by going to the Kan Al-Khalili marketplace and bargaining for souvenirs. The boys were much better at arbitrage after their experience in Kenya. Hours passed, and day led into night.

Twenty-three

It was almost 9 p.m. when Hunter, Imam, Ashley, and Sabah, with curios and souvenirs in their hands, came back to the Marriott, as suggested by Hunter. He wanted to change his clothes. It was evident the Nike bag lacked appropriate attire.

The 'gang of four' as they decided to call themselves, walked through the customary security search, came into the hotel lobby and serendipitously ran into David and Diana. The last people in Egypt the boys wanted to see other than Omar Al Nassar.

Diana couldn't let them pass without engaging the girls. She approached the four of them in a quiet and unspoken way putting pressure on the boys, and her curiosity about Imam and Sabah got the best of her. Ashley and Hunter already worried about the awkward pleasantries of the girl's meeting their mom were surprised, however. Dad was always socially on the spot, but mom could be off the wall at times. Both boys just stared at their mother and waited to see which version of Diana was there tonight.

She stepped forward, took both girls by the hand and said, "Sabah, Imam I am Diana Russell. I have heard so much about you. The pleasure is mine. Your beauty so classic and understated, it overshadows the queens of Egypt. The kindness and hospitality you've extended my sons is genuinely well received."

David coughed. The boys were stunned. Diana just laughed at the three men.

She looked at them and said, "I could not resist. My sons have made David and I feel you are our daughters. Their joy is ours." Before David could say a word, Diana interjected again, "Don't feel you have to fill our time. Go share the evening with each other. We will retire to older friends who are fraught with dullness, and are not enjoyable, and who render us bored." She kissed each girl on the cheek. "Have fun."

David said, "How can I follow that? And by the way, we left messages on the answering machines upstairs. We also had itineraries placed in your rooms. Tomorrow is a working day. See you. Hope the four of you have fun."

Ashley said, looking at Sabah, "I hope it's not presumptuous and forward of me to ask if you want to come up to my room, but I am edgy about this itinerary stuff. Sabah, I want time to be with you tomorrow and the rest of the trip before we have to go home."

He almost said, "Before we go to New York," but he wanted to save that for the anticipated romance later tonight.

The four went up to Ashley's suite. Checking through the itinerary was like an appointment book. Day one: a list of meetings and conferences. Day two through five: were unexpected and not well received. A Nile cruise for the boys had already been booked, and an asterisk had been placed next to it stating t it was obligatory, no discussion. A flight at 7 a.m. to Luxor, visit Karnak, the Luxor Temple, and the Valley of the Dead. Board the Sonesta, a five-star Nile cruise barge. Visit the Temples of Edfu, Homo Omo, and the Temple of Philae. The disembarkation point was Aswan. A 7:00 p.m. flight back to Cairo. There were two free days at the end. Diana and David would be in Jordan by then.

Hunter stunned the three with the proclamation that he and Imam would see Ashley and Sabah later. He grabbed her hand in a demonstrative manner; there is something I want you to see. It was his way of being alone with her at long last.

Before Ashley could say a word the suite door swung shut. Sabah startled him by unbuttoning her blouse while standing directly in front of him. She slowly pulled it over her head and threw the white silken garment to the floor. She then rapped her hand behind her back and undid her bra strap. Her full breasts with darkened hard nipples were ripe with anticipation. Ashley pulled her on to the bed and said don't say a word, let me do the rest, as he pulled her pants down her long legs and over her feet. Her loins were wet with lust as he entered her. He was gentle and aware of her every need as they made love for more than an hour and a half.

In a panicked voice she said, "What time is it? We can't be late and disrespect my father. Ashley, we can't be late! We have to call Imam."

He looked at her and said, "It's cool, it's only about 12:30' but you're right, we better call. Do you think Hunter got lucky?"

"She is my sister. What do you think? She is an Al Nassar, is she not?" she said. "Imam may seem shy and cold but when it comes to men she will be a full woman to your brother but I am also sure she is aware of the time, we must call and tell them we will meet them down at the lobby. The two of you must walk Imam and me to the car. Khaled my daddy's driver and spy will be waiting. We can't be late."

Years later in reflection it was the best day of their collective lives. The five-day cruise was torturous for both Ashley and Hunter. Even though, Hunter, the pseudo-Egyptologist, saw unimaginable and wondrous archaeological sites his thoughts of Imam and her olive skin and her firm body was ever present.

Ashley couldn't utter a sentence without saying Sabah's name. Raging hormones of the nth degree made the anticipation of two days with the girls in Cairo all they could think about. They would have 48 hours, two unbelievable days of lovemaking and occasional Cairo sites.

During these two most wonderful days of their lives, as 'the four' would call their pleasures in Cairo, the boys filled in Sabah and Imam about Diana's plans for setting up the family business in New York.

The next three months of separation, semester recess for Imam and Sabah in Egypt, and planning for Hunter and Ashley's New York move inched by very slowly.

In concert with Omar Al Nassar the boys traveled to Cairo in late August and shepherded the girls back to New York for the beginning of school and the beginning of the *those people* operation.

Twenty–four

During the flight, the boys talked to Imam and Sabah about their collaboration on the project.

Ashley seated next to Hunter leaned towards Sabah and said, "We never told you about what happened in Nairobi and our near death experience, did we?"

She gasped, "Oh Ashley, what happened?"

His eyes were peeled and his chin jetted straight out as he related his tale of horror.

He said, "We had just left a political rally where my dad's friend Martin was speaking. On our way back to the hotel, we almost got killed by those f-ing animals. A group of them attacked us on the street. About thirty of them were opposite us at a major intersection and one of them began yelling some shit we couldn't understand and all of a sudden they rushed toward us throwing stones and wielding knives and stuff. They were all in some type of trance or something in the pitched fervor. All I know was they only had death in their eyes. We took off running to get the hell away from them. Good thing the hotel was only a couple blocks away and we are in shape or we would have been dead. Man, were we lucky! The hotel guard started screaming at them and raised their gun and those animals backed off. We were really lucky. They wanted to kill us, but they were not frightened by the guards. It was as if they knew they would not be shot and they were tolerated as long as they didn't go any farther."

"And the most disgusting was once inside the hotel the manager apologized for what happened and asked if he somehow could make things right. It's as if this shit happens all the time. They should have killed those fuckers not apologized for them."

Ashley looked at Hunter and said, "Did I forget anything?"

"My little brother tells the understated truth. We both almost shit in our pants. It was a lot scarier than Ashley makes it out to be."

Sebah related what happened to her friend Heba and her boyfriend. It was a similar story but those people were Egyptian.

She said, "It's exactly the same thing, the chanting, the aggression, and their disregard for life. Heba thinks they would have been dead if the guards at the nite club had not come to their rescue."

It was personal. They all had a real stake in getting to the truth of *those people*. *Those people* touched their lives and not in a positive way.

Ashley said, "They are not fucking human as far as I am concerned. It is real important that we never intellectualize this. We aren't just going to study them we have to rid the world of them."

None of the group took his macho talk as hyperbole. They all felt the same way.

The boys had a keen awareness of the girl's insights and what they could bring to the table, but they were taken aback by the fact that it was personal to them as well. They would build a working relationship on the equally shared foundation that they were dealing with a less than human species. The excitement of working together was evident. The 'gang of four' would function as an interlocking directorate with multiple responsibilities. The agenda discussed was totally concurrent with their mindset. They all knew the potential danger of *those people*. Their visions of how important *those people* were and how they would define them was easily agreed upon. They would have to deal with how they discovered their emergence, and what effect those people would have on future financial and socio-economic events.

Imam's and Sabah's viewpoints held significant sway with the boys. They had a different mindset but were of equal intelligence and prowess. The seriousness of this work was not lost on the four of them. They discussed approaches to series of complex questions on how to deal with *those people*. How would they set up an organization? What resources were needed? It was as if they were in a University study group cramming for a midterm or final. It was readily apparent Imam's strength was science and Sabah's strength was organization. The two girls had no tolerance for either intellectual or workplace laziness. They were both product driven.

Imam said, "We should create a methodology and models that are based on social game theory. I know we are just throwing out ideas and setting parameters, but I think we should be less mathematical in our approach. We are testing acceptable scientific constructs and arguing that other people exist. Do you know how crazy that sounds? We are not anthropologists looking for a new sub=species of human. We have no credibility. What do we do with our findings if we really find something? We have to figure this out; there is a tremendous responsibility here."

Hunter expressed a similar concern. He said that there were limits to the scientific method. He gave an example of following existing conventions and rules and how this could limit the outcomes of their research. He wanted to do research outside the box, even if it made credibility problematic.

Ashley and Sabah expressed organizational views. How could they set up an office? Where would it be? Who would they hire? How could they create an organization that expressed originality and creativity? Politically, who would they enlist for support if those people did exist, another human form? If they existed and were a threat to society, what options were available in the political arena?

"We just can't kill them can we? I can't believe I said that" Imam uttered with a straight face.

Imam said, "We should create a methodology and models that are based on social game theory. I know we are just throwing out ideas and setting parameters for our vision, but I think we should be less mathematical in our approach. We are testing acceptable scientific constructs and arguing that other people exist. Do you know how crazy that sounds? We are not anthropologists looking for a new sub-species of human. We have no credibility. What do we do with our findings if we really find something? We have to figure this out; there is a tremendous responsibility here."

Hunter expressed a similar concern. He said that there were limits to the scientific method. He gave an example of following existing conventions and rules and how this could limit the outcomes of their research. He wanted to do research outside the box, even if it made credibility problematic.

Hunter stated, "Ashley started by searching the internet, but soon found the United Nations Environment Programme (UNEP) had done years of research on subjects of pollution and global warming and environmental disruptions. In 2005 they published a book, "One Planet, Many People." We found the following information showing areas where pollution was the worst. Here is a small report, but by all means it's just a beginning."

Mining Locations: <u>*Powder River Basin, US*</u> – *Core area of coal and natural gas production in the US;* <u>*Ok Tedi Mine, Papua New Guinea*</u> – *this area was very isolated, sparsely inhabited, and ecologically pristine. Satellite images reveal the tremendous environmental impact the mine has had in 20 years. The uncontrolled discharge of 70 million tones of waste rock and mine tailings annually has spread more than 621 miles down the Ok Tedi and Fly rivers, raising river beds and causing flooding, sediment deposition, forest damage, and serious decline in the area's biodiversity. In fourteen years the area changed completely.*

On the other hand, <u>*Mining Ekati, Canada*</u> – *As of 2001 the Ekati Mine was North America's only operating diamond mine. Located in north central Northwestern Territories of Canada, the mine yields raw diamonds from a sparsely inhabited sub-artic region. Air transport connects mine personnel and supplies year-round, while a single winter ice road provides the vehicular access just ten weeks per year. Wildlife officials have collared and tracked caribou, in a herd ranging from 350,000 to half a million, to monitor their movement and behavior in* *proximity to the mines. Historical information about the herds comes from Dogrib and Inuit knowledge obtained from elder natives who still inhabit the NWT, and who have depended on the caribou for centuries. These miners have kept the area clean and also in <u>Weipa Bauxite Mine, Australia</u> – Now replaces topsoil or stockpiles it for later use.*

<u>Mining Escondida, Chile</u> – Open-pit copper, gold, and silver mine and also the largest copper mine in the world. Isolated in the barren, arid Atacama Desert in the country's far north, the Escondida Mine relies heavily on external well fields for the water used in its mining operations. Unlike similar mining operations, however, Escondida has a redeveloped tailings impoundment, which helps reduce water consumption and enhance water conservation, two areas where mining activities typically fall short. The Escondida Mine also minimizes the impact of its operation on the environment by means of a 106 mile underground pipeline that carries copper concentrate slurry from the mine to the port of Coloso. This underground scheme is efficient and ecologically sound, as the copper travels downhill without disrupting the environment. This mine has expanded but at the same time continues to minimize negative impacts from its mining operations on the environment.

Now we come to the culprits -- <u>Mining Copsa Mica, Romania</u> – In one year up to 67,000 tonnes of sulfur dioxide, 500 tonnes of lead, 400 tonnes of zinc and 4 tonnes of cadmium can be released by the city's two active smelters. The affected area is huge: in excess of 180,000 hectares of land are affected by air pollution and 150,000 hectares of agricultural land are untenable. 31,000 hectares of forest are also unacceptably polluted.

In 1989 Copsa Mica was exposed as one of the most polluted places in Europe. It has the highest infant mortality rate in Europe, 30.2 percent of children suffer reduced "lung function" and 10 percent of the total population of 20,000 suffer "neurobehavioral problems." The soil and local food chain probably will remain contaminated for at least another three decades.

Mining The Black Triangle, Europe – The so-called Black Triangle is an area bordered by Germany, Poland, and the Czech Republic and is the site of extensive surface coal mining operations located primarily in the Czech Republic. Air-borne pollutants from coal extraction activities tended to become trapped by the mountainous terrain to the northeast and were concentrated in the area around the mines, eventually causing sever deforestation along the border between the Czech Republic and Germany.

The implementation of anti-pollution technologies, including circulation fluidized-bed boilers, clean coal technology, and nitrous oxide emission burners, appears to have reversed some, albeit not all, of the environmental damage experienced by the region as a result of the mines.

So although mining is one of the most severe polluters, not all mines are deadly. And one of the worst polluters is technical manufacturers. The high tech boom has been accompanied by E-waste, which represents the largest and fastest-growing type of manufacturing waste product. Recycling E-waste involves major producers and users, and the shipping of obsolete equipment and other products to Asia, Eastern Europe, and Africa where recyclers, such as the people in Nanhai, China.

The disposal and treatment of waste can produce emissions of several greenhouse gases that contribute to global climate change. Even the recycling of waste produces some emissions, although these are offset by the reduction in fossil fuels that would be required to obtain new raw materials. Human footprint is a quantitative analysis of human influence on the Earth's surface.

Human interactions with the environment leave many traces. For much of human history, human impact on the Earth's surface has been relatively minor. In the last several hundred years, however, that impact has grown tremendously. Change brought about by human activities can now be objectively measured, it can even be seen from space.   A study by the national Aeronautics and Space Administration known as the Human Footprint is a quantitative analysis of human influence across the globe that illustrates the impact of people and their activities on the Earth.

Evidence of change is not always visible on the landscape. Change also occurs in the atmosphere, in the soil, and in the oceans and other water bodies. In these environments, evidence of change can still be "seen," however, by detecting and measuring things such as rising average global temperatures, the concentrations of certain gases in the atmosphere, and various chemical contaminants in water.

Hunter continued, "We need to start searching the highest pollution places for *those people.*"

He said, "I'm exhausted. Let's revisit this later. I'm going to walk down the aisle and stretch and use the restroom. When we get to the airport, Mom won't be there to help us," and he just laughed.

Hunter told Imam and Sabah of the unbelievable and unexpected treatment at the Cairo airport.

Sabah looked at him and said, "Cairo is the in Middle East. It happens to us all the time. Our father always says wealth has privilege. New York will be a different story for us. We will need to get a taxi from the airport; Father does not like us to have a limousine in the U.S. He feels we would be looked upon with suspicion and envy. At home it's important for people to know your station in life or your clan, for they provide safety. People would be foolish to suffer the wrath of our family if we were in danger. Here it is the opposite. The knowledge of who we are could put us in danger, or at the least, make us uncomfortable. We are NYU students and should act accordingly. By the way, how are you getting to your new home? We can't wait to see it."

Hunter looked at her and said, "We had a limo, but no more. If Ashley's going to attend NYU at night, we'll have to give it up." He had a look of exasperation on his face. "See, Ashley, look what I do for you? We'll get a van."

Ashley asked how far it was from Chelsea to the girls' apartment.

Imam said it was a 10 minute walk. "We should share a van together. We are closer to NYU than you are. We have a flat in Washington Square. It's about one block from the campus. The university is very different, it is urban. It is nothing like anything you've seen before."

Sabah said, "Maybe we can just drop off our bags and have the van wait for us a little while. When we come out, it won't be five minutes; we would like to see your place. I can't believe you have a flat so close. Do your mom and dad own it? I can't believe tomorrow is orientation for Imam, and I as well have something to do. I have to talk to Dr. Waters about an internship at JP Morgan Chase. If we can work together on the project, I will give up the position. At J.P. Morgan, I think I will be on the platform reviewing small commercial loans. Dad knows people there and he can get me on the loan side of the bank. He says that's where it would be best for me. I didn't know dad was getting me the internship; it is supposed to be prestigious. I am only 20 years old and my father thinks I'm a businesswoman already. If we work together, I will have to tell him of our project. I must tell him the truth. In our family, it's always a matter of honor and trust. I must tell him what we are doing.

There could be a major difficulty, he usually wants input. It can be a problem. As we say, too many chefs in the kitchen... too much salt in the soup?"

Ashley said, "Your father trusted us in a social setting in Cairo, so he will trust us, if we present things correctly. Let me think on it. I promise I won't come on strong and sound arrogant like a young punk again."

Your father said to me, "Once is once."

"I will be careful and respectful. My father said that Omar Al Nassar was a valuable asset in any future business, and this sounds like the future to me."

Arrival at Terminal 4, Gate 37, and clearing a US passport station, the four were off to the baggage area of British Airways. Hunter and Ashley had met Imam and Sabah in the Cairo airport after the girls checked their own bags. They were not aware and were staggered by the volume of Louis Vuitton bags traveling with the sisters. The boys secured four pull carts, but that was just a start for all the luggage pieces, so they had to solicit services of the sky cap with two large four-wheel baggage trolleys.

After going through the customs line they said, "Nothing to Declare."

They entered the main terminal of the airport and searched for the ground transportation desk. They found the kiosk and waited in line alternately for 20 minutes and finally hired the services of Speedy Transport. In 15 minutes, a Ford Econoline Van waited for them in front of the terminal.

They were at the designated curbside with two bags for the boys and 17 bags between the girls.

Hunter said, "I can't believe you have Louis Vuitton bags. Why so many? They must have cost a fortune, and your father doesn't want you to be ostentatious and stand out here in New York? Those stick out like a sore thumb."

Imam said, "The bags are knockoffs purchased at the bazaar in Cairo, but my mother and father have the real ones. We got these because if something happens to them, we don't care, we can just throw them away."

Ashley said, "When the van arrives, you guys get in, Hunter and I will help the driver arrange the bags in the back. I hope it's a big van."

Hunter and Ashley paid $42 per person and two dollars per bag for the trip to the city. The boys had never been to New York before and were transfixed looking out the window on their way to Chelsea. The 55 minute ride was not similar to the one in Nairobi from the airport to the city and hotel, none of *those people*. The traffic was better than Los Angeles. They couldn't believe it was so easy getting into uptown New York. They were excited about the city and Chelsea and were looking forward to being with the girls that night.

Twenty–five

Imam and Sabah's excitement at seeing friends and fellow students and being able to share Hunter and Ashley at a pre-school function was novel. The girls felt privileged and proud of their new boyfriends. Both had American friends, but none were of a romantic bent. After introducing Hunter as her boyfriend at the NYU Mechanical Engineering Society gathering, Imam was viewed differently. Her beauty was never questioned, her academic achievements were impeccable, her mental acumen was held steadfastly as superior, but a boyfriend was not expected. It was as if, after a three month hiatus, a beautiful girl bloomed into a multi-dimensional woman. Her social and emotional status as a graduate student with boyfriend now had empowerment.

Hunter was more than acceptable, he was viewed as a west coast hunk by Imam's female friends and her male 'big brothers' were impressed to the point of being happy for her. Everyone at the gathering felt it, but as per east coast social code, no one expressed it outwardly. She became an equal member of the group. She would no longer be the unassuming foreign interloper of different social norms.

Beautiful people who did not date were perceived as socially flawed, even if that was the practice in their home countries. Enculturation to American ways made young people at NYU feel more at ease.

Sabah's friends at the party were her study group; they were social as well as academic companions. Sabah and her cohorts were members of the Honor Society, the NYU business fraternity, Alpha Theta Sigma, and were all vying for internships at major investment banks. It was customarily the case at top-tier school's fraternal undergraduate order. Her announcement of having a boyfriend and introduction of Ashley was taken with trepidation at first.

Heather Smith, a transfer student from Magdalene College Oxford, had asked if she had lost her mind. It was so unusual for Sabah to have a boyfriend. Ashley's handsome appearance and the way he handled himself was out-of-sync for Heather and her classmates. It was disconcerting. He was too perfect. It was the first time Sabah was not totally study immersed in the company of her American friends.

Hunter expressed to Imam his underlying concerns about the social setting at NYU, "Your friends are nice, but they seem like they could be a cold crowd. It's either that or they're boring. They are a little younger than me, they are so judgmental. It's as if they have eyes fixed on my every movement. When I went to UCLA, which, by the way, is probably a better school than NYU, or equally as good, my friends were not as serious, and certainly not as nerdy. There were a lot of Asians and foreign students at UCLA. Not all white kids like NYU. But we were friendlier."

Imam stopped him and said, "Please don't feel put upon. They are very protective of me. I am looked upon as the younger, geeky, nerdish sister, because Sabah and I never dated. They are really nice, but protective. Don't be judgmental. Everyone here is a student. They have no experience except education. All they have ever done is go to school. None of us have real jobs, but we all have extreme social viewpoints and opinions. None of my friends have ever worked other than part-time jobs, and none in engineering or science. My friends have an unsophisticated technical standing, because their expertise is lacking, but they will see things professionals do not. They have a nontraditional approach, a non-diminished platform to analyze things. Their eyes, as well as ours, are fresh. You want to be different. My friends are, and some of them are brilliant. Hunter, the people I want you to meet are definitive about everything that is socially significant and unwavering in their principles. They can't be bullied by authority or convention. Professionals we assemble for our staff will not be better than them. If we need some of them in our project we can use them. If we don't, that's fine."

Her friends had never seen her have a drink before, even if it was just a glass of Pinot Grigio. When someone asked if she and Hunter wanted to go to a club later that night she responded, "Sure, we always go to clubs in Cairo." A response never uttered till that very night.

There was a metamorphosis in Imam that was greeted with affirmation. She was coming of age. Hunter must be of special stock to deserve such a prized and beloved friend, Heather Smith said to herself, as the evening wore on.

Twenty-six

At 6:30 a.m., the phone rang in Hunter's and Ashley's Chelsea flat. The thunderous sound of the cell phone after a night at the Club Burgess with the girls was enough to kill the spirit of awakening. Its piercing sound, coupled with the early morning light shining through the nearest window, was jarring. In Hunter's murky mind, a violation had taken place, and he wondered who would call at such an early hour, such a sacred hour.

Hitting the green upper right key, Hunter blurted out, "Hello? This better be good. If you are a solicitor or someone of insignificance, this is not appreciated." He abruptly hung up.

Within seconds, the cell rang again. His automatic reaction was that of all young people, to pick up the phone and answer it. The cell gravitated to his hand. He was wired to say, "Hello."

Before he could utter another word, he heard, "This is Omar Al Nassar. Is Ashley there?"

Hunter clumsily tried to apologize and said he would get Ashley forthwith. This man, Al Nassar, made him feel very insecure. "Ash, wake up, its Sabah's father."

In a state of blur and confusion, Ashley said, "Tell them I'll call back."

Hunter didn't have to be persuasive and handed him the cell.

"Mr. Al Nassar, I am honored to hear your voice. To be honest, it is early for me and I must clear my head for a second. How can I help you, sir?"

"Ashley, I know it is early. This is my way of advantage. We are six hours later here in Cairo. I can call back if you wish, but this call is about business. If we are going into business together on the research project, I wanted an early conversation with you. I have given Sabah and Imam my blessing in their commitment to your project, but I want to expand its scope. I should say that David, Diana, and William and I want to expand its scope. We will be aligned investors with the four of you and secure the seed money of $15 million dollars. It is a very large sum of money, young man. I hold you as principal in this project. Our money is where your mouth is as we say to ventureists who use our capital for their own gain. I know this is not for your personal gain and it is for things bigger than all of us, but Ashley I hold you responsible for all of this. That is large for a young man but you called for it. Bend in the wind my son, don't let the weight of the air break you. Your parents and William and I will be responsible for $5 million each; in total, it will constitute 40% equity of the entire project. Imam, Sabah, you and Hunter will have a 60% apportionment -- 30% for the brothers and 30% for the sisters. The direction will come from you. It will come from a business plan and prospectus developed solely by the four of you, but we will oversee the resources and have business practices oversight of the company. Staffing matters will be viewed by you but we will have final say. We want to make this doable. We feel the matter of *those people* needs a set of fresh untarnished minds to lead the project. That's you. Diana feels this is much like her youthful participation in Kenyan independence. There is one caveat: We, the elder investors, will not let you plunge into areas that are illegal or immoral. Your mother confided in me about her past. It is similar to my family's involvement in the overthrow of King Farouk and the Turks who led to a colonial free Egypt. I did not participate, but we Al Nassars, as a family, have a social obligation to do what is right for our people. Suffice it to say it is important for the four of you to be passionate."

He continued, "You will have a briefing with the board of directors, which consists of David, Diana, William, and I, every 30 days. There will be progress reports. The $15 million dollars provided is a sizable amount of capital. I can't overstate that. If we feel it is not enough, we can have other rounds of selected solicitations to bring in more money. If you take us down the wrong path the project is over. You must be a profit-making enterprise. You will sell collateral materials generated from research of *those people*. Profits are imperative, for we will have outside investors. A business plan and investment materials must not discuss *those people*. There are many political and environmental consultants and forecasters who are profitable with capitalization of $10 to $15 million dollars; comparable to your funding. You will be a large player in the independent consultancy business. We can be profitable, we must be profitable. Our Board of Directors can generate many clients from foreign countries to purchase investment information.

This information will pertain to political and environmental issues related to their foreign investments. This will be your core business. The research of *those people* must be kept in-house, one last thing, Ashley. May I thank you for being good to Sabah, and thank Hunter for his warm attention to the Imam. Our daughters are the center of our world. They say things of joy when it comes to you and your brother. I trust they are not deceived. The girls see special things about the two of you, but you have to prove it to me. You may call me Omar when we discuss family or personal things, I would like that, but for business, it will always be Mr. Al Nassar. I have called you this morning to inform you of our business union. So, my friends, go back to sleep. I will be watching like the falcon from on high. You have much to do to show me you are a man worthy of my youngest daughter.

The phone call was over. Hunter looked at Ashley, "Man, is he long-winded. You did not say a word." Hunter was going on, "What did he say?"

Ashley looked at him and said, "It's all good, all I have to do is prove I am worthy of his daughter and run a twenty million dollar business, not much more. I'm going back to sleep. We'll talk later when I get up."

In the subsequent hours there were calls to Sabah and Imam. The conversation Ashley had with the girls' father was discussed. Both boys thought it was strange that their mother's name never came up. Omar always referred to her with reverence and love, but the discussions never centered on her opinions or parental guidance. This discussion had been man to man or as Ashley put it, your dad to me. Their mother's role in the family was dissimilar to Diana's. Both women loved their children, but their input in their children's upbringing seemed dissimilar.

At 9:30 a.m., a call from David was placed on a landline from Dubai to the boys. He and Diana were staying at the Jameria Tower Hotel. The phone rang. Ashley picked up his cell.

"Ash, put the phone on speaker so the two of you can hear this. I have just talked to Omar Al Nassar and William, and they are both interested in your project."

Hunter said, "Mr. Al Nassar called twenty minutes ago and talked about the project. Ashley listened and Al Nassar did all of the talking."

Ashley added, "He blew me away by the large sum of money you're willing to put into the project. Plus we had a little man to man. He put a lot of pressure on me in regards to expectations, that's cool, I deserve it."

David said, "We want the four of you to be successful and learn from this project -- kind of a living inheritance. Success begets success. Do well on this one and you can look forward to others. We don't want you to fail, so it was agreed to make it a priority, even though you are young, and only Hunter has real work experience. He has worked for Russell Company for almost two years. He has relationships with some of our associates and has a knack for picking-up things quickly. There is great importance to *those people* project, but you must not be viewed as extremists or crackpots. Over time all investors will be told of *those people* project. We will only take money from a pool of like-minded investors who share our concerns about *those people*. A few words of advice, and then you will be quasi on your own. One, be lean and nimble. Two, only hire people who feel it's a privilege to be with you and be part of the project. Three, loyalty is the most important commodity. Make sure everyone is loyal to you. Four, simplicity bring things down to the lowest common denominator, Occam's razor. The simple answer is the best solution. Five, never lose sight of the journey. You should always be unbiased, respectful of knowledge and respectful of our investors' money. If any of your staff have a personal agenda differing from your mission, when you have defined it, they must immediately be jettisoned. No ego is larger than your goals. There is enough satisfaction in this project to be shared. Making money is a short run evil that will lead to knowledge of *those people*, but this is a long running task, don't loose your patience. We will not interfere unless extreme measures are necessary. That will be more pressure on you than you can imagine. It's like when you respect someone and they have a request of you, you always overachieve because you want their approval. You do more for those you respect than you would do for yourself. It will be more difficult if we keep out of your project and better if we do not inject our wisdom and experience. Hear these well, guys: what's important is that you might be successful in this project. We hope you are, and we will make sure you four of are on the right path. You will not fail if you pursue this to the best of your abilities. This project will be the hardest thing you've ever done because you're conscientious. This is a way of life in business. Do your best and never get big headed. Make every day a masterpiece. When you get home, be proud of what you did that day. You will be powerful if the vehicle you create let's all people around you be successful. The farthest you can fall is upon us and our monies. Money for us is currency of doing business; it is lost and gained without emotion. Omar has discussed with you a business plan and investors materials. I have one last request -- we need a timeline."

The difference between his father and Omar Al Nassar was a world apart but he respected both men. Ashley had the best of all mentors, one cerebral and caring and the other brutally honest. Hunter was steadfast and kept his distance from the emotional side of business. He would let his younger brother deal with his dad and Omar Al Nassar.

Twenty-seven

"We only have a few days before your school begins, so we should get started on the organizational plans," Hunter said. "Early tomorrow morning is when we will start. I know that the two of you have put a lot of energy and thought into the project as he looked at Sabah and Imam. So, thanks before we start. We should develop some type of matrix for information gathering and analysis. I think we should start with *those people* part of the plan. I think it will be more fun, and we can use it as a learning curve for the core consulting and forecasting business. Then we can develop some investors' materials."

Imam looked at him and said, "It sounds like you want to lead this planning group. It's okay with me. Sabah, Ashley, is it okay with you two? Hunter seems organized and he can put our talents together in an efficient manner. Hunter and I will develop a scientific approach to this project and the two of you," pointing to Sabah and Ashley, "will set up the business plan. Are you fine with that?"

Everyone seemed amenable.

"I will set up an agenda, or as dad says 'time line,' and keep notes." When Ashley was serious, he was very organized.

Sabah lent her opinion, "Its fine to delegate us into groups, but each team must have input on the other's work. A redundancy of different systems doing the same thing is important and may yield different results."

Everything was in place for the first round of planning and organization. At 8:30 a.m. the next morning, Imam and Sabah, with Starbucks coffee and scones and their academic toolkit of computers, iPhones, legal paper and pencils knocked on the Chelsea flat door. The fourth floor, 2200 square-foot loft was large. Its dining area, kitchen, living room and three bedrooms and baths were atypical for New York.

Sabah again asked Ashley and Hunter how their parents procured these quarters in such a short period of time.

Ashley said, "Mom and Dad are distinguished donors to the University. Dad was made a member of the graduate school of real estate advisory board, which might be the most connected in the country. I think a million-dollar donation or something like that was presented to the school as a gift, with more to come in the future years. For NYU, that is a substantial donation. NYU is not like Harvard or Stanford or Ivy League schools with many billions of dollars in endowments. Columbia probably has an endowment fund of eight to ten billion dollars, but NYU was late in the game. It has less than $1 billion in donations. So Mom and Dad's donation is meaningful and distinguished. I think that's how we got our loft. It's amazing how many things they are into, and how much money they throw around. Sometimes it's hard to live up to, but man, what benefits we always get."

Imam said, "Our father always says 'Plant seeds where they will grow best.' I think our parents are very similar. I know that donation will generate much business. Anyway, your loft is just great. You're very lucky."

Ashley had purchased an immense white board on wheels -- 40 by 60 inches. It came with colored marking pens and an eraser. Sitting in the living room, a view of the Empire State building in the background, coffee in hand, the four started hashing out ideas. It was agreed *those people* would be analyzed in three different categories. Number one, define *those people*. Number two, discuss the emergence or etiology. Number three, discuss their effect on society. Ashley placed the three categories on a horizontal plane on the white board and stood with marker in hand. As the four developed and discussed subcategories, a framework of general to specific developed. No specifics but generalizations in a macro point of view. Micro analysis would be developed by experts. The analysis would go from big to small. This methodology would create clarity and would not allow the matrix to be diluted by research minutia. Too many variables with mutually exclusive data would not be corresponding to the categories. Simplicity was best.

Hunter said, "Let's discuss the definitions first."

Sabah said, "The lack of life in their eyes was definitive. I am afraid of them, and they create hatred and even a respect, because they are so dangerous. They changed my life when I had even marginal contact with them."

Ashley wrote down "eyes" and underlined it and the words, "fear" and "respect."

Sabah said, "They are violent, but I don't know if it's a definition or an effect on society? She mentioned, "They're wanderers and aimless."

Ashley pointed out there are similar people in Los Angeles who are also violent, sex-driven and have a disproportional amount of children. They have a different way of bringing up their kids."

He continued, "I'm sure they're on welfare. They're different than *those people*. They are an underprivileged class; no franchise, no support and therefore, poor. If they are different than us, it is cultural. They are not like *those people*. *Those people* are entirely different. I don't want to sound like a bigot; so I must differentiate between the poor and *those people*. *Those people* kill with no guilt they're animals. The poor aren't, they're just different by circumstance. *Those people* are all sex and guns, and no reflection on morals or consequences. I know I've seen *those people* eyes in Appalachia and the South, they're all over. They're every where. You know, poor white trash, like Billy Joe Bob but it's hard to tell them from the poor and we have to be careful.

Hunter suggested, "*Those people* are extremely tactile, both in a physical and sexual orientation. They're aggressive. They're not cerebral. They like sounds to be loud and primal. Their sense of sight is different. It is discontinuous; quick bursts of imagery, nothing sustained. Like a MTV video. I have to turn away if things move too fast and lights and colors flash too bright. It sometimes makes me feel dizzy and I know what a person with epilepsy feels like in front of a flashing light. *Those people* only assimilate quick bursts of sensory stimuli."

Imam said one last thing about sensory stimuli, "It's evident they have short attention spans. They have no focus and maybe a different comprehension because of the way they receive information."

Ashley asked, "Is there anything else before we go on to etiology or emergence. Sometimes it amazes me how smart I am. I must sound like Einstein."

Sabah said, "I'm not totally clear on this, but I'll give it a try. They seem to have limited verbal skills. Maybe vocabularies of little children; they don't have a way of communicating complex ideas."

Hunter entered in, "Sabah, I remember reading about chimpanzees at Stanford -- one called Coco. She was 16 years old and had a vocabulary of eight to nine hundred words and she could relate to multiple complex ideas. Coco signed, and it took her three years to learn her vocabulary. The article went on to talk about an example of Coco and complex thinking. Coco was given a kitten as a companion and signed she wanted to have her own baby. How incredible is that? The article also stated the typical American had a vocabulary of 1800 to 2200 words. The lower the number of words, the harder it was to communicate. More importantly, the lower the number of words, the more frustrated people become, and with very limited vocabularies, they become agitated and violent. An example of sending a young tech savvy teenager with raging hormones to a hardware store and have them ask for a tool he had never seen or used before was given. You know when you want something and say, 'I want this thing; that what'm a call it. I can't explain it. I can't articulate it, but I want it.' You feel dumb, and the sales person looks at you like you have no clue. You feel awkward, you feel stupid. I mention this because those other people will never be able to verbally express or understand complex ideas. Sabah, I think you're totally correct. But we have to be careful. Some of this stuff might be a cultural interpretation, not a new type of person."

Sabah responded, "I know there are gray parrots and dolphins that are as smart as eight to ten year old children. They all function in an orderly way. You guys saw elephants in Kenya that might have more control over their environment than *those people* have over theirs. But *those people* are different. I think they're not as smart as these animals. There's nothing there. It's not that *those people* are just poor; it's that they are different. We have many of them in Egypt, especially near the brick making factories and the irrigation ditches. Perhaps it's something in the soil? Is it something in the water? I don't know. Actually, I think there's something else, too. I'm not sure, but it seems people like this don't live very long."

Then Imam looked at her and said, "Sabah, remember Abdullah at Cairo University, when he was going to medical school? He talked about all those young people dying. He talked about how they looked different. Remember when they were going to set up a business and sell their cadavers and sell the skeletons, but they couldn't because it was illegal? I think you're right, we should look at early death as another variable."

Ashley said, "I'm just joking, but maybe we should shoot them all. They are no doubt different than us. We won't let them join us; so maybe treat them like Indians."

There was no response to Ashley's jocularity. "Hey, I said I'm just kidding. I thought I'd be funny. Dad said that was my gift, deprecating humor."

This did not go over well.

Ashley was just beginning to learn how really serious the undertaking would be for all of them.

Twenty–eight

Ashley shrugged, "Okay, let's discuss causes and the emergence of *those people*."

"Raging hormones," Imam said, and just smiled. "I read that people have more testosterone now. The article said pollutants may push our bodies to produce more hormones. The body reacts to some man-made substances that mutate genes or something and causes some reaction like raising hormone levels."

Ashley said, "There are heavy metals for sure. Look at lead and mercury; there are even trace elements that cause problems. All that stuff about China and lead and how it affected children. You know in the long run, whatever chemical it is, can cause big time problems. Maybe *those people* are industrial mutants? I read about some stuff called dioxin, that's an industrial byproduct of dying paper white. It's supposed to be the most toxic man-made substance. There must be untold numbers of chemicals that affect our genomes or our DNA. What about all the mining processes and the arsenic that pollutes the ground and problems with run-off when it rains? It passes the stuff for miles. Rivers distribute the pollutants. I think it's something we should look at in terms of how the stuff is moved around. It seems like it's a virus."

Imam picked up the theme, "Evidence of change is not always visible on the landscape. Change also occurs in the atmosphere, in the soil, and in the oceans and other water bodies. In these environments, evidence of change can still be "seen," however, by detecting and measuring things such as rising average global temperatures, the concentrations of certain gases in the atmosphere, and various chemical contaminants in water.

"Ashley, you should put down chemicals and industrial pollution, elements, and virus. I'm not sure if we should be more specific like listing actual industries. Defining them by name, like paper milling or whatever it's called. Maybe we're being too specific. We should be more general in our framework," Sabah said.

"We're not trained in any of this. Maybe it sounds elementary. You know what? I think what we're doing is simple and clear getting away from the core basic idea. With too much science, we'll lose direction. We will not be able to find out about *those people* if this gets too complicated. I feel comfortable with what we are doing," Sabah continued. "Scientists are academically smart, but most of them are actually stupid. They can't apply their knowledge. They are too caught up in discovering and can't do anything with it. We might be really unsophisticated, but I think that's good. We are going in the right direction."

They all agreed. They felt good about what they were doing. Their lack of training and the way they attacked the problem was not a disadvantage.

Imam held, "I'm thinking, natural radiation, radiation caused by fission and atomic reactors, and don't forget the byproducts, should be viewed as a cause. We should look at the dispersion of Grennoble and its affect on the environment."

They discussed petrochemical fertilizers. Non-metals like polymers and ceramics and the replacing of iron and aluminum were thrown around.

Imam looked tired; she looked like she was in a trance. She was in a fixated state. She raised her head and said, "I've got to say something. None of us ever mentioned outside causes like space or aliens. Why, are we afraid, or is it totally outrageous and a non-factor? I think the chances of *those people* being aliens are zero. But let's discuss it."

It was evident before she got the word "zero" out of her mouth that the gang of four was in unanimous concurrence. They all felt that aliens were not a factor. The childish or unsophisticated notion of that causality was dismissed out of hand.

Hunter then said something provocative, "We seem to be saying this is caused by pollution, what about global warming? The ecosystem and the hydrological cycle that pushes this stuff, it might move like the flu virus. It might move in a particular pattern. It starts in Southeast Asia and over time, approximately a year; it has traveled to South America like the migration of some birds. We should pinpoint where *those people* are and see if there is any kind of pattern. Ashley, there is a lot of stuff on the cause side of your white board. We might have missed something that is evident, but I don't see it. Does anyone have anything else to add? Between all of us, we came up with a lot of reasons, but why does it feel so simple? Do you think we are missing something major? I remember taking an environmental economics class to meet a requirement and the professors said, 'The solution to pollution is dilution.' It sounded like stupid stuff that Jesse Jackson would say. But if we saturate the environment with pollutants, that might be causing the problem. More pollution might trigger more changes even faster. If industrial pollution is the problem, then things will speed up. This is frightening, but do you think species can mutate or evolve faster? Do you think *those people* are our evolved family? Is that too difficult to think about? Well, what about the landfills and the barges that dump garbage into the ocean trenches? They have to fill up someday. What effects will filling them have? Can saturation of the environment cause things to change much more rapidly? There is so much to think about it is overwhelming."

Imam said, "I think you're on the right track. Ashley, why don't you put "timeline" and "saturation" on the board; and how about faster or "geometric progression"?"

It seemed odd that the four of them had so much information and recognition to the potential problems they were discussing. Ashley wondered if professionals were that much different in their understanding of things. "Let's make a list of the research projects to go after."

Research Information

1)   How does a virus circulate around the world?
2)   Copsa Mica, Romania
3)   Ok Tedi Mine, Papua New Guinea
4)   Powder River Basin, United States

5)	Nanhai, China Tech Dump
6)	Oceanic Dead Zones around the World
7)	Water Distribution and Pollution
8)	Tropical Forest Changes
9)	Agriculture Development and Cropland
10)	Tundra and Polar Regions Pollution and

Warming

"Enough, Enough, Dude," Hunter exclaimed. 'Let's work with this. We can always add to this list."

Twenty-nine

Ashley, still standing by the white board, asked, "Everyone who wants to continue discussing the effects of *those people,* stay seated. Everyone who wants to go eat, stand up."

The hours had flown by. It was 4 p.m., and they hadn't even had lunch.

Hunter said, "Why don't we finish up? I'm not tired. Imam, what do you want to do?"

She said she didn't care and asked Sabah what her feelings were.

Sabah said, "I want to go with this until we finish. Why don't we stay here and eat later?"

She continued, "I think the most important factor of *those people* is their cost. They don't seem to add to society, and the numbers are increasing. I also think they cost society considerable amounts of money. They are violent, so there is that cost. It costs someone for their housing and food and medical. I am sure there are more costs, as they don't pay taxes. Society pays for them."

Ashley inquired, "What about the social cost?"

Imam spoke in a concerned voice, "What about the violent nature? How will it affect society because of legal retribution? Will we become police states? I don't know what it's really like in America, but in Egypt, we don't have time or resources to deal with them, so the local police are really brutal. They don't shoot them, but they are beaten up badly, and they are always relocated if they're in the wrong areas. Most of the time, where they live or where they congregate is lawless areas, and the problems are settled by the army, or they are just left alone. The problem I see is that they inhabit larger and larger areas because of neglect."

Hunter said, "It is not a clear line for me. Sometimes the gangs in Los Angeles are so animalistic towards each other I think they're like *those people*. I might be mistaken, but the gangs are so aberrant I think *those people* could just be beginning to emerge. *Those people* are not clustered near environmental sites or near waste dumps. There are so many people who fit the description of *those people*. I don't know if Latino and black gang members are *those people*. It seems like it, but I'm not sure. I think they're probably different than *those people*, but the gang kids are so much different than us, I don't know what to make of it. The level of poverty in America is great, but I'm not sure if they fall into the category of *those people*."

Ashley points the board and says, "A case study by NASA and UNEP shows Dead Zones around the world. The large region of oxygen-depleted water – a dead zone—spreads across nearly 15,080 km2 (5,800 square miles_ of the Gulf of Mexico appears to be an annual event NASA satellites monitor the health of the oceans and spot the conditions that lead to a dead zone. Sediment-choked water from the Neuse River flowing out into the Gulf of Mexico near the states of Mississippi and Louisiana."

He continued, "The oldest and most well-studied marine dead zones are found in the Gulf of Mexico, the Black Sea and the Baltic Sea. In 1995, the most severe case of hypoxia was in the Baltic Sea, in which about one-third, or 38,000 square miles of the water was reported lifeless."

Imam asked, "Does that mean more damage or does the satellite data of Arctic regions showing warming taking place there at an accelerated rate. The anomalies range from $7^{\circ}C$ ($12.6^{\circ}F$) below normal to $7^{\circ}C$ ($12.6^{\circ}F$) above normal. The data reveal that some regions are warming faster than $2.5^{\circ}C$ ($4.5^{\circ}F$) per decade. Atmospheric temperature and chemistry are strongly influenced by the amount and types of trace gases present in the atmosphere. Examples of human made trace gases are chlorofluorocarbons, such as CFG=11, CFG-12 and halons. Carbon dioxide, nitrous oxide, and methane (CH_4) are naturally formed trace gases produced by the burning of fossil fuels, released by living and dead biomass, and resulting from various metabolic processes of microorganisms in the soil, wetlands, and oceans. There is increasing evidence the percentages of environmentally significant trace gases (green-house gases) are changing due to both natural and human factors, and contributing to global warming. Global warming is recognized as one of the greatest environmental threats facing the world today. Global warming is gradual rise of the Earth's average surface temperature caused by an enhancing of the planet's natural greenhouse effect. Radiant energy leaving the planet is naturally retained in the atmosphere thanks to the presence of certain gases such as water vapor and carbon dioxide. This heat-trapping effect is, in fact, what makes life on the Earth possible. Global warming, by contrast, is an intensification of the Earth's greenhouse effect, the Earth's average surface temperature, which has been relatively stable for more than 1,000 years. The nine warmest years in the 20th century have all occurred since 1980: the 1990s were probably the warmest decade of the second millennium.

Sabah reflected on Europe. "I don't know if I've ever seen any of *those people* in Europe. It might be where our family travels and what we do, but I see no evidence of them."

Ashley stoically expressed, "When we do find what looks like them it is not clear; there are gray areas. You think the gang members act antisocially and are hyperactive sometimes, but does that make them *those people*? If the gang members are different in their behavior and are so antisocial, could they be crossbreeds? I'm not saying all gang members are those kinds of people. I've always thought society made them the way they are because of inequity or injustice or lack of opportunity, but can it be crossbreeding or inbreeding, if they really do exist. This is very difficult. It's going to be hard to distinguish between actions and definitions. Boy, this is getting hard. I'm feeling like a racist again or something. We are white and rich, and it feels like we are blaming the social problems on minorities, solely on them. The reality of gang membership is it's a tool for social survival. Their subhuman actions on society are not all their fault. We can't lump them together with *those people*. Social costs of repression and non-assimilation of gang members may be understandable. I'm starting to feel like a racist. This is not where I want to be. Some of our problems with people are because they deviate from social norms, but it might be rational for us to do it if we were in their situation. *Those people* are different. We must be careful. I think a major cost might be the recognition of whom and where they all are. We may have to segregate them from society if they are some type of subspecies. Action should not define the species. I know this might be all scientifically incorrect, but you know what I mean."

Imam wanted to say something else, "If they exist, what do we do with them when we have determined they're out there? I think finding them, will determine the cost. We must create a whole set of scenarios from educating them if possible, to not letting them breed."

Hunter said, "It sounds like apartheid in South Africa. How did we get onto this path?"

Sabah said, "They could be like my dog at home in Cairo. Mom got a dog for Imam and me, for the family compound. We love him. He's a German shepherd. We used to sleep with him. The whole family believes he is Imam's love of her life. Sorry, Hunter. But still he is a dog. You could spend countless hours and great sums of money and you could not teach him to speak or write or read. He is just a dog. *those people* may be the same. They're not lovable like a dog, but they may not be able to be human either."

Up until the discussion of the effects of *those people*, the four were having a stimulating, engaging set of discussions. The reality and seriousness of what to do if *those people* truly existed dampened their moods and made each of them feel uncomfortable. It became clear that this could be serious. The human race might have only a few decades to change things.

Thirty

After completing their work, Ashley said, "Now it's really time to go out and get something to eat. I'm so hungry. Let's get out of here. Man, am I hungry. I have never worked so long or hard in my life except for sex."

They all laughed, he did have a way with words. They all felt the same way about sex, but Ashley had no couth. He always said what was on his mind"

The four went down the hall to the elevators that took them to the lobby. Exiting, the doorman, Richard, said, "Good night to you, Ms. Sabah. Good night to you as well, Ms. Imam." He said nothing to the boys.

Hunter looked at the other three and said, "That's incredible. He met you guys once and remembered your names and didn't even acknowledge us. Either you're really something special, or we're not very memorable."

They walked for two blocks in the old brownstone neighborhood. Chelsea was like Soho and Tribeca, it was the new European cosmopolitan experience. Its mixed use of residential living in high-density apartments or flats with retail was an exciting way of life. Most people in Chelsea have the luxury of what was called "domicile next to revenue." Translated it meant, "Live near where you work." Each little neighborhood had an array of retail shops, local markets, and restaurants. They were all small, mom and pop business ventures. The idea of close proximity to everything you needed was alien to Hunter and Ashley. They had no functional need for a car in New York. In Los Angeles, cars were a live or die necessity. Everything was close at hand here, and if not, the subway system was easy and accessible. They were envious of the urban life. Cabs were at their disposal all hours of the day and night, or short walks would take you to places of importance in a few minutes. The city as a whole was an overwhelming experience. People everywhere, but they had purpose and were friendly. What they had heard about New York from their Los Angeles contemporaries was not coming to fruition. The negative stereotypes of New York people, the congestion, and the lack of personal space was not the case. The phrase was "It's a good place to visit but I wouldn't live there." was their friends' typical assessments of New York. To Hunter and Ashley, New York was wildly enjoyable. They mastered and embraced urban life in an instant. It felt natural to have everything at hand. Having girlfriends and walking down the street to find an eatery was blissfully natural.

On 6th Street, a couple of blocks from the flat, was an Asian fusion restaurant. Standing in the doorway, viewing the contemporary style restaurant and its trendy bar, Sabah said, "Let's eat here."

As was the case of most restaurants in New York, it was small. A capacity of 50 or so, but its food was to die for. By the time they finished dinner and paid the bill, it was 11:30. Hunter asked Imam to come back to the flat before going home. She grabbed his hand as if to say sex would be a great finish to this long productive day.

As they walked down the street, Ashley said, "It's been an amazing day. We worked all day, and we've been together since 8:30 a.m., and I am just blown away by all this.

He looked at Hunter and said, "Dude, how are you doing?"

Then looked at the girls and said, "Do you guys want to come back to our place for a while before you go home? It will be worth it."

Imam had already said yes, it was now Sabah's turn. She smiled and said, "What were the sex habits of *those people*?"

This was to be the first of many nights spent in Chelsea by Imam and Sabah. Richard the doorman was correct remembering their names. It would take a while for him to properly recognize the boys.

Thirty-one

"Mission statement, G.O.F.E.M. (Gang of Four Engineering and Management) will be a world-class organization with scientific research and academic staff at its disposal. Its goal is to determine if other human forms exist and what effect they have on societal, economic and geopolitical institutions.

"Sabah, it's amazing it took so long to condense our goals to one simple statement." Ashley continued, "There is so much depth and importance to our mission and we are so general. There has to be more to it."

"Ashley," replied Sabah, "the second we use the phrase 'world class,' it suggests who we are and our commitment to the project. It means people of unquestioned credentials, maybe Nobel winners -- the best. We need total transparency and world standing if we discover anything that deviates from acceptable thought. 'World class' means double blind studies, the best technical equipment, the best research campus or access to the best campus, and on and on. We need the best public relations firm and lawyers and the best political lobbyists, each part costs millions. We don't have the vaguest idea how to run an organization of this magnitude, so we have to hire the best administrative staff and delegate. We have a vision and we hire the best to carry it out. Let's call Imam and Hunter and share some of our thinking before we get too far. I think they will like what we are doing and I have an idea about a C.E.O. I'll call Imam."

Hunter and Imam were coming out of the elevator, and heard the other two talking.

"Before you do," said Ashley, "I know there are a handful of successful young people out there. The guys at Google and Yahoo and Bill Gates and Steve Jobs thirty five years ago are prime examples, but we are not them. They created something new. They were visionaries. I don't think we have to reinvent the wheel, but if we have all other people's knowledge at our disposal and are a little unconventional, I think we can be successful."

"I heard my dad say 'there are two different mindsets out there: The ones that invent because they see things differently and those who use things differently'. We have to use existing conventions and rules and push them to the limits is my guess. Let's not forget who is really in charge here. It's our parents and their money but we are the ones who unearthed *those people*. Let's feel fortunate that they let us run with it. We should be competent enough and old enough to add real value to the project. If we define the roles properly and use their experience and their resources, this should work out. Everything is always dropped into our hands and we are usually the beneficiaries of our parent's wealth and power. Let's show them we can contribute. That's real important. This is our chance. I want to be proud of what we do and make our parents proud of us. I don't want to feel like a little rich kid given a new toy and not appreciating it until it's broken or gone. I am ready for this, I don't want any illusions of what we can do but I know we can make this work. Many people are going to look at us as rich indulged brats over our heads and not worthy of this, but screw them, we're up to it. I am only 23, I drink too much, and sometimes I'm inappropriate in what I say and who I say it to. Oh, and I use too much profanity. I'm certainly not perfect but I'm up to this. I know we may get a little over our heads, but if we bring in the right people we can do this."

"It's more than being successful, like I said before, it is personal. Those f-ing people tried to kill us once and they will do it again. It is not like they are being orchestrated by some ruler to come after the four of us in particular but it is in them to just fucking kill randomly, that is what is so frightening. We have a chance to do something really important let's not blow it by being arrogant or lazy or even worse stupid by not knowing our places."

The room was quiet, Hunter and Imam were standing in the doorway, "Jesus you're a little dramatic, but that sums it up," said Hunter.

It was evident all of them felt the same.

Thirty-two

"The four of us haven't been together for a couple of days, so we were just fooling around with some stuff," Ashley said. "Sabah came up with the name for the LLC. It's going to be called the Gang of Four Engineering and Management. G. O .F. E. M. It's an acronym but it almost sounds like, you know, 'New York, Gotham city.' If you and Hunter don't like it, we will come up with something else he said to Imam. We also wrote a mission statement."

Sabah gave them a copy of the one sentence statement. "Again, we were just playing around. So if you guys don't like it, then we can always change it."

Imam and Hunter were at ease with the business minds of the group putting forth these ideas. Hunter said, "We feel completely comfortable. You guys know the business side; just set it up and we will give you input. If we hash it out like we did a couple nights ago, we won't be much help. Even though I worked for Dad, I feel much more comfortable letting you do the business stuff, and we will be involved with the scientific stuff. I can always give you help, but the two of you should do a better job because you have a better feel for it. Dad said I did a real professional and important job on what turned out to be the financials for William and the Al Nassar group. I did not like the work and felt like a mechanic. I had no passion or ownership for it. It was just work. I know this business stuff means much more to the two of you."

Imam said she was ill equipped to understand the business side and therefore felt the same way.

Ashley and Sabah wanted to show them a tentative business plan, but more importantly, an organizational structure for G. O. F. E. M.

Sabah said, "We feel that the organization must be small and nimble. This was Omar's position in business. It will give us the ability to change direction and course at any time. Our core business and the business of *those people* will have some overlapping areas. We must become profitable. Our investors' participation is predicated upon those profits. We will have two distinct organizations: our core business and *those people*. The employees on the business side will be of a geo-financial nature but will have research expertise like people at the big think tanks or the major government agencies. Our researchers will extract data from them and compile it in some ways so it can be valuable for financial reconnaissance firms. Under *those people* project we will need geneticists, virologists, anthropologists, environmentalists, and maybe mathematicians and even some physicists. I have looked into all the fields and maybe there's a need for other scientists but that's up to you two. We will develop a scientific model to detect *those people* if they do exist and explore their proliferation and evolution. If we can find them, then we study the ways they behave and forecast their physical and psychological makeup. This will let us determine if they are a threat to society or an opportunity for society."

Ashley said, "Our structure will be twofold. On the technical side, Hunter, you and Imam will oversee it. On the business side, Sabah and I will oversee it. We will need a CFO who acts as a CEO. He or she will determine policies and directions and implement them. Our staff should be Spartan, you know like the movie 300. Our major costs will be for expertise and their research. I think we should limit hiring time for durations on a project basis, one year maximum. We should give options for future employment with full benefits and bonuses if the business side meets certain criteria. On the *those people* side, remuneration or pay will be different. There will be no profits, so we can't judge efficiency or value. No bonuses, only good salaries. Sabah has another idea. I want her to pass along to the two of you."

Sabah said directly to Imam, "I know you're going to like this. I think Fatma should be the chief financial officer/chief executive officer. She is aware of *those people*, she is Egyptian isn't she? She has been threatened by them just like us and she has no equal in business, that's what Daddy says."

Instantaneously Imam said, "That sounds perfect, but you know we must pass it by Dad first before we ask Fatma if she would like to participate."

Sabah said, "He is the one who suggested it."

"Let me tell Hunter about her," Imam said. "This is going to sound strange and out of character because you will think this is my dad's way of controlling us. Fatma was our nanny. She worked for Mom and Dad because her mother was Dad's nanny. She and her mother lived with us on the family compound. She was our companion and bodyguard. She went everywhere with us. When she got older, Mom and Dad sent her to university in Cairo, and she has a Ph.D. in physics. She brought us up. She is like another mother to us. Fatma is loyal to the two of us, not solely loyal to the family or dad. She will not report to dad. She will work for the four of us. Later, Dad sent her to the United States, and she got her MBA from Columbia. She worked with Sharif and the family for years. You can have your father talk to Sharif. She will only do what is right for us, and she is a brilliant business person, and of course, she is technically sound. She is perfect. You are going to have to meet her to see for yourselves what we're saying. If you don't agree, we will understand. We know she is perfect for the job. All her conversation was directed at Hunter. We would like you to see her; how about next week?"

Ashley said he had agreed earlier once Sabah passed the thoughts along to him. Hunter would become to accept the idea Fatma. The final decision was in place.

Hunter asked if there were any other matters, and immediately had a thought, "We should use Dad's firm to do all of our background staff screening. If *those people* become a sensitive issue, we should not have to look over our shoulders. There could be leaks, or someone that works for us may have a different agenda. Who knows? We have to be careful, this is really involved stuff, but dad's people will know what to do."

Ashley said, "If Fatma works with us and she's that good, then she can oversee the background checks. I have another thought. I think we should be unconventional. Dad had mentioned Wall Street. He wanted us to be in ZIP code 10005. He wanted us to have status. I don't think that should be the case. I think we should either be in Soho or Chelsea where it's less financial sounding, and I think we should be next to the slaughterhouse district near the Chelsea market. Hunter, Imam, would that affect the kind of people you guys want to hire to do the scientific work? If Omar and Dad are going to bring clients, would being in the Chelsea district have any negative effect? By definition we will have to be a world-class organization because of our client list. I think location should be of little concern. I think our product is what's most important. If we hire the best, we should pay the best. Warren Buffett only has 12 employees and has offices in an old-fashioned building with a diner downstairs. That should be our guideline - small, but world-class. We will have the best minds in the world around us. We don't have to spend a fortune on rent just to impress people."

Sabah chimed in, "I don't want to have another round of investors. If we are going to hide the real purpose of the project, the research on *those people*, then the first goal must be profitability.

The first goal has to be profitability. Your parents and Daddy and William are the only major players so far. They might have partners in their investments, but no one we have to report to, other than our fathers, Diana, and William. If we can do this on $15 million, and I think that's a lot of money, we'll have to report to no one else and we can be almost totally autonomous. If we are nimble and flexible and independent, we will have the ability to accomplish a scientifically meaningful study of *those people* and hide it in our core business. We won't have to be worried about what I call outsiders. We will have no interference, and no one can tie our hands and discourage us or tell us what to do and how to do it, except our board, and we know who they are. If you guys want to look at the financials, we have them on an Excel spreadsheet."

Both Hunter and Imam said they were impressed with their siblings and partners.

Then Imam said, "There's no need to view the financial matters even though Hunter has experience. Hunter and I feel really confident about what you're doing, and Hunter is willing to give up the business side to solely focus on the scientific side with me."

Thirty–three

Fatma Kassar arrived at Kennedy at 10:30 p.m., one week after discussions with Sabah and Imam. Her functions and responsibilities, as they related to the girls, were acceptable to Omar Al Nassar. Simply put, they were of a business associate who would sever all ties with the Al Nassar group and have total commitment and resolve for her future employer, G. O. F. E. M. Her role as guardian and protector would be unwavering. The girls first, *those people* project, and the Al Nassar's family would be prioritized in that order. She would not report to or dispatch any business-related matters to Omar Al Nassar in any correspondence other than quarterly statements or responses to requests of a business partner nature.

As was her way, she was prepared. "Be prepared to the furthest extent." was her adage. Sleep was her enemy. She could be consumed by a commitment. She had boundless energy, but it was always outwardly harnessed. She was cool and unflappable at all times.

After her initial discussion with the girls she conceptualized an approach to the *Those People* project. The core consulting business was a simple matter of business as usual because of all the partnerships and relationships of David Russell, Omar Al Nassar, and William Mkabi. It had to be a home run. Failure in this endeavor would be because of negligence or a lack of resources directed to its execution. The need for geopolitical information as it related to political stability, taxes, subsidies, world court rulings, the WTO, foreign exchange, economic forecasting, and legal international trade policies, were all existing parameters for global investment. It would be her job to assemble a small team putting all this data under one roof and expedite its assimilation into usable consulting proposals that had market value. None of the major consulting houses had anything more than an area specific field of expertise.

This specialization was their weakness. G.O.F.E.M. would be a house for all information fields leading to a comprehensive analysis of any market or economic geopolitical considerations for foreign investment.

As for *those people* project, Fatma felt a new approach was necessary. She always held scientific convention could lead down a predetermined path and could extricate meaningful results, therefore blunt, not expand knowledge. She always looked at stochastic variables and extraneous roots as results not to be thrown away.

These could be the prizes of science; they must be viewed as such. In a scientific analysis, an aberrant result would be lost because it was so egregiously invalid that it would be disposed. Fatma felt there was scientific relevancy to this disregarded slag, and it should be taken into consideration. She held that science, not opinion, was of the highest order. To throw away any generated data without totally understanding its value did not set well with her. Just because an authority had an opinion on junk as she called it, his or her opinion held no credence by itself. Most authorities, in her mind, were blowhards. She would work with people that were humble, open to common sense and had opinions that were only fact-based. Research and results spoke for themselves. "In the data," was her credo. The unbiased model that could be replicated was the scientific truth. Convention must not hold back construction of models, and therefore, results.

Her scientific mind was in full gear for a week and peaked on the flight from Cairo to New York. She completely forgot her new employers and cohorts were the girls and their to be introduced boyfriends. They were children, and she had complete knowledge about them from childhood. Now she was to meet their first real boyfriends. The delicate oversight of the project and well-being of the girls became a stark reality on the jet way as she left the plane and saw the gang of four awaiting her at Kennedy. Fatma's maternal instincts would hold in check the impending scientific work of her lifetime. Gazing upon the girls holding their boyfriends' hands with young love's pride was an image stopping time and warming her heart. The ride to the girls' apartment across from Washington Square farmer's market was joyous. Imam and Sabah were able to show their affections of love as adults in front of Fatma, whom they loved and respected. They were all of a sudden young women, not teenage girls, and a heartwarming experience to Fatma.

After the traditional introduction and kisses from the girls, she said, "It is late here in New York, but I am still on Cairo time. Am I the only one that's hungry? Can I convince anyone to eat with me?"

She was Nubian and rich with beauty. Her very nature of being dark and tall made her seem mysterious. Her accent was almost English because of her education and because the Al Nassars made proper English the first language in their household.

"We must have this night for family, and I must be immersed by the four of you. I am truly proud of the project on which you embark. I know you arrived here a little more than two weeks ago. I myself packed your belongings for your journey and stay here in New York. I truly missed you when you departed. A few weeks seems like an eternity when you are gone. I must become reacquainted with the both of you,"

Looking at Hunter and Ashley, "to bestow my acceptance. It is customary for me, a mere nanny, to talk to you in ways Sabah's mother and father would find inappropriate. There's no pretension to my protection and love of my girls."

Then Imam spoke up. "Fatma is uncontrollable in her ways. Father always says when it comes to us; she is strong-willed and refers only to her instincts. She is like the mother."

She said, "I don't embarrass easily when we speak of family but enough of this. Let's talk about the four of you and tomorrow you will interview me and we will speak of business. I know you're going to do your due diligence, and your father has investigated me and will pass along an assessment," she said to the boys. "

"Tomorrow is business; tonight we share the fortunes in your young hearts."

It did not take Fatma long to understand why the girls loved Hunter and Ashley. She took the two of them by the hand. Hunter's right hand to her left and Ashley's left to her right and said, "Whatever your parents did with you, I applaud them. You are right for my lovely daughters. Even though I am a surrogate mother, my eyes see like a falcon and I see treasure before me. I don't have to say this, but my duty is to Imam and Sabah. Then my duty will be to you and your enterprise. I am rich knowing my girls are in such good company. I feel honored and privileged to be here. This is not a slight, but your age is ill-defined for you act older than you are and treat family and friends with the dignity and respect that is fitting for adults. It does not matter what your decision about our intercourse tomorrow will be. Tonight my heart is full. Business is business and family is family. We must indulge ourselves in the delight of youth, for tomorrow the nature of our mission may not be so joyous."

Thirty–four

"Hunter, I feel funny about our meeting with Fatma later today. She is so perfect for the CFO/CEO job, she is so f-in smart. It makes me understand that I don't know enough to even be part of the project. She did not discuss business last night but shit I know we are, especially me, over my head."

"Ashley, I worked for dad for almost two years and I feel the same way. It's been fun working with Imam and Sabah, discussing *those people*, developing a simple business plan, it's been great. But you're spot on, we're not very sophisticated. It's been more like a game than a scientific pursuit. First off, for us to be executives is simply out of the question. Man, it's way out of our league. Ash, as you would say, no fucking way. Here's what I think we can do. Whenever Dad gets in over his head, he hires the best. Fatma seems to be that person. We don't even have to interview her, she is so good. We'll have Dad's assessment before we meet her later this afternoon. Let's assume we hire her. She runs the show, with us helping in whatever capacity. I think we can help. We also need the help of Mom and Dad and

Al Nassar and William. Without their help, we are deceiving ourselves."

Ashley said, "Dad would not put us in a position of failure. He must want some kind of oversight. Listen dude, he is so controlling and he just thinks things through before he jumps into something. He wouldn't let us fuck up. We'll be all right. Let's talk with Imam and Sabah and tell them how we feel. I don't want to fail on this project. This is too important."

At 4 p.m. David's affirmation of Fatma's qualifications arrived by e-mail; "She is more than they could ever expect.... Dad." At 4:30 p.m. Fatma showed up at the flat in Chelsea with a laptop in a Tumi leather shoulder case with four copies of her employment contract, a business plan, and materials for Hunter and Ashley to read and later to be given to Imam and Sabah. The meeting was under the thumb of Fatma. She was in total control. She knew it, the boys knew it. It was what the girls had envisioned.

Hunter invited her to sit down and offered her a coffee or water, which ever she preferred, and said, "Ashley and I want to be honest. We feel you are more important to us than we are to you. We feel in over our heads. We don't want our mom and dad to run the project, but it's just too extensive and sophisticated for us. We know we need your help and theirs. At first I thought I would be a Bill Gates or Steve Jobs, young visionary, able to run a company. That was a pipe dream. I want you to be honest with us. If our parents and Imam and Sabah's parents were not rich, this would never happen. No way in a million years. Let's be honest here, just know we understand that fully. Let's be real. How can we not make fools of ourselves and do something meaningful, is the question?

Fatma said, "You just made my job easier. I was going to tell you almost the same thing. But that's good. If we know what we are we can make it work for us. No one is going to listen to you because you're so young. They will listen to the scientists you hire. Their credibility comes from results. Your status would be predicated on how you disseminate information and to whom you disseminate it. People will listen if science contributes. I have thought this through, and you will eventually be spokespeople for the project. But your strength is in the fact that you are not scientists. But that's premature. We have much work to do before we get there. You saw *those people*, roughly defined them, and think you know they are mutations and threats to civilization. So we will have scientists prepare position papers of a general nature from their research that you can understand. It will be condensed and made intelligible to you. You will digest it with theirs and my help. Then we will create a vehicle so you can be a spokesperson for it. I will filter all materials and prepare them for your eyes. I'm not being condescending, but your strength is you are not scientists. Hunter, I know you and Imam feel secure about being scientific. Your lack of graduate education makes it impossible at your ages. You're not Stephen Hawking. Your advantage is you're scientific enough to find the correct path for explaining *those people*. You won't be intimidated. You know enough to know what you don't know. It will be easier for Sabah and you, Ashley, because the business expertise needed is relatively easy. Your greatest strength will be your managerial and motivational skills. Guiding a team well is important and you both have innate skills in that area. Manage by example, your enthusiasm is infectious. We will make this work. At first your assembled team will think you are just little rich kids and pacify your parents by coming to me. That's fine. Over time your skills will shine if you have them. I think you do, your parents think you do, only time will tell you do truly have what it takes. It is up to you. You say this is important, we will find out if you are good enough to stick around and help me. Your families will not jeopardize their money and more importantly their reputations just to please you, they are not stupid people. They have clearly thought it out with their associates and think it has merit. They are successful for a reason and are pulling all the strings for a reason. Enough be said, they, that means I am in charge. Your success is dependent on your contributions and work, my standards, not yours. I can run G.O.F.E.M., but I am giving up much of my life. I will run you it for you, but I'm giving up a lot. My opportunity cost is not being with the Al Nassar groups as well as my emotional investment. I could do many things, but I really think this is important. A major consideration is I truly want to be with the girls. You are young and a lot will be in my hands, and of course, we will need your parents. You must speak to them the same way, in the same truthful manner that you have confided in me. Now, enough of this let us get to the science."

Fatma continued as if she never had to flex her power. The gang of four all knew she was right and felt the pressure of this huge undertaking. "We will need a geneticist to educate us. The five of us will be prepped or tutored tomorrow. If *those people* really exist, we need a framework for this scientific endeavor. Genetics is the vector or direction where the truth lies. We must prove that DNA changes or mutations caused *those people*. There will be a learning curve on genetics. The more we know, the cleaner the science. We will not be experts, but we will not be in over our heads, as you so aptly put it. We will begin tomorrow. Genetics will be the cornerstone of *those people* project. We have an appointment with a company called Genetics and Genealogy. A company we may purchase to do our genetic studies. They have a market value of two million dollars and are under funded. We can be a white knight, a friendly bidder as we call it. We'll talk tomorrow after they give us a tutorial on DNA. If we own the company we will have total security and control over a large portion of the science needed to prove *those people* really exist."

Fatma had come in running, they all wondered if they could catch up.

Thirty—five

At 8:30 a.m., Imam, Sabah and Fatma picked up Hunter and Ashley at their Chelsea flat. The limo ride to Genetics and Genealogy Inc. in Manhattan took 25 minutes.

William Steeleford, lead genetic engineer, would guide them through an elementary discussion of DNA and its role in genetic genealogy. Proper testing could map out a person's past as far back as Lucy and her emergence out of Africa. Tracing one's ancestral patterns through DNA analysis could be key to understanding *those people* and their evolutionary path.

Mr. Steeleford greeted them and insisted, "I have some perfunctory words for you. I hope I'm not too elementary. If I am, speed me up. If I am pedantic or too fast, slow me down. Make me explain things in ways you can interpret and assimilate. When I speak about DNA sometimes I get carried away," he smiled.

"Let's start, if I may, let me explain the process so you might have a total working construct. Then I will answer any questions. It will take 15 to 20 minutes to run through our approach here at G and G."

Steeleford started off by saying, "We use DNA markers to search for DNA linkage of known groups and specific geographical areas. All living things, including humans, are made up of cells. Humans are made up of many different kinds of cells, including skin cells, blood cells, basal cells, muscle cells, fat cells, and many more. Most of the cells in your body with the exception of red blood cells have a nucleus. There are nuclei in all our cells, it doesn't matter what cell type. Nuclei contain chromosomes and are responsible for storing our hereditary. Chromosomes are made up of DNA. DNA is like a blueprint because it holds the informational codes for all of a person's genetic information. The DNA for each individual is unique to that person. With the exception of the egg and sperm cell, all of the cells in a body contain 23 pairs of chromosomes, 46 in total. One chromosome from the pair is inherited from our mother and the other is passed down from our father."

He showed them a picture of the chromosome in each cell. "Both males and females have 23 pairs of chromosomes. However, in the male, the 23rd pair consists of an X-chromosome and a Y-chromosome, whereas females have two X-chromosomes. The Y-chromosome is special because it carries ancestral information regarding a male's paternal line. DNA looks like a twisted ladder and is often referred to as a double helix. The double helix consists of two complementary chains of DNA twisted together. If we were to hypothetically untwist DNA and lay it flat, it would look like a ladder. The two sides of the ladder are called the DNA's backbones. The steps inside the ladder represent bases. There are four types of bases in DNA: A for adenine, C for cytosine, G for guanosine, and T for thymine. In the DNA strands, A always pairs with T, and C always pairs with G. The unique sequence of A, C, T, G carries genetic information. DNA is deciphered by genetic testing. The DNA code can be written in the following manner: AGCT GGAC AATG G... etc. No two human individuals are the same, except for identical twins. None have exactly the same genetic code, and that's what makes everyone unique. However, all males with a similar background who originate from the same common lineage could share the same or similar DNA code. We will be looking for that code. A male inherits his Y-chromosome directly from his father. The Y-chromosome that a man receives from his father is very special because it holds a lot of valuable information about his ancestry and is passed down along the male line, relatively unchanged from generation to generation. We will try to look at these changes and mutations. Males who are descendants of the same line will have the same or nearly identical chromosomes. When a Y-chromosome genealogy test is performed, the laboratory examines specific regions that are called 'markers.' These features, called hyper variable regions, are regions or areas where the chromosomes can differ. Where a difference occurs, this is called an STR, standing for short tandem repeats. These are small chunks of DNA and are repeated over and over again. The following example of a Y-chromosome marker is called a DSY19. This section of DNA that repeats itself is TAGA. Thus, someone with a DSY19 marker of six will have TAGA repeated six times. Someone with a DYS19 marker of four will have TAGA repeated four times. By testing Y chromosomes, a DNA laboratory can provide you with a Y DNA marker which is specific to an ancestry because all males of the same ancestry will have the same DNA markers. You can enter your Y DNA marker into a gene base to solve questions about ancestry to conclude links between families and to discover distant relatives and mutations. When a Y-chromosome test is performed, up to 40 Y-chromosome markers are analyzed generating a unique profile for individual males with the same lineage have the same forefathers and will have similar profiles. Obviously, the more markers tested, the more powerful your test becomes, and the more information you can obtain and compare with our large gene database. All living things are made up of cells, and from cells we can discover details about DNA, from which we discover heritage or linage, and the mutation or evolution of sub species."

Thirty-six

Steeleford suggested, "There is another way to look at evolutionary change. During the pre-Cambrian explosion, about a billion years ago, life forms evolved from single cell organisms to multi-cell organisms, which precipitated into what is called "the sexual revolution;" organisms having sex with each other. Sexual reproduction, not single cell replication, allowed for more variation of species, which allowed mixing and matching genes. Contrary to the right-wing religious doctrine and its "intelligent design," evolution took over, and each organism generation was better suited for survival than the preceding one. There were more individuals of each species than the environment's ability to provide for survival support; hence, survival of the fittest. The natural selection process led to change in species. This process took hundreds of thousands of years, but better equipped organisms were able to cope with the ambient environment. We call this "sexual revolution to natural selection evolution." Each species has its own timeline for change, depending upon its survival environment. The process can be followed by DNA analysis over a time continuum."

Steeleford continued, "If we gather different people's DNA and match it with our existing database, we can measure these evolutionary changes or mutations. We don't expect to see any new species, but subspecies may be detected with enough matches of DNA along the Y-chromosome helix. With better more sensitive equipment we will be able to detect micro-chemical changes and measurements, or incremental deviations of the nth degree. We can revolutionize genetic studies of humankind. Coupled with new methods of measuring CO_2 and nitrogen levels of cells, we can place a person in a region anywhere in the world and map out his or her evolution. We can trace evolutionary variations all the way back to Lucy. We have everything in place for scientific breakthroughs taking us back to the origins of human beings. Refinements will come with second-generation spectrometers, cryogenic freezing units, new centrifuges and mainframe computers with enough memory and speed to simulate cell division over an infinite time span."

"We are able to see evolutionary changes let us forecast what nature has in store for us. Couple our science with global warming models, and we can follow ourselves into the future."

He paused. "Ms. Kassar, I am sorry. I must be overbearing in my presentation. Sometimes I get carried away and speak science talk. Do any of you have any questions?"

This was too much to digest.

Hunter said, after trying to absorb all of this, "It's impossible for me in one sitting. I do have further questions, but my brain is on over load. Is it possible that I can get back to you later?"

Imam, Sabah, and Ashley were quiet.

Ashley said, "I know I could not repeat all of this, but I do feel it's clear to me. Where can I get some reading materials so I can sound informed enough to discuss these things without coming off like a moron?"

The limo ride back to Washington Square, where all five would have a light lunch, was filled with energy and anticipation of the great scientific hunt awaiting them. A total affirmation of *those people* had been driven home by Steeleford's seminar. They would boldly move forward on their errand of knowledge.

Fatma said, "That was certainly a good first step. We have many organizational questions to address concerning your time commitments, your functions and responsibilities to G.O.F.E.M. Hunter, Ashley, do you still feel in over your heads? Or did Steeleford light a fire under you?"

Washington Square was one of New York's many small urban parks. Its proximity to NYU and student life, people of many colors and ethnicities felt comfortable to Fatma. The day was bright with late afternoon sun and the hustle and bustle of the streets seemed natural. This was to be a good home for Fatma. She fit into New York urban life. It was not much different from Cairo's wealthier crust where the Al Nasser's lived. The enlightenment and energy the five brought back from their meeting with Steeleford superseded any food or drink. The gang of four, plus one, was ready to get started on their journey.

Thirty-seven

Fatma called a meeting of the principals of G.O.F.E.M. Her vision of the organizational plan, with positions and titles for Imam, Sabah, Hunter and Ashley, was laid out.

She reiterated, "We don't have the luxury to just set up a for profit business, that is relatively simple. We can never loose sight of the danger of *those people*,"

She passed out a copy of atrocities committed in Angola where thirty people had been beheaded as hundreds stood by and chanted some unintelligible garble. They all looked at the fact sheets with a callousness coming with an overload of information. It was as if, I have seen this before, let's get on with business as usual.

Fatma told Hunter and Ashley they were to commit 40 hours a week to the endeavor. Special dispensation and accommodations for Ashley's classes in NYU extension were taken into consideration. Their responsibility was data collection and DNA evaluation. The task would include purchasing Genetics and Genealogy Inc., agreements and contracts with scientific centers that had appropriate databases, both public and private, and the actual collection of DNA from peoples of particular interest.

Because of time restraints, Imam's and Sabah's directive was supporting the project. They both still had educational commitments. Imam had a 20 hour schedule weekly. She worked on setting up a team to accumulate data and oversee its product.

Hunter would oversee Ashley in his acquisition of assets and purchases of information, even though business was not his first love he was much more knowledgeable than his brother when it came to financials. He would also be charged with the personnel decisions of each operation. He would have input from Sabah per her schedule of 15 hours a week. If actual physical collections of DNA were needed, Hunter and Ashley would work in tandem in the field.

Imam and Sabah would provide support by setting up travel accommodations, finances, communications and freight forwarding samples back. The four would be policymakers on an advisory board and they would be in the trenches with the scientific information collection to determine if *those people* really existed.

Fatma scheduled experts from different fields of study to better inform the 'four' on nuances of business and science. An interdisciplinary approach would give them the greatest chance of accomplishing their goal of finding *those people*.

"We are in the process of leasing a building in Chelsea," Fatma said. "It's small, about 3,000 ft². It will be our headquarters. I've already interviewed people, and we have the staff in place for our core business. We will have everything together in three to four weeks. In the meantime, I will have a cadre of scientists bringing you up to speed on how to approach *those people.* Tomorrow we will have an anthropologist from Columbia. His name is Dr. Renault. He will propose a way of analyzing the presence of any other subspecies of humans in our environment."

The afternoon meeting with Dr. Renault did not interfere with the academic schedule of Imam or Sabah.

"Well, let me begin by saying I'm here after having a preliminary meeting with Dr. Kassar. I would like to direct my remarks to our aforementioned discussion."

Imam and Sabah were not familiar with the pronouncement of Doctor; it had always been Ms. Kassar or Fatma. Things had progressed in their awareness of Fatma's professional recognition and stature.

Dr. Renault continued, "I'm going to present a view of competing human subspecies. Our existence as a distinct species dates back approximately 1.8 million years. You've heard of Olduvai Gorge and John and Mary Leaky and the findings in Tanzania and Ethiopia? They all date back to a similar time frame. There is, of course, Lucy and human migration out of Africa. It is all about 1.8 million years ago. This is all common knowledge. Some of us anthropologists theorize that in mankind's 1.8 million year journey, there have been many episodes of competing subspecies. We can take Neanderthal man that lived over 200,000 years ago cohabiting with Cro-Magnon man in sub alpine Europe. There is no evidence of genetic compatibility of the two subspecies. There are minority theories that expose very limited cross breeding, they surmise our DNA might contain 1% Neanderthal co-mingling but the majority of scientists express that the DNA shows two completely mutually exclusive species. They did compete for control of the same environment.

Neanderthal died out about 30,000 years ago, and we are the next successful evolutionary product. Mitochondrial DNA shows there are distinct differences between us and Neanderthal. You're looking at the possibility of a new subspecies of humans on the earth right now. If there are, their evolution is significantly faster than anything in the evolutionary history of primates. Our conjectures are the following; are we incorrect about their existence, or has something speeded up the evolutionary process to a hyper drive? We can show some subspecies crossbreed, mules are an example, but it may be what is called 'sum zero proliferation of competing subspecies.' Offspring of interbreeding can not reproduce. Let's look back on Neanderthal; they could have died out because of airborne pathogens, in other words a virus could have wiped them out. Maybe they couldn't crossbreed, or they died off because they could not compete for food. We don't know the exact reason or cause of their extinction. We just know they no longer exist, and we are the last subspecies of humans, and we have been around 25,000 to 30,000 years. If there are other subspecies, they cannot cross fertilize with us. We have no evidence of mixed genes. Competing sets of Homo sapiens were common throughout history, but we've never had cross-fertilization or a mix of genes. If there are *those people* in our midst, then why have they emerged so rapidly? It's important; we must look at the causality. I would venture to say that industrial byproducts and the creation of synthetics are the evolutionary cause of *those people*. We must be careful not to equate deviations with evolutionary change. There are many children with diseases like autism and Asperger's Syndrome. *Those people* may have some similar characteristics, in truth, they may not be a different subspecies at all, but have a medical condition or mental anomaly. They may be non-responsive, they might not have anything behind their eyes, as you say, but it might just be a mental illness, not a class of subspecies."

"I'm not trying to minimize their differences but they probably are the same as us. Environmental degradation may be the cause of new human subsets. I don't know. I generally lean toward your position. I do not know why, but as a person, not a scientist, I feel they are out there. Our tools for analyzing something of this nature are old, and they are more of a social science than a physical science. Our margin for error is great and our ability to prognosticate or forecast is limited. We are not analytical enough to actually determine if *those people* exist, but we can build models or guideposts for computer analysts. We in the private sector don't have enough computing power to replicate evolutionary changes and then follow them to a logical extension. I think IBM's Big Blue mainframe computer that costs more than $100 million, and is used by the Department of Defense to simulate a nuclear reaction in plutonium grade weapons to see how much they have degraded, can do the job. It has the capacity to image the division and subdivision of cells hundreds of billions of times if not trillions of times to follow the logical progression of human evolution and the advent of new subspecies. Anthropologists no longer just dig for bones and categorize them. Now we build programs and virtual models, and we try to enter data of our physical findings. There is something else of importance: anthropologists' personal agendas. There are many people and scientists with their own agenda, and it's an agenda other than knowledge. We must be careful, they are like the Crusaders and they do not compromise. Let me finish up by saying, I would love to help you. Even if it only means I can pass my opinion on to you and maintain a relationship so you can bounce ideas off me. You need an advocate. I'm not soliciting employment or remuneration, but I want to be on board in some way. I truly believe in your questioning of *those people*."

He paused. "Just one more thing, lay out a foundation for action. The easiest part of the science world is discovery. Its application and the ability to adaptation to real life is called the devil's work. The layers of an onion is a good example. The discovery is just the skin; it is the meat that makes it sweet."

Thirty-eight

The modest office with Spartan support staff was incongruous with the amount of product and revenue generated by G.O.F.E.M. Position papers formulated for foreign investors were a profitable endeavor. Operating income was the blood line of *those people* project. First-quarter profits were $38,000, with projections of $110,000 in the last quarter of the fiscal year. In her weekly board meeting, Fatma expressed optimism for how well the core business was performing. Most business endeavors are not breaking even operationally in the first 18 months. Our financials will be exceptional she said.

Routinely in weekly meetings, past business was discussed. New orders of business forwarded, and outside consultants offered their expertise.

Dr. Rosalina Gonzales from the University of Mexico was an authority on string theory and general physics. In the beginning, her remarks were taken with skepticism by all members of the advisory board. But in a matter of seconds, it changed to acceptance.

"Let me express my underlying theories of physics and reconcile quantum theory to the theory of relativity to explain the nature of all known forces and matter," she began.

"This is called string theory. Everything in nature is made up of loops of vibrating atoms strings. An apparent particle difference can be attributed to variations of vibrations. Objects, for example, humans in our discussion, can be broken down into atoms, which can be further broken down into electrons and quarks, which can finally be broken down into vibrations of strings loops. These strings can be on parallel planes. What this means, for us, is we can have two human types cohabiting the earth or any state at the same time. Using string theory, physical science can prove the existence of human subspecies mathematically. We can also approach competing life forms with something called Game theory. Game theory, simply put, is a mathematical framework for making choices. It analyzes any situation involving a conflict of interest, with the intent of indicating the optimal choice, that, under given conditions, can lead to a described outcome. The outcome for *those people* and the human race can have many variances. There could be cross breeding, and a mutation could result. There could be social or physical competition eliminating one subspecies -- us or them. There could be a mutually exclusive existence and segregation. There are many variations in Game theory that describe the outcomes in an unbiased way."

"Lastly, we can view *those people* in a system called Chaos theory. Again, a definition is necessary. Chaos theory describes the behavior of certain dynamic systems. Systems whose states evolve with time, may exhibit highly sensitive initial condition dynamics. As a result of the sensitivity which manifests itself as an exponential growth of perturbation in the initial condition, the behavior of chaotic systems appears to be random. This happens even though systems are deterministic. Meaning their future dynamics are fully defined by the initial condition with no random element involved. This is called dynamic chaos. What it means in simple terms, is we can prove or disprove mathematically that *those people* exist or do not exist. We can give you a new analytical tool for discovery and study of *those people*."

As was the pattern of board meetings, questions and detailed explanations followed. Fatma, looking across the table said, "Thank you, Dr. Gonzalez. This was not only informative but thought provoking as well." Her scientific interests were peaked.

But Hunter, Imam, Ashley, and Sabah were at a loss for words. This was over their heads. Fatma said, "I will get back to you."

Dr. Gonzalez's departure stirred conversation. Imam was the first to speak. "I followed her line of thinking somewhat, and it does lead to the conclusion we can prove *those people* exist by hard science."

Fatma said, "If we put it together with our other scientific body of knowledge, we can get somewhere. We can develop a tool to prove and forecast the future outcomes of *those people* and their influence on the human race."

Ashley said, "Every week we get another approach and they all say the same thing. We're at a point where we can build models to prove the existence of *those people* and share our findings."

Before he could say another word, Sabah said, "Who are we going to share our findings with if we determine them to be a threat to humankind? If *those people* are competing with us, is it not like war? Do we open them up to be slaughtered? We must look at the potential reactions of our findings. Is there a rationale for law and order people to kill them; or a reason for tribal killings to be acceptable? We have to be very careful who we employ and with whom we discuss this."

The meeting was adjourned. Food and company did not lighten the burden and gravity of their work.

Thirty-nine

"We just have one more expert session," Fatma said. "We will meet with representatives from Scripps and Caltech of the West Coast. I have talked to David, Diana, and Omar, so we will be meeting them in California on the 14th of October. We have two weeks to prepare a presentation that shows your parents our work warrants their investment. It must be informative. We will lay out our long-range planning. I will be responsible for the business side, all financials, income statements, cash flows, and pending contracts. It will be your responsibility to develop an overview of *those people* project finalizing a systems analysis and narrative of the operation."

Sabah said, "My dad is coming to California to see us?"

Fatma replied, "He's in the process of signing an agreement or letter of intent for purchasing the Laguna, California Ritz-Carlton Hotel. It's close to San Diego. Before I came over to the G.O.F.E.M. Group, we had lined up investors for this purchase. The financial problems in California's residential real estate market have put pressure on income properties, and your father can purchase the hotel at a discount. It will cost approximately $170 million or about 300,000 dollars a room. He wants a walk-through. He will be part of the due diligence process. He will visit David and Diana, while he's here and, of course, his lovely daughters."

Imam and Sabah were ecstatic.

Fatma said, "We will not mix family with business. We will be prepared beyond your father's expectations. When I say 'we,' I mean 'you.' You will please your father by exceeding his dreams. You must be seen in another stage of life, not as daughters, but as women of respect, for you are your father's daughters and professional women, no matter what your ages. Hunter, Ashley, the same goes for you. David and Diana have expectations. They think of themselves as enablers. All American parents think that they enable their children. Their help is needed for their children to be successful. We will dispel that notion. You will be seen as independent and worthy of all responsibilities bestowed upon you. Their involvement in this project will not diminish your stand-alone skills. Your closeness to them, all four of you, will have nothing to do with your worth. You will impart value to the project because of your skills, your passion and your vision. If not, you will failed. I know you are right for the job regardless of family connections. Now just prove it. In Egypt, there is a passage of wealth and power from father to oldest son, it is called primogenitary. Your parents have passed opportunities to the four of you. You will take the greatest advantage of what you have been given. You will prove up to the task."

Ashley said, "This may sound out of place, but you are so amped up you remind me of a coach, someone trying to motivate a team. I know you don't understand, but Hunter does." Yet again his smile lit up the room.

Fatma did not understand, but she knew he felt close enough to her that he could be himself, joke a little and a bond was forming. She would have four children/adults under her wings. Her shoulders were strong, and her heart was open. They would accept her tutelage, her ways and be better for it. They would win their parents over by hard work well beyond their years. The gang of four's transformation was in progress.

The flight to Los Angeles was scheduled to leave at 10:30 p.m. Eastern Standard Time and arrive LAX at 12:45 a.m. An LAX transportation van would pick them up and take them to David and Diana Russell's home in Bel Air, West Los Angeles. The Russell home was large enough for three extra guests. The Mediterranean-style home's casitas, with its three bedrooms and living area and small kitchen, would be adequate for Imam, Sabah, and Fatma. The casitas was off the courtyard of the 12,000 ft² main house. The house set atop Balagio Drive overlooking the Pacific and Catalina Island. The Bel Air country club golf course lay directly below.

David and Diana were waiting for them with a breakfast large enough to feed an army. It was natural in the Russell household to show respect and comfort by having food and conversation in the casual setting of the backyard pool area with its spectacular view. Diana, the ever doting mother, was interested in seeing Fatma's influence upon her sons. She was maternal. In one minute, any fear of competition was gone. Her appreciation for Fatma being a surrogate parent to her soon to be adult sons was expressed. The breakfast would be short.

A meeting with a climatologist/meteorologist was scheduled at the Russell Group's office at 12:30 p.m. The meeting was one of two scientific briefings scheduled for the three day stay in Southern California. Later, they would go to the San Diego Scripps Institute for an environmental science seminar. At 12:30 p.m., Dr. Cynthia Teicher, a recent Ph.D. in meteorology recipient from the University of Chicago and a climatology associate professor at Cal Tech, stood before them. She was small in stature; she looked no older than a teenager, but had an attention commanding voice. Her voice was a powerful tool for communicating because it held one's attention with its deep resonance and atypical cadence.

She started off by saying, "Much of my work is unconventional, and after discussing with Fatma, I can show how *those people*'s physical spatial displacement can be charted and forecast.

She said, "We have some sophisticated climate and weather forecasting models at our disposal. They show how the hydrological cycle carries water around the globe. The National Weather Service and the National Oceanic and Atmospheric Administration computer models are forecasting hurricanes and weather patterns and present a perfect technological template to assemble data on *those people* and derive their patterns of inhabitance. I feel industrial pollutants are concentrated in certain global regions because of weather patterns. These patterns can be studied; ergo *those people* locations can be determined. Pollutants are the major cause of mutations. After discussion with Dr. Kassar, it became apparent that *those people* live in areas other than northern temperate climate zones, except for urban pockets of pollution or areas of industrial concentration. The Southern Hemisphere is the location of greatest population of *those people*, and it is driven by climate change caused by greenhouse gases. In Europe and America, their population is driven by the toxicity of the environment. Climate and toxicity cause genetic mutations rendering a new subspecies of human. The combination of the two, high concentrations of toxins and climate change causes an incubator effect. Incubation causes *those people*s rate of development to be much faster. I hate to look to Al Gore and his movie, *An Inconvenient Truth* because it's so simplistic, but when he showed the exponential growth of CO^2 on his six foot screen, it was almost vertical in the last time element. It expresses the high levels of toxicity in the atmosphere. His famous Nobel Prize graph shows CO^2 as a cause of global warming and its attendant problems. Well, *those people* are a major attendant problem. To speak of global warming, we must discuss protocols, fingerprints; number one, heat waves and usually warm weather, number two, ocean warming, number three, sea level rise and coastal flooding problems, number four, glacier melting, and number five, Arctic and Antarctic warming. Environmentalists also discuss the harbingers of global warming; number one, the spreading of diseases, number two, early spring arrival, number three, plant and animal range shift and population changes. I will come back to this. Number four, coral reef bleaching, number five, heavy snowfall, flooding, drought, and fire. These are major problems caused by global warming. We will look at plant and animal range shifts and population changes. *Those people* fall into that category. We have seen there has been an atypical evolutionary pattern for amphibians, frogs in particular. We can use their hyper evolutionary changes as a map for *those people*. We can build models of warming patterns, pollution movements and show causality of *those people*; and what happened to the amphibians is now happening to humans. Let me use the hydrological cycle as an example. All water eventually collects in the oceans. Because of gravity, small creeks flow into streams that flow into rivers that flow into the ocean, from high to low. If water is trapped and can not flow, the law of gravity is no longer applicable; therefore, evaporation will bring water to the oceans. All water ultimately collects in our oceans. Now we look at the second law of thermodynamics or entropy. High pressure seeks a normality or low pressure regions, which causes wind patterns. An example is, let air out of a tire and it seeks the ambient atmosphere. You hear the hissing and feel the wind. The Gulf Steam is a pattern of air that follows a particular course. Evaporation causes clouds, they gather at the equator and the winds move them in fixed or recognizable patterns deviating only if temperatures change. Because of CO^2 gases or greenhouse gases and carbonation of the great mountain ranges, we have global warming and different weather patterns. I emphasize that industrial waste particulates follow the same pattern as precipitation, and therefore combine into the same wind patterns. If industrial pollution causes people's genes to mutate and bring about evolutionary change, we can find *those people* if there's an exaggerated level of pollutants or toxicity in the air. We can find *those people*, and we can create a working model to find their geographic location. I am simplifying things, but it does work like this. *Those people* are there. We can find them. We can forecast their spread, and we can determine a timeline for their concentrated arrival."

Forty

Omar Al Nassar arrived LAX at 12:30 p.m. and was taken directly to the Beverly Wilshire Hotel. He cleaned up and made ready to meet his daughters, Fatma and the Russell's for dinner. His flight was long, but the anticipation of seeing his daughters made the ten-hour journey more pleasant. Omar had refused the Russell's' invitation to stay with them. He did not want to intrude and felt it would be better for Imam and Sabah and Fatma. He was worried they might attend to him too much. A parental separation as it were, they were no longer in his nest.

"Tonight we have reservations at the Ivy restaurant on Robertson at 8:30 p.m.," Diana said.

"That should give you enough time to rest by the pool, if you like, and get ready for dinner. We will meet your dad there," she directed this to Imam and Sabah.

"The Ivy is like all Westside restaurants, a little trendy, good food, and the paparazzi are always there. If the four of you want to be by yourselves after we eat, Omar and Fatma and David and I will understand. There are some nightclubs nearby. But, and there is always 'a but', tomorrow morning will be early. We fly to John Wayne Airport in Newport Beach, from there Omar is nice enough to let us walk through the Ritz Hotel with him, and finally to Scripps where we interview Dr. Jonathan Williamson. Fatma said, "Dr. Williamson is a possible technology project manager. He will help us with *those people*."

Diana was the consummate host. Her planning for everyone was almost anal, if not totally controlling, but it was done for her guests' pleasure, not her own comfort.

After dinner and the exit of the younger set, as Omar liked to call them, the adults could talk. The terms "daughter" or "children" made Omar feel old and paternal. "Younger," the term he liked to use, equated him with them, and he could live through their actions and experiences more easily. Their stories, even though couched, made Omar feel his youth. Imam and Hunter, Sabah and Ashley felt parity existed between themselves and their parents when they could sit and share experiences and stories. No lines of age blurred their relationship. They were friends and now, colleagues, in the pursuit of *those people*. The passage of power and position in their families would take place soon enough.

As Diana put it, "You kids are no longer children. Very soon you'll be taking care of us. Not in a financial way, but in life terms and vicissitudes." She liked to use her extensive vocabulary.

After the four left, the talk of children and their own ambitions led to what was next for *those people* project. Sitting outside at the Ivy and watching the young West LA crowd, as they were called, was as far removed as one could be from *those people* and the matters of social importance.

Omar wanted to express an idea. "I know you have just recently opened an office in New York for our children. I cannot express my gratitude and thanks enough. The children are well suited for each other, and matters of the heart are central to the young. Accepting Fatma as a mentor and administrator was wise, but more importantly to me, she is a lifeline to my daughters. I could not have asked for as much. You did not do all this solely for me and my investment. I know that. I know some regard for my family was taken into consideration. I will never be able to express my appreciation properly. I have a suggestion, though. I would like to move the operations of *those people* here to California and leave the Chelsea office in New York for their core business. Fatma has brought the operation to a point where we can have someone else manage it. We can bring in our own people, and it will stand on its own. It will fund *those people* project. If I may express my indulgences, please hear my request."

If I can express my indulgences, he stood up. Please hear my request. I want my children nearer to you.

He stood up, "I want my children nearer to you. It is apparent that scientists and technologists can be brought to Los Angeles and our operation will not be the lesser for it. You and I know Fatma can make this work. The three of us will need to be more involved. I'm asking for more direction on your side, and, of course, more oversight of my daughters. If I am intruding on your family and its ways, I am truly sorry. If you want to have your sons in New York for reasons other than Imam and Sabah, a thousand pardons. I am going to buy the Ritz-Carlton Hotel and I will spend much time in Los Angeles. I will have need for a home here and I thought our children would be better cared for if they were with you, and occasionally, me. If I am stepping on lines drawn by your family I shall step back. I will, of course, honor your plans and desires."

Both David and Diana were taken aback. It was like an out of body experience. Listening to someone else express their hidden ambitions to be closer to their children and be more connected to them as important. The idea of working with Hunter and Ashley and Omar's daughters was euphoric; the narcotic of love's proximity to one's children. Diana, who made all decisions, big or small, with respect to the children, was in total concurrence. Only the logistics had to be worked out, which was her forte.

She said, "Omar, what of Imam and Sabah's last year at NYU, and of course, their friends? Have you discussed this with them? I do not want them closer if it means too close. They have to grow up. I don't want to smother them."

Omar said, "My dear Diana, the project will smother them and make them old beyond their years in short order. We can somehow arrange for their school later. This experience and its outcome are much more important to them and to me."

David said, "I may be able to help you with school. I am on the Graduate School of Real Estate advisory board at NYU. I agree with you in every way. But as Diana says, there is always a 'but': the tension between their work on the project and our increased oversight is always tenuous. We must be careful and clearly delineate ours and their functions and responsibilities, not only in business, but in family. I don't yet know our role in all this."

Omar replied, "It will come to the light. Answers always surface for people like us. Diana, I will sound presumptuous, but you must play a major role in this project. Your passion and skills in bringing together all elements of society are extraordinary. Sharif has told me of your charitable work and the political groups you have led and your constant involvement in affairs of community. We are just businessmen, David and I, so if we do find *those people*, it will be you who must give us direction in presenting our findings. This will not be an easy task."

It was getting late and Omar needed to get back to the Wilshire Hotel. He was mindful of the early flight to Orange County, and jet lag was creeping into his conscience. He had to address a clause in the letter of intent to purchase, before tomorrow when he would walk through the hotel and interview the management staff. He had to mold it all to perfection before the actual deliberations took place tomorrow morning. As was his mode of operation, he wanted bring to his attention every conceivable circumstance that could possibly unfold.

David said, "Omar, we will have the car for you tomorrow morning at 7 a.m. It will take you to Van Nuys Airport. This is the largest private airport in the world by flights per day. We have a King Air that holds eight plus our crew. It is a workhorse plane for short flights. It's a turboprop and very comfortable, but it's slow, maybe 300 knots per hour. We will arrive in Orange County after about 40 minute's flight. Vehicles will be waiting for us. They will drive us to the hotel which is approximately 30 miles away. It might take 30 to 40 minutes, depending upon traffic. Is this okay with you? If not, we can make arrangements at any time you wish."

"David," Omar said, "this is what Sharif likes so much about you. He told me, 'Leave everything up to David.' I am most comfortable with that. See you tomorrow morning, my friends."

As David and Diana were driving home after dropping off Omar, David's cell phone rang. Diana knew it was something important from the look on David's face. William was calling from Kenya.

Imam and Hunter and Sabah and Ashley were sitting in the trendy Sky Bar club in Hollywood. Hunter's cell phone rang, he didn't want to answer but saw it was David.

David sounded disturbed, "Hunter you guys need to come home immediately."

"Dad, what has happened?"

"There has been an incident in Kenya. William just called. Please come home so we may discuss this before tomorrow."

"We're leaving now. Everybody, let's go," Hunter turned to the other three and grabbed the bill, paid and started walking.

It took a few minutes for Sabah and Ashley and Imam to understand something was happening, but soon they were following Hunter out the door to the valet and their car.

As Hunter drove he explained the call from his dad. He would never make demands to come home immediately, if it were not serious. They were all four nervous and excited by the time they reached home.

Diana was holding the door open as they walked from the garage. "Come on kids we have to talk."

David sat in the living room looking very serious. "William just called me about an hour ago. In the outskirts of Mombassa there has been a pack of *those people* harassing, raiding farms for food and just being mostly annoying, until tonight. There were about fifty farm workers being housed on a large plantation who were murdered in the most brutal ways. They were ripped apart, eaten, and left as carrion. There is a back lash coming from the tribes who have banded together to wipe out *those people*."

Diana continued, "Surely there will be other countries watching this unfold."

Ashley wide eyed, "Do you think we are too late to do something about the problem?"

"This is just one incident but it will be an example of what can happen. Maybe, we'll get more help with our research." Imam stated, shaken but still constant in her diligence.

The family and Al Nassar girls talked well into the night about the ramifications of this incident.

Forty-one

Morning came early for Imam and Hunter and Sabah and Ashley after a night of clubbing at the trendy Sky Bar in Hollywood and the late night assessment of the Mombassa incident. The early flight and transportation to the Ritz-Carlton was uneventful. The beauty of Laguna Nigel's beaches where the hotel stood atop a horseshoe cliff was magnificent. The recently refurbished Ritz Carlton was one of three five-star hotels in Southern California. There were only a few top tier properties of value in San Diego and Orange County area, and the Ritz was its jewel. The $170 million price tag in a down market was a substantial discount for Omar because his business dealings were in Euros. The value of the Euro relative to the dollar since 2001 had appreciated 47%. He had to buy the property for no other reason than it was so inexpensive and in the long run it would be handsomely profitable. He could not walk away. Needless to say, Imam and Sabah loved it regardless of its business value. Its beauty in Southern California could not be matched.

The drive to Scripps was 45 minutes along the California coast. The deep blue Pacific was lovelier than any waters the girls had ever seen. The sight of surfers, skate boarders, and tourists in October was not a familiar sight to Omar and his daughters. They drove through Carlsbad, Solana Beach, and Del Mar and its race track before reaching Scripps Institute. The only place the girls could relate this drive to was Sharm El-Sheikh on the Red Sea. The Scripps Institute, overlooking Tory Pines and Black Beach, was next to the University of California at San Diego campus. It was another of California's beach treasures. Its beauty could not be surpassed.

Dr. Williamson's office was adjacent to the aquarium and medical research center on the Scripps campus. Fatma led the contingency into a conference room where Dr. Williamson was waiting. David, Diana, and Omar did not know what to expect. They only knew that Fatma's decision making was beyond reproach. They would be spectators, not participants, in these proceedings.

Dr. Williamson introduced itself, "Let me tell you a little of my background. I asked Dr. Kassar not to discuss me with you. It would prejudice your opinion of me and my talents, if I really have any, he smiled. I am an environmentalist, first and foremost. My actual function is that of the project manager. I was lead on the United Nations Millennium Project, I have worked on disparate endeavors, from the Mars Explorer landing vehicle at JPL, to leading Operation California, a nonprofit agency providing world disasters medical relief. I was a provost at the University of Michigan. I just run things, and I do so rather well. My discussion with Dr. Kassar makes me believe we are on a path of epoch discovery. I have been peripatetic all my career; bouncing from one scientific activity to another. But my resume is full of successes. It had been my desire to embrace as many different scientific endeavors as possible. But this one stands out. *Those people* project will have my complete attention and interest. It would be my honor and privilege to be involved. Dr. Kassar, may I call you Fatma, has assembled a team of experts without equal. Dr. Steeleford, DNA, Dr. Renault, anthropology, Dr. Gonzalez, physics and mathematics, and Dr. Teicher, climatology. With your permission, may I add one more member to our staff to be named later? But it's not a scientific member. We will need someone to navigate the scientific waters when we unveil our findings. Yes, I say 'when,' for I believe you're 100% correct in your assessment of the other human subspecies on the planet Earth. The science is not sophisticated, it is easy. But it is costly, it is very expensive. You know from your discussions that we are close, very close to finding *those people*. The first 90% cost 10% of your money and its costs 90% to find the next 10% and the longer we wait in science the costs rise exponential. To reach 91% it costs 15% more, to reach 92% it costs 23% more and so on. So we must start now. Hunter, Imam, Sabah, and Ashley, your definition, your discussion of discovery and the impact of *those people* is first rate. It's good science, to say the least. We will change the format but you have distilled our quest to its very core. The specialists you have hired are all on the mark. It is my job to use all this information developing a model which can withstand the scientific method and prove the existence of *those people*. As I said it will be very costly, very dear in dollar terms. Then we have to put our findings to work. Let me give you a couple of scenarios. We can lease a supercomputer or mainframe with enough power, or we can develop a simple connectivity of many smaller computers; with either one of these I.T. set ups, we can simulate the genetic linkage that leads to *those people*. We will plot their development and their spatial placement around the globe. We can forecast the clash of human subspecies in a timeframe. These findings will be replicable, our best science. Then we go out to tell the public. How can this be done? Is it by scientific journal, or by a Washington DC lobbyist? I don't know. Do we inform private foundations and organizations. Or just bring the government, whoever that is, into it? Our problem is to disseminate the information. If we tell the southern countries, say Zimbabwe or South Africa, how will they react? Ex-President Mbeki of South Africa thought AIDS was a lie and later a US plot to kill Africans. A global conspiracy, he thought. How would you react to this if your country had the highest percentage of AIDS victims in the world and you were totally ignorant, and now someone, a white scientist tells you about *those people*? What if Robert Mubabe of Zimbabwe, a vitriarchal and mendacious man of total depravity, is told that *those people* exist? How do you think he will react? If you said to him, 'Your people are not really your people, they are *those people*', what would be his thinking? If they were his followers, would he give them more land and bounties of corruption? If they were the opposition party, would he kill them all? In either case, there would be no regard for the real problem facing humankind. Tell Jesse Jackson that we have to exterminate blacks. Tell him that the black community has many of *those people*, and what do you think his reaction will be, even if science proves it to him, then what? We would be viewed like Shockley at Stanford. We would be viewed as racists no matter what the science. Tell Rockwell of the KKK and he would feel the same way, even if we showed him evidence of his neo-Nazi's evolving into *those people*. What would he think? I could go on and on. The science is costly, but easy. It is the world recognition of our findings that will tell the tale. I truly believe that we are understating those people global danger. They must be stopped or humanity as we know it will cease to exist in less than 50 years. Our findings are monumental, and I'm not exaggerating the science. How is that for being forthright?"

Forty-two

Two weeks passed before another meeting was scheduled with Jonathan. The meeting scheduled for general business would pick a West LA home office site location, and new business prioritizing research to be conducted. The Russell group's boardroom was the project meeting place until new facilities could be found. In attendance were Jonathan Williamson, Fatma, Imam, Sabah, Al Nassar, Hunter and Ashley.

Jonathon passed out the agenda and said, "Let me start off by discussing our meeting of two weeks ago. I believe through impetus brought trying to import caution and apprehension, I appeared rough and negative, about the political consequences of our work. Let that stand for the moment. We will address it when we have conclusive evidence of *those people.*

We must send teams into the field for collection of DNA. We can hire outside consultants and contract them to collect what we call live DNA, or we could have the four of you expedite its extraction yourselves. If there is involvement of the four of you, this will be a delicate proposition.

Our new findings show live DNA can present different results than extraction of DNA from dead subjects. Mutations of DYC37 on chromosome 17 six markers are different between live and dead subject's DNA samples. Mutations are obfuscated in dead samples, and readings are not indicative of the true machinations. The DYC37 may not replicate itself fully, not the six markers, but a fraction less, say, 5.99999 markers. This causes the mutation. A nano-change or mutation brought about by carbonic acid will be differentiated enough to be detected. Not just carbonic acid, but any synthesized substance. If cells escape the human body, they reconstitute fully back to DYC37 6 markers, even if there are mutations. Mutations or evolution will not be noticeable.

If we can biopsy DNA samples in sutro, which means within the human body, then we may show provable changes in DNA. This must be done at 40°C, or the DNA will reconstitute itself and will show no changes. That's where the four of you come in. Scripps Institute developed a probe which extracts and freezes samples of DNA within a human body. You plunge it into the designated part of the person's brain. We can analyze this sample. It must be extracted from the frontal lobe of the cerebral cortex, where cognitive recognition or consciousness takes place. It's the brain area where activities initiate in response to our environment, judgment about everyday activities, control environmental responses, language, memory, and motion activities. We feel frozen DNA samples will prove *those people* DNA in this area of the brain is different.

These samples must be retrieved before they leave the subject's body or they become oxidized and reconstruct themselves. I want you to look at DNA as a memory performing plastic. These plastics will always go back to their original form when heated. Like a hair brush. If we heat up and bend a hair brush, it always goes back to its original shape. It is the DNA oxygenation by carbonic acid causing the mutations. If the DNA isn't in sutro, we cannot show there have been changes. We must study DNA in a frozen state of animation before it reconstitutes itself.

There are four known major human groups who have life spans of more than a hundred years. We will look at them and compare them to *those people*. There is one of these groups living in Loma Linda, California, one near Papagayo, Costa Rica on the Pacific side, another at Okinawa, Japan, and lastly, one in Sardonia, Italy. There is information available from these four groups of over one hundred year old people. The life span of humans is one hundred and seventeen years at the outside margin. When we talk about expanding a life expectancy, it means we are approaching the limit, not extending it.

Our preliminary findings show that *those people* don't live very long, outside margins of 50 years. We can compare people that will live a hundred years to *those people* that live 50 years. We must get live frozen samples of *those people* and compare them to live frozen samples of different cohorts."

"But how will we get the samples?" asked Hunter. "I don't think they will volunteer them."

"It won't be easy," replied Jonathon. "Most people will not want to give their DNA samples. This is self-evident. We must develop teams to capture targets, hold them defenseless, extract samples, and do analysis; all of this will be done in an illegal manner.

We will be viewed as Frankenstein's if we are detected, and God forbid, caught. Surreptitious by definition and insidious by deed will be our credo. No accountability directed to us, for we will have no way to explain our actions. If we are caught, we will be viewed as Joseph Mengelas. This must be done in secret, in total secrecy."

Forty-three

Jonathon continued, "I know we've discussed a lot, are there any more questions?"

Hunter was first to respond, but he was cut off by Fatma. "Mr. Williamson, I will not let my charges break laws or do anything immoral. I know things have to be done, but this is not the nature of our involvement. I have made other arrangements"

Hunter said, "Jonathan, if we do what you suggest we will be criminals. We will be kidnappers, or at least, party to it. If we extract the DNA as you've suggested, that could be attempted murder or something like that, people could even die. This is hard stuff. Things are never simple, there is always risk. Usually there are unintended consequences of illegal activities. I'm just a kid, but it seems way too risky to me. We are not covert operators; we have no skills for this kind of stuff. In reality, we are little rich kids, the four of us, we are not streetwise, and we do not have a criminal mentality for this kind of work. I feel we would be in danger." Excuse the language but I want no part of the illegal crap.

Hunter's remarks were echoed by Ashley, Imam and Sabah. They were frightened. They really did not know what to do, but there was excitement about the romantic notion of working undercover. They did know their limitations, and Fatma wanted to make sure nothing would happen to them. There would be nothing illegal or dangerous for the five of them.

Jonathan listened intently before countering with his proposed plans for action. "I know fully that you are not qualified. You do not have the stomach for this work, therefore, we will hire field agents to do the heavy lifting. I have discussed these matters with Blackwater, a security organization. They are sending some associates to discuss and present a bid for their services. Very soon you will be introduced to Mr. Jones and Ms. Smith, absolutely pseudo-names to keep their identifications and involvement secret. If you think about it they are a pretty scary outfit. They will discuss the logistics of getting DNA and our involvement. Fatma, I have exceeded my authority, but I think you will concur with Blackwater's appraisals of the operation when you hear it. Sometimes I am a hard charger but that is my nature, I won't apologize, it's just me."

On cue, Mr. Jones and Ms. Smith came through the conference doors. He was 6'2" tall, and chiseled. His strength was apparent by the way his clothes hung on the massive frame. His size was physically unsettling to people, this gave him a clear advantage over an adversary. His posture was erect; his movements were smooth and deliberate. His suppleness made him look lethal. He reminded Ashley of the leopards they had seen in Africa. The cool, collected nature of his demeanor made him seem bigger than life.

Ms. Smith was beautiful in an exotic way. She looked Euro-Asian, large black olive eyes, high cheekbones, and the muscled back of an Olympic swimmer. The athletic proportions of her body hid her size. She was 6 feet tall and 180 pounds of tempered steel. Her beauty and physiognomy also gave her the advantage of intimidation.

The pair's polished presentations opened the group's eyes to their intellect and tactical professionalism.

Mr. Jones spoke. "We've given you a general overview of our company's capabilities and resources. I will now begin my analysis of extracting DNA from two tribal peoples, the Quecha and the Aymara in the highlands of the Ubamba River Plateau region in Peru. These people have little or no contact with outsiders. They live in an enclave. Their DNA will be virgin, as we call it. I'll base my assumption on the fact that the four of you will be operatives in an ancillary way. You will not directly participate in any covert actions. We must have a cover for you. You will be given proper identification, passports, driver's licenses, credit cards, degrees and credentials if needed. A body of published works will be attributed to you, so you have a history. Hunter, let me start with you. Because of your photographic background, you will be an associate explorer for National Geographic magazine. We have to retrofit you with photographic equipment."

Hunter thought he had the best camera equipment available but was mistaken and taken aback by his lack of knowledge relative to real professional photographers.

Hunter broke in and said, "How do you know about my photography? I've never taken a class or published anything."

Ashley spoke up, "Man, that's pretty intense, do you guys spy on everybody?"

Mr. Jones said, "Look at these materials. We have tracked the purchases of your photo equipment on-line at BH Photo in New York. We followed up at Bel Air camera and Samy's camera in Los Angeles. We have good recognition of the level of your photographic skills. You will need some tutorials. Our staff will prepare some scenarios with Lia Roberts of Shutterbug Magazine and bring you up to speed. She will equip you with a new camera of choice by professional photographers. It is a Hasselblat H^2D. Imam will be a technical and logistic adviser, as this would be consistent with her engineering background. She will be helpful in preparing a geological and geographic component of the photo shoot story you have written for National Geographic. We have a copy here that you could view. You're going to do a photo shoot of the Quecha and Aymara, they are of Mestizo origin. Sabah and Ashley, because you are younger, it is more plausible you work for an online magazine. We picked Slate Magazine. You will, also have new identification. Here are some of your works." He gave the group a folder.

"The four of you will be accompanied by a team who will do the actual DNA extraction. Here is a tactical and logistical analysis."

He gave them another group of papers. Mr. Jones laid out more materials that accompanied the PowerPoint presentation which was to follow. He finished his segment of the presentation by saying Ms.

Smith would answer any questions to fill in the gaps with each of the four impending participants on an individual basis. Jonathan thanked them for their time and information. Mr. Jones and Ms. Smith gathered their materials and left.

"Well," said Fatma, "this is why we make money. Blackwater is the best. You are a hard charger as you call it, thanks for the all the preparation. However did you engage Blackwater. They are impressive. If we interact with them, we will get our intended results."

Jonathon responded, "Just one question, they are military in the middle east, are they not?"

Ashley said, "This sounds like black ops. If we are involved, I want absolutely no guns or weapons. Shit, give me a gun and I would probably shoot myself. And I sure as fuck don't want guns around Sabah." This was a bold statement of affection from Ashley as he looked toward Sabah.

Ashley continued, "Fatma, it's your job not to let this get out of hand."

Jonathan said he had expressed the same concerns with the Blackwater group about violence and potential illegal activities. Mr. Jones had assured him that Ms. Smith was the only lethal weapon needed.

Jonathan added, "Any illegal activities will not be borne by the four of you, and you will never be in harm's way. The Blackwater group has a remarkable history of successful operations in Iraq that should translate to success for this simple DNA extraction. Any forged passports or papers for you four will be for business consumption and will only be used for the vagaries of conducting negotiations. The documents will not be carried by the four at any other time. The false papers will never be presented to anyone at a governmental official capacity. Hunter, Imam, Ashley, and Sabah will be camouflaged for Blackwater's operations, if the proposal were accepted."

Forty-four

As Sabah and Ashley were exiting the conference room, she grabbed his hand and said, "That guns and weapons thing you said was sweet. Did you really mean it?"

"Of course, I meant it. I would blow my head off if I had a gun. Just kidding."

That smile once again lit up the room. He squeezed her hand and said, "Of course, I meant what I said. I would lay down my life for you. Hopefully it will never come to that, but I don't want you to be in danger, especially over the *those people* project, or anything else."

Sabah said, "I think we are in safe hands with Blackwater."

"Why?" Ashley said, "Do you know anything about Blackwater?"

She responded, "I do. They are infamous in the Middle East. They are the US security guards in Iraq. They are responsible for the security of all US diplomats and all Iraqi national politicians. They are professional mercenaries, and control the Green Zone in Baghdad. And they were the first responders in New

Orleans when hurricane Katrina devastated that city. Actually not bad for an Egyptian girl, is it?"

Ashley was impressed. He said, "Do all Egyptian beauties know this stuff, or only you?"

"No, really, Ashley, they are known all over the Arab world for their ruthlessness and extra governmental powers. They are a country unto themselves. No responsibilities to any government, only responsibilities to those who pay."

"We should talk to Fatma and Hunter and Imam. I really want to do this, but probably for all the wrong reasons," Ashley said. "I think it will be cool, and I really think it will be safe. I think Blackwater will protect us."

The five were in conversation at the elevator when Jonathan walked up.

He said, "I know that was a lot to digest, and it really sounds dangerous, but we can farm it out totally to Blackwater if you wish. We don't need physical involvement if you don't want us to be. Isn't it interesting no one wanted Fatma or me to go with them?"

Blackwater had presented a scenario where only the four younger members of the team would be out into the field as they called it. "Are we too old? Again, if you think it's too dangerous, then we will just send them. Why don't we meet tomorrow and discusses the details, and, of course, let's think about discussing this with David, Diana, and Omar. Fatma, is that okay with you?"

Fatma responded, "Listen, Jonathan, I am only the money person and scientific overseer, and, of course, the girls are my total responsibility; so if they go, I go. Blackwater will have to change their operations."

Jonathan said, "Does that mean that I'm left behind, they left me out?"

Ashley smiled and said, "Let's vote on it. Just kidding. I think we're all a team, and if the four of us go, you two should also go. But I can't imagine the two of you together. Again, just kidding."

While looking at everybody, Ashley said, "What do you all think?"

It was unanimous. Jonathan was now part of the gang of four plus two.

"One more thing," Jonathan said, as the elevator door opened. "Thank you; it will be an adventure of a lifetime. Let's look at the Blackwater reconnaissance and discuss it. See you tomorrow, and again, thanks."

The next morning after breakfast at La Marmaton in Marina del Rey, the six decided to sit outside at the common's and discuss the Blackwater proposal. They were very mindful of being in a public place.

Fatma said, "After reading all the position papers, I'm in agreement that the Quecha and the Aymara people are perfect. Their tribal territory is so remote and they are so xenophobic that I now know why their DNA is called virginal. No industrial contaminations can reach them in the Llabamba rain forest where they live and where they gather food. They are so primitive. They are gatherers, not even farmers, and of course, there is no tribal intermingling, making their DNA pure. I like the idea of comparing their DNA with that of *those people*. We will compare other cohorts with *those people* also. I think we must have 25 different comparisons to give the research total validity. We will pick DNA from 25 *those people* from diverse places around the globe. Each DNA will be compared with

25 virgin DNS's. That means 25 times, 25 comparisons."

Imam said, "Oh, you mean 25 squared, or 625." She smiled.

Fatma, looking at Jonathan, said, "You are the environmental expert, but I like the model I have developed. What do you think?"

He said, "I think you have thought this through and on first blush it seems good to me."

The six left the commons and walked to the fisherman's village, a tourist attraction. Marina del Rey, the largest small yacht harbor in the world, was at its best. The clear sky coupled with 70°F windless temperature was perfect. The six of them walked through the marina to world famous Venice Beach. Conversation passed to the beautiful beach, the exceptionally strange inhabitants of Venice, California, and matters of the heart for the group of four. Fatma and Jonathan were strangely feeling the pressures of socialization outside *those people* context. It was as if they were courting as they walked on the Strand towards the Santa Monica pier.

The next afternoon, a call was placed to the field office of Blackwater affirming G.O.F.E.M.'s desire to engage their services. All contractual materials were to be viewed by outside counsel as the procedure at G.O.F.E.M. Blackwater's in-house counsel had written the contracts and any changes would be ironed out. After a few minor changes, a per-assignment fee was agreed upon with proper confidentiality clauses. The fee would be $225,000 for the Ubamba project which would extract DNA from the Quecha and Aymara people. Fatma's financial prognostications of $2,000,000 - $2,750,000 for DNA extraction for cohorts starting with the Peruvian venture were within *those people* budget. Some extractions of DNA were intricate and dangerous, and therefore expensive, and some were as simple as a fee-based simulation of clinical trials; simple and inexpensive. Project Ubamba would jumpstart the cohort analysis phase. Three weeks were established as the time frame to make the necessary changes to the Blackwater plan with the inclusion of Fatma and Jonathan.

Forty–five

"This is Fatma, meet me at Jerry's Deli near UCLA by eight o'clock. This is important. I got a call from your mom, and she is incredulous about our participation in the extraction of DNA and our trip to Peru. Your parents, or as your mom puts it, the principles of G.O.F.E.M., want us to be at their house immediately. I held them off until 9:30."

She placed a call to Jonathan. He did not respond so she left a voice mail. It was returned in two minutes.

"Jonathan, I got a call from Diana, and then a call from Mr. Al Nassar. We are scheduled for a conference call at 9:30 at the Russell house in Bel Air. The six of us have to be there."

"I guess you were on your cell when I called; Diana Russell called to inform me about the meeting at 9:30. I've never been talked to that way in my life. Her disdain and anger were so measured, she was in perfect control, and it was frightening to be talked to that way. I told Ashley and Hunter we would meet near UCLA at Jerry's Deli at eight o'clock. The restaurant is close to the Russell house. We should discuss our reaction to her anger and indignation. Jonathan, I have worked for the Al Nassar family for 25 years and lived in their house all my life; altogether I have known Mr. Al Nassar for more than 40 years. He has never given me an order, he has never told me what to do. In this case, Mr. Al Nassar ordered me to be at the Russell house with Imam and Sabah. He said no more. It makes it harder when he never said why we were to meet. It is implied, and we know why, but it is heavy on my neck, as we say in Egypt. I have seen him do this in business; he wants an advantageous position in any event of importance. Being that these are his daughters, and that I am entrusted with them and I'm supposed to oversee them, he has every right to be agitated and angry. I will collect the girls, and we will see you at eight o'clock, if not before."

All parties were at Jerry's Deli by 7:30. After finding tables in the deli's outside area, calm started to prevail.

Hunter said, "Well, what do they expect from us? Dad always says stand up for what you believe, and I believe we should go to Peru."

Fatma looked at the group and phrased her words very carefully. "We all assume they are angry at our decision to go to Peru with Blackwater. We must present a rationale on a basis they cannot refute: our emotions. Something to this effect: it is our calling to do this, or we have to because it's the right thing; something of a psychological viewpoint. You can't argue with someone's feelings or emotions."

Everyone accepted Fatma's interpretation of how they would proceed.

Jonathan said, "I just have to say this. When I agreed to work with you, I looked into and did research on the Russell Group and Omar Al Nassar. It became clear that Diana Russell was an accomplished heavyweight in Southern California. Her charitable work and her political connections are notable. She is a powerful woman. But she is more than that. I told Fatma of an abbreviated conversation I had with her about the project, and she is formidable beyond description. We will most likely have to deal with her rather than David or Omar. She is angry. She is hurt by the lack of supervision of her children. But more importantly, she is a mother. I don't want to sound sexist, but that is a combination of great power and strength."

Ashley said, "I always heard Dad call her 'the mouth' when they get into arguments. He would put his hands together at the palms and open them up menacingly like a crocodile when they have a heated discussion. He would inevitably say, 'I can't argue with you. You have too much energy, and this means more to you than it does to me.' He would usually just quit. He would just sit there, until she just ran out of steam, kind of like a balloon when all the air leaks out. Maybe that is a bad picture of mom, but you get the idea. I think he knows her words are like knives. Dad would wait calmly and then present his position without emotion and she would listen. She was a different person after she got it out. From that point on, they were on equal ground."

Sabah said, "It's getting late and we certainly must be on time. Ashley, can you get the check and let's get out of here."

The formal living room was opened, and the Russells were already seated when Hunter, Imam, Sabah, Ashley, Fatma, and Jonathan entered. Nothing was said, but all eyes were on the speaker phone on the large coffee table near the couch.

Diana finally said, "We will begin when Mr. Al Nassar calls. It should be 10 minutes or so. Does anyone want coffee or tea? I will go get them."

No one accepted her offer. The 10 minutes seemed like a lifetime.

Omar Al Nassar called promptly at 9:30 a.m. David greeted him by saying, "My friend, we are all here. It is important for us for you to be part of this dialogue."

Omar said in perfect British English, "I would not be tardy or absent from any such discussion of my daughters' welfare and safety. Is Fatma there?"

"Yes, Mr. Al Nassar, I am here."

He said very clearly, "Fatma, why? Be careful what you say."

Imam leaned to the speakerphone as if it were a person and said, "Fatma, this is not a matter for you. It is a matter for my father and me. Father, this is for your older daughter and you, not Fatma, she is not responsible for our decisions. She made her position known and we rejected it. We are Egyptian women of the Al Nassar clan. We speak for ourselves, and we will defend our actions. Fatma had nothing to do with our involvement in going to Peru. She, in her role as guardian, agreed to go to Peru against her will. Knowing that we were wrong, she would still go to protect us. You have put her in an unfair position. Sabah and I will are the ones to talk of your angry. We will go to Peru because this is how you brought us up. No more, no less, we are Al Nassars. It is in our hearts."

Diana was sitting on the edge of her chair like a female lion ready to strike. "Omar, may I interject something? I too asked myself, why? But just as importantly, why did you, Jonathan, and Fatma, not act as responsible adults?"

Imam interjected, "We will respond collectively. The four of us are of one mind. Jonathan and Fatma may stay here, but they will not be party to this discussion. If you wish, at a later time, you may discuss this with them on an individual basis. See fit to do so, but your children will not be part of that conversation. Your protestations are with us. Fatma and Jonathan were not the decision makers. We were and we are responsible."

Every imaginable rationale, trick, threat, or recrimination came through the speakerphone by way of Omar Al Nassar. It was as if he were sitting on the table, leering at his daughters.

He started by saying, "This is not done in our family, what will your mother do if something happens to you, you are not mature enough, you will embarrass our family, you are mere children and not up for this, this is not acceptable, I forbid you…"

Hunter waited for an interlude or break when Al Nassar would take a breath. When he finally broke to collect his thoughts, Hunter said, "Mother, you now have the floor."

Al Nassar knew he was talking to deaf ears, so he stopped. Diana started off by saying, "We did not fully discuss my past, but you cannot make the same mistakes I did. It has haunted me all these years and will until my last days here on this earth. Not just that, but why can't you just hire mercenaries, that Blackwater Company. Why do you have to do this, why do you have to be there? You will just make it harder for the professionals if you are involved. You don't have to do this. We brought you up, sent you to the best schools and did the best for you so you can do this? I don't think so. I don't want you to go to Peru. If you insist, we will cut off the project no matter how important your immature minds think it is."

Hunter's eyes flashed as he sat there stoically. He did not react and merely said, "Father, it is your turn."

David said, "I will pass for now."

Hunter shot back, "You say something now or never to us as a group. It is our lives. I am setting the rules for this discussion. We will clear this up now, or we will never discuss it again, even if it means canceling your participation in the project. We will do it on our own, even if it takes a life time. And, if we have to we'll do it on our own."

Hunter's parents could not believe what they were hearing. He continued, "You called this meeting but you have to listen to us. I will place our cards on the table, and then it is your turn."

They had never expected this. In business everyone deferred to them, but this was different and totally unexpected.

"You told me in Kenya I would someday oversee meetings and presentations and consultancies, well, I'm starting now. This is the most important decision in all of our lives; yours and ours, all nine of us. Say something now, or we will not respond later."

David looked at Hunter and saw a man before him wanting to control his own destiny. "Hunter, I pass. I throw my cards in without comment. The floor is yours."

Hunter said, "I'm going to speak for all four of us. I know your daughters feel the same way, Mr. Al Nassar. Mom, I am going to say this for you. Ashley and I know all about Kenya. We know everything you and Dad did and why. We know about the deaths, the imprisonment, the convictions, but we also know you freed millions of Kenyans from British rule. It was awesome, but now it's our turn. You can't take this away from us. What you called stupid and impetuous back then was neither impetuous nor stupid, but it was the correct thing to do. You would do it again to get the same results of freeing people and giving them dignity, even knowing the pain and guilt you have suffered. It was worth it. That cause was bigger than you, even though there were horrible consequences. You had to do it! It was a life's' imperative. You can't take this away from us. No one can. We don't have to go, but we do, just like you did, and just like Dad did. It defined you and made who you are. To ask us to do less, with all you have taught us, would not be right. I know how much you suffered. You have tried to make up for it your whole life. You have tried to be perfect to hide your pain or guilt or what ever you call it. That is your problem. Don't make it ours. Well, you wanted us to be honest. And furthermore, yesterday by the elevator, Ashley told Sabah he would lay down his life for her. It didn't sound corny, it sounded noble. We are no longer children. You can't stop us like your parents couldn't stop you. You can't stop Ashley from loving Sabah and wanting to protect her. You can't stop my feelings for Imam and you sure as hell can't stop us on this project. You always did the right thing. You try so hard to be perfect because of the situation in Kenya when you were a kid. It was horrible then, but look how you made the world a better place. Your pain and guilt have shaped your lives and certainly affected us but look how much good you have done. I'll take the chance. I'll speak for us, we will all take the chance. If we have to suffer your pain to make the world better, we will. It's just that simple. Now is our turn to do the right thing. We will go. We would like to go with your blessings. It would be great if you would be with us to help guide us, and you could share all you know, so we don't mess up, but our going is out of your hands."

David knew he was right for not saying anything and passing. He saw men and women of conviction before him, and he was proud. Omar was lucky as well in David's mind. These four children were truly exceptional.

Omar said, "I have one last thing to say to my daughters. In our home, you were seen but not heard as children. But you have spoken clearly, and by the grace of Allah, I will be at your side in your decision."

Forty–six

The prep work and briefing the gang of four plus two was conducted in Moyock, North Carolina at the Blackwater operational facility. Mr. Jones and Ms. Smith would lead Operation Urubamba.

Mr. Jones presented a narrative. "The Quecha and Aymara villages are nestled in the Phuyupatamarka portion of the old Inca trail. In the early 1200s to the 1400s AD, the Inca people ritualized symbolic physical activities that had to be observed for adulthood or, as it was described, their passage to maturity. That meant young boys had to climb the Inca trail, a path from the lowlands of the Urubamba River Valley to Machu Picchu. It had to be completed in 6 days by boys of 14 years old to prove their manhood. Young Warriors traveled through the rainforest of the Llabamba, to the highlands of the Palamayo Mountains to the old Inca capital of Machu Picchu. This trail's topography changed from 6500 feet at river's edge to 12,700 feet at the highest areas of the mountains and down to 9000 feet at Machu Picchu. The total time needed for the proposed trip was six days, but the conditions of sweltering heat and humidity caused by torrential rains made it almost impossible to finish in the prescribed allotted time. The penalty for failure was death. The journey was filled with many dangerous predators, both animal and human. There were many obstacles to the coveted prize of manhood. One of three died on the trail to maturity. Tribal animosity made the cannibalistic rituals of offering a sacrificial adolescent to one's enemy an acceptable appeasement to forgo actual warfare between tribes. This practice was to insure the peace between the Quecha/Aymara and the Inca peoples. Many young worriers gave their lives for the security of their tribal brothers. One life taken in the most inhumane manner was better than total warfare. Cannibalism was an anticipated practice. It occurred many times on the trail.

The Incas are known to have abandoned Machu Picchu in the early 1400s AD. The trail was not used for hundreds of years. That means no cohabitation of peoples or mixing of the gene pools during that period. Quecha/Aymara DNA is pure or virgin. The Quecha and the Aymara have lived uninterruptedly all these hundreds of years. They've had no contact with the world outside, and their DNA is not compromised. This is where we're going and why. We have to train for mountain trekking at 12,000 feet. We need your cardiovascular systems able to function efficiently on the Incan trail. Per our preliminary talks, you will be representatives of National Geographic and Slate magazines," as he pointed to Hunter, Imam, Ashley, and Sabah.

"Fatma and Jonathan, you will be husband and wife trekking by yourselves. We will create a situation where both your touring companies' guides will have to be paired with us. Ms. Smith and I will be Inca Trail enthusiasts. We will meet your two groups by chance at a touring office in Cusco. The six of you will be forced to visit the village enclave together because you'll be forced to share a single guide. Jonathan, you and Fatma will fake being put out, but you will go to the village. The visitation at the village will be approximately 5 hours. Ms. Smith and I will effectively forge on to Machu Picchu by ourselves. Hunter, you will take your pictures. Your guide will act as interpreter and you will go about your interview, all photos and interviews will be scripted." Mr. Jones handed them a folder.

"Ms. Smith and I will not be with you. But we will travel back to the village and extract DNA. You will have done the reconnaissance. Your pictures on a CF card will be left for us. We will go exactly to the correct subject in the village and extract DNA. The six of you will eventually make it up to the Machu Picchu Lodge, and we will be close behind. We will meet up with you the next afternoon. Nobody will notice our association."

He laid out an itinerary. "We will leave from Miami on separate planes to Lima. The four of you, pointing to Hunter, Imam, Ashley, and Sabah, you will fly into Lima and stay at the Sheraton Hotel in central part of the city near St. Martin Square. Fatma, you and Jonathan will not lay over in Lima. In Cusco, you will stay at the old Savoy Hotel, which was the favorite of President Fujimori and his famous Cadre Organization. Hunter, Imam, Ashley, and Sabah, after one day in Lima, you will fly to Cusco and stay at the Hotel Las Marquesas in the center of the old city. Cusco is the oldest city in the Western Hemisphere. We will have a day excursion set up for the four of you, so you can fully acclimate to the altitude. We will train here in

Virginia, but it is not exactly the same. The temperature swings between night and day in the Andes are impossible to replicate, so you will train there for an additional four days. That should be ample. Fatma, you and Jonathan will be in Cusco for five days, and your guides will come from Northern Lights, a US tour company that Blackwater has relationships with. That will give you one extra day to train. The six of you will be in separate groups in Cusco. We will meet with you by prearrangement, and we will advise you if there are any changes in the operation. Our training here will be extensive and last for three weeks. Are there any questions?"

Hunter had a question, "I want to start off by saying I want the truth where ever that takes us. What is our real role in all this? Are we going with you because we are paying for this adventure and it's a way of appeasing us?"

Mr. Smith said, "You're hardly eye candy young man."

Hunter did not know how to interpret that.

"All of you are going to be our eyes and ears and collect Intel for us at the site of operation. You will not be in harm's way but you will be important to the success of the mission. Being there will give you platform for oversight of our future collections. Your role is not a make it or break it deal for us doing our job if that's what you are asking."

"But, and I say, but, you will not be eye candy and being in Peru will be the hardest thing you will ever do. Do we need you? Of course not, but you need to be there for a true appreciation of what we do? Hell yes you will be safe. Is that clear enough?"

Hunter wanted to stand his ground to this macho woman or whatever she portrayed herself to be but he thought better of it just in case he needed her in Peru.

Forty–seven

"Dad, its Hunter. I had some time during our training and thought I would call."

"Hunter," David answered the phone. "How are you? How is Ashley? Are they doing their job and running you into the ground?"

"Dad, it's unbelievable. We are at the gym at 7:30 a.m., a lot of weights, and tons of cardiovascular. Ashley almost passed out on the treadmill yesterday. I know you are always in the gym or working out at home, but this is really intense. Ashley got his heart rate up to 185, that's almost what tri-athletes do. We wear, I can't really think of the name, but, they are like oxygen masks and they measure our CO_2 levels. Our goal is to be fit and not let altitude sickness affect us. We are working our butts off. They even have us on a diet. It's all protein, low-carb, a lot of nuts, and we get a supplement, you might have heard of it, co-enzyme 10, it gets oxygen to your heart. They might even give us an epigone. We are training like big-time athletes. Imam and Sabah and Fatma and Jonathon are also doing great. But the reason I called is to thank you again for your support the other day. That was really hard, but you were there for me, so thanks. I know you and Mom have reservations about what we're doing. I want you to know we will really be safe. Our training and our preparation is rigorous, but that will make it much safer for us. We train from 7:30 to 11:30 in the gym every morning. It's really structured. Then they brief the six of us on the mission. I take photo lessons. Imam is schooled on the geography and the geology of Peru. Ashley and Sabah are actually taking lessons in journalism and they're extremely thorough. Everything is laid out for us. This should make you feel better. Not only are we prepared, but we will be safer because of our preparation and planning. Our job is that of reconnaissance only. You know the general operation, but my specific mission will be to take pictures for Mr. Jones and Ms. Smith that they can use with their satellite reconnaissance to coordinate their extraction of the DNA. Can you believe we still don't even know their names? We call them Mr. Jones and Ms. Smith. Anyway, we will be a day and a half ahead of them on the Inca Trail. They go back on their own to the village, and we meet them later at Machu Picchu. We will never be with them until the end of the operation, so we will really be safe. The only danger is the trail itself. Every morning training, we have a virtual hike through the trail. It should make things a lot easier for us. We are hiking the trail, it is not a climb. It should be real easy if we are in shape. Nothing dangerous, but it sounds more adventurous than it probably is. Dad, really, we will be safe, I promise, we will be okay."

"Hunter," David said, "we did not talk much after that meeting the other night. It seems like the four of you got out the door and ended up in Virginia. I want to say something. I have never envied anyone in my life. If someone did something I wanted to do or I could not do because they were lucky or rich or just in the right place at the right time, if they were good people, I was always happy for them. If it meant everything to me, I would someday sacrifice enough to follow suit. I would do it, I would buy it, or I would be it. If they were jerks, I would not let it bother me. But I envy of the four of you. I have never said that before. I know how you feel and how important all of this is to you four. I know the adrenaline; it's almost like a drug. You can't get enough and what makes it even better is that you're correct in what you are doing. This is why I supported you. This is how your mom and I felt when we were in Kenya. I envy you for this. I did what any father would do for the two sons he loves. I want you guys to live your dream. I know what you're doing is noble, it's something bigger than you. I can't explain it, but you can feel it. Hunter, go to Peru. It's important. Your mom and I know you will be safe. We really do. Just call Mom, tell her what you told me. Love you, talk to you later."

The Russells had used considerable influence and money with the Blackwater Group and were given assurances their children would be safe. The four's role in the extraction of DNA in reality would be secondary and safe, but they would feel their participation was central. They would be useful but not in harm's way.

Forty–eight

After three weeks of operation Urubamba's training and briefing, the three couples took separate flights back to Los Angeles. Different airports and different embarkation times were used not to leave a trail from the Moyock operational facility. Communications and activities were held to a minimum for their staggered stays in Los Angeles. If their training were to be investigated in the future by any organization or even the government for what ever reason it would be hidden by a web of cover-ups. Lodging and food purchases, shopping excursions, and credit card receipts placed the group at different locations at different times. Blackwater formulated and constructed viable documents for all their transactions. Every expenditure was sent through a back channel, third parties were solely responsible for financial arrangements. Transactions were developed and expedited. Dollar disbursements could not be traced back to the G.O.F.E.M. group. Operation Ubamba would be the template for all DNA extraction around the world. It had to be by definition a black operation. Their stay in Los Angeles was a brief one.

After a two week stay while they formulated the operation, Hunter and Imam left LAX, and 4 1/2 hours later, landed at the Miami International Airport. They traveled on American Airlines in coach as did all National Geographic correspondents and adventurers.

Their counterparts, Ashley and Sabah, were three hours behind flying on Delta Airlines. They met at the American Terminal 14, Gate17, and flew on to Lima. Once in the capital, both parties made arrangements through their respective magazines for a day's sightseeing and travel on to Cusco. Expenses were only traceable to the magazines, placed on magazine expense accounts. From Lima, they flew to Cusco and registered at the hotel with their false identification. They triumphantly went to dinner in the old city. Sitting outside in a bodega picked by Mr. Jones and Ms. Smith, they openly discussed their fictitious employers and assignments to bolster their cover. They felt no threat of their work exposure and needed to blow off steam and congratulate each other. All the preparation felt good and they knew it would translate into success. They were psyching themselves up for *Those People* and where ever it would take them.

The next morning they made travel arrangements with a local guide company, Transportasiones Del Sol. Guides and porters were Blackstone operatives, as was Fatma's and Jonathan's Northern Lights Company employees. The prearranged loss of a guide and merger of the gang of four plus two was accomplished smoothly, as if it were a sleight of hand trick. It was rational and acceptable the group of six would travel to a tribal region and visit the Quecha Indians. Four porters carried the camera equipment, as well as provisions.   The   Mestizo   Indian   guides   who accompanied them were surefooted, moving along the trail in their sandals.   They wore woven alpaca hats, wool pants and bright solid red shirts. Poor indigenous people all over the world wore bright colors.   It represented closeness to nature.

Ashley and Sabah contrasted to the garb worn by their guides.   Their trekker's outfits which were purchased at A 16 Adventure, a camping store in West LA. Their Northface pants, Bug Be Gone shirts and blouses, English Tilley hats, and Timberland boots were fresh out of a scene in a travel magazine, and of course, they were not suited to the Inca Trail. They were color-coordinated in their drab khaki green.   Hunter and Imam were more to the professional standards of National Geographic magazine in their slightly worn long-sleeved cotton shirts, lightweight Levi's pants, baseball caps, and army surplus boots but they still stood out in their minds as a little too cool for working outfits. They all were equipped with DEET bug repellent and were well clothed for the trail. But before they would set out on their adventure, they trained four more days in Cusco.

The training of Hunter, Imam, Sabah, and Ashley continued under the guise of day trips and excursions outside Cusco.   Jonathan and Fatma continued their training in the Ubamba Valley 30 miles east of Cusco. They all trained in their resplendent outfits per their instructions from Mr. Jones and Ms. Smith. All details of Operation Urubamba were an exact science. Preparations were completed by the group, who began the trail at 5:30 a.m. the morning of the fifth day in Cusco.

Imam was confident, "Sabah, I never thought we would be able to do this. I feel positive it will be easy on the trail. We are in shape, and I even feel like a geographer and technical assistant. It's amazing we got to this point so fast. We trained and we were briefed for three weeks for a five-hour visit to the village. At first I thought it was excessive and I still do, but it is better to be prepared and made to look like real professionals, just in case someday, someone might look into this. I hope it never comes to that, but someone could investigate *those people* project if we make a mistake. If they said we were not prepared enough, what would we do then?"

"Imam, don't worry. This is like a cause to help the poor or a political cause. We are either in it or out of it. I feel we are in this for life and you know what, I am glad. Don't worry, this can only come out all right, I feel what we're doing is something we have to do, you feel the same. I know you do. This would not mean anything, if we were not worried or scared. It feels important to be scared. Let's go meet Ashley and Hunter. This is our last night."

They all met at the Pasado restaurant next to the hotel in the old sector of Cusco. Ashley was in his effervescent, self-deprecating best. "Well, I might not be ready, and I might not look like a reporter or, excuse me, a blogger, but this will be cool. Let's kick ass tomorrow on the trail."

They laughed because in their hearts they knew the trail would be easier than originally anticipated, and they were well-trained. They knew that their level of expertise for the interviews with the Quecha Indians was over the top. Blackwater's need for detail and attaining the last percent of perfection for a mission's success was appreciated in an after-the-fact way, now their training had been completed.

Ashley brought up Mr. Jones and Ms. Smith. "Do you think they are together? Do you think they do it? You know, get it on? They can't be together and not know each other's real names. I think they do it."

They all joked about how stoic and how serious the pair was.

Hunter said, "It was unbelievable that they were never out of character."

But the overriding consensus was they were safe in the hands of these two and the trip was going to be easily doable. It was if G.O.F.E.M. paid a lot of money to be prepared and do too little of the actual work. Cover for Operation Urubamba was fine, but in their hearts, they knew it was an appeasement of sort. They still felt important. Blackwater would do all of the pushing and extracting of the DNA. This was totally acceptable to them. It was all right. They would be out of danger's way, but they would see how serious the job of extraction was and how it was to be done. Better to have firsthand knowledge of such an important part of the quest for the causes of *those people* than just bystanders. They were not disillusioned by their roles. It would be the greatest adventure of their lives, even if it was in a secondary role to Blackwater.

"Do not make more of the situation than it really is," Hunter said. "There are real places for us in *those people* project. It's our discovery and oversight, not the extraction of DNA that's important. Since we have been here I have diminished my role in all this and it still is the most dangerous thing I might do in my life. We are safe, I am convinced of our safety and I actually think we are helping Mr. and Ms. Perfect. Things will be better for the project because of our involvement."

They all agreed. No illusions just pride to get this far.

Sabah sounded a little like Ashley, saying, "This is going to be cool. Don't sound so serious, Hunter. We're in this together, and you are with my sister, isn't that enough?" and she laughed.

They all knew the sex that night would be the best, Sabah would later say of her entire life. The next six days would form their souls. None of them would ever be the same. Their young hearts would swell with convictions and accomplishments. They would wait until morning light and instructions from Mr. Jones and Ms. Smith. Jonathan and Fatma would meet them at 5:30 a.m., and the merged Transportaciones del Sol and Northern Lights expeditions would be one of just a few adventure groups to transverse the Inca Trail in early December.

Forty–nine

In consolidating the excursions, the rendezvous point was to be the office of Northern Lights on Avenida de Las Estrela. Four porters, a guide/interpreter, and a 1998 Ford station wagon were waiting in front of the lighted building at 5:30 a.m. The gang of four was prompt, as per operation, they were early by 25 minutes. Fatma and Jonathan were conspicuously late by 10 minutes, as scripted. A 55 mile descent off the Cusco plain down to the Urubamba River led to a train station where an old steam engine train took the trekkers to the Llaltapata highlands and the Inca Trail's beginning. Dense foliage looked familiar along the stone paths, because of their virtual training; but the contrast to the alluvial plains below was a surprise.

After 20 minutes, Jonathan started to experience a nose bleed. Altitude sickness was discussed in training but didn't truly describe the volume of blood streaming from his nose. He applied pressure at the bridge and put a small piece of cotton under his upper lip. The blood coagulated quickly, but his breathing was hindered by clots of blood in his nostrils. The guide suggested as a precaution they should all put Vaseline in their noses to eliminate the chance of anyone else getting a nose bleed. They rested for a few moments. Jonathan felt a little embarrassed, but everyone understood. For Jonathan, being the oldest, it was a point of manhood, not to be the frailest.

Their guide, an American of Peruvian dissent, Jorge Estrada, was holding court during the respite. He told of numerous times he had led treks up the Machu Picchu trail, but this visit to the Quecha Indians would be an infrequent one. It would be an honor to visit the tribe. He was fluent in the Mestizo dialect. Arrangements had been made with the tribe, the price of the visitation was cotton goods to be delivered at a future date. They would reach the village in three days. He talked of other excursions he had led for Northern Lights all over the world.

"Jonathan, don't worry about your nose. It happens all the time. We are at 7,500 feet and will climb to 12,500 feet before we descend down to Machu Picchu, which is 9,000. Your nose will be okay, just use the Vaseline. I should have mentioned it before we started. Sorry, I forgot. Let me tell you a story. Three years ago I was in Tanzania climbing Kilimanjaro, not actually a climb, but a trek, and altitude sickness stopped me dead. I trained just like you. I was not prepared for it, even a little bit, though I am a guide and experienced. So it can happen to any of us. I was at 18,500 feet on the last day at the glacier level, about 1 1/2 hours from the peak. You climb at about 300 to 400 feet every half hour, and during my ascent, the capillaries in my eyes broke, just like your nose, but blood poured from both my eyes. I was blinded and had to be taken down the mountain. I had not heard about blood vessels or capillaries popping in one's eyes and thought I would be blinded for the rest of my life. It scared the hell out of me. I know it's not the same, but its okay, believe me. It won't get any worse. That's my story. I know it's bad habit to tell stories all the time. If it bothers any one, just say something. Everyone let's get ready; let's get going."

"Jorge," Sabah said, "Ashley and Hunter were in Kenya this summer."

Looking at the two, he said, "We will have time to talk about our trips; that's what adventurers do. I sometimes think we travel so we can tell stories. It's amazing how much better our stories are than the actual adventures. Tonight after the porters set up the camp and cook a hot meal, we can talk, but for now we have to get going."

The pace was steady, about a mile's distance every hour with a rest of 20 minutes. Jorge was ever persistent in pushing the group to drink water and eat power bars or fruit. The lack of nutrition and dehydration was the enemy of all trekkers.

At a stop on a ledge overlooking the Urubamba River, Imam asked, "Jorge, if these foot paths have always been here, why didn't someone discover Machu Picchu before 1914?"

"Ms. Imam, we don't know for sure, but the Incas terraced the hillside slopes for cultivation of what we call potatoes. The paths we are on were laid down about the same time, maybe 1200 AD. The igneous and pumas rocks were set down as trails between five different Inca cities, Machu Picchu being the furthest out. The Incas left this region around 1400 AD as best we can figure. It was because of poor agricultural production or a lack of water, we don't know. Some people cite illness like Dongle Fever, a hemorrhagic illness, or some unknown disease as a cause of the mass migration. Whatever it was, something panicked the population. In any event, the trails to the cities were abandoned about 700 years ago. The vegetation totally overtook the terraces and the foot paths. The last 40 years, physical fitness people, or adventurers, you know, the eco-tourism types, cleared the paths. The vegetation has receded because of the heavy usage. The path still exists because rocks don't wear out. The Incas were incredible architects as you will see six days from now. Machu Picchu is an architectural masterpiece maybe you could not even replicate today. It is as amazing as the pyramids of Egypt. You will see."

After 6 1/2 hours of hiking with frequent stops, they reached a foot print of 80 x 100 m laying on the hillside overlooking a deep lush valley. This was to be campsite 1. The porters had surged ahead and set up tents, a fire for cooking, and dug a hole behind a cluster of small trees so anyone in the group could relieve themselves in private. Leather bags of Ubamba River water were hanging on trees with chemical purifying agents to assure a safe water source. The trek was over 8 miles, and the gang of four plus two were smitten by the first-day accomplishments. Jorge had stories to tell, Imam and Hunter were spellbound by the stars in the night skies, Ashley and Sabah were entertaining each other by discussing the prowess and skills needed to climb the trail, and Fatma and Jonathan were ever closer to courtship, which met with unanimous approval.

Jorge said, "I must discuss something important; there is a high chance of us being robbed tonight.

Highwaymen may sneak up on our site and break into our tents. They will try to steal money or cameras or anything of value. Usually, the porters are in arrangement with them and share the bounty. We think this will not be the case because we picked our porters very carefully. But there could always be a chance. The robbers will not harm you. They will just run away if we catch sight of them. They're very quick and very effective in cutting your tents without being noticed. They do not want physical confrontation. They steal and run."

The briefing at Blackwater told of highwaymen, but not so matter-of-factly.

Fifty

"I will wake you up at 7 a.m. We will have one hour for breakfast and whatever else you want to do. Don't venture off during the night past the tree area if you have to relieve yourselves. Be sure to zip up your tents all the way to the top, there are large centipedes and sometimes a monkey or two. There are big cats up here, but they will not be a problem. I also want all of your valuables, I will take the cameras and the computers from the porters, but I also want your watches. I will have everything in my tent. This way if we have intruders, they will just take stuff of no value. They will not come to my tent. If anything happens, just yell," Jorge warned the group. "I know I sound like I'm overdoing it and making too much of the highwaymen, but better safe than sorry. Have any of you ever heard about the midnight train from St. Petersburg to Moscow?"

Fatma said she had.

"They have thieves on the train all the time," Jorge said. "The same exact thing here. When it gets dark in the summer in Russia, the nights are only a few hours long. Tourists on the train are staked out by the porters, and thieves will break into their sleeping cars. It is all set up by the porters when the tourists get on the train, same thing here. No one is hurt, but Bam, Bam, Bam, it's over. Well, I want you to be aware, in any event. You all did a great job today. There are two more days until we meet the Quecha at the village. Goodnight everyone, sleep well," as if that were possible after his pronouncements of highwaymen.

The stars were brilliant. The night skies were as clear to Hunter and Ashley as were the savanna nights in Kenya. With no moon, the brilliance of the Milky Way made this the most romantic night any of the six had ever seen. The three couples felt the spirituality of the Andes and the magic of each other. Hunter had read about spiritual places but with total disdain and discount. He now knew why humans held such places in reverence and awe. Africa was primal and held adventure at every step, but this trail was majestic, an out of the world experience. His readings of the young warriors on the trail seeking manhood and his extensive training at Blackwater were trifles compared to the depths and complexity of this wonderful place.

It struck Imam that they were here to destroy the equilibrium of these Indians and their lands. She said, "How can we masquerade as photographers and then extract DNA from these simple people who live here among the gods? I am fearful we might be doing something wrong."

"Imam," Hunter said, "they will not be hurt, and this is bigger than us. If they have misgivings about us, how do you think they would feel about *those people*? I know I sound like I'm being intellectual, but they would never understand. We need the purity of their lives. All the locations of pure DNA extraction, as far as I'm concerned, are pre-industrial places in the world. It really strikes home how much the so called civilized people have brought the world to the brink of destruction. We have to do this, now I am surer than ever before. He looked at her and said, Imam we are doing the right thing."

The three couples went to their tents, waiting with bated breath for the highwaymen. At 3:30 a.m., Fatma let out a scream that could have curdled the blood of a dead man, as Jorge later described it. In an instant, a knife tore into her and Jonathan's tent, a hand grabbed a backpack, and only the patter of feet could be heard as someone fled into the darkness. The camp's quiet was broken by the scream. All six appeared out of their tents fully clothed in an instant. Not one porter reacted, and Jorge was the last to leave his tent with an 'I told you so' smile on his face.

Ashley holding back a laugh said, "Well, Jonathan, Fatma, looks like we know who the porters thought would be easy prey. It would have been embarrassing, if it were any of us. Did they get much? I hope you had a lot of crap in that bag."

The tension slowly abated; they talked for a short while and went back to their tents. Ashley felt Blackwater probably set up the whole thing to make the trip more adventurous and make them feel they were getting the greatest value for their money.

Seven a.m. came early. Hiking the trail on a few hours rest would be taxing, but it proved to be within their acquired skills. The many days of training paid off. Their covers as reporters and photographers were to be tested when they finally got to the village. But they felt confident they would be up to the task. All their work and training would be justified; Blackwater was well worth the price. They were trained as professionals and felt as such. The next two days took them through the rain forests to the Palamayo Mountains where the tribe was waiting at the top end of one of the most beautiful valleys any of them had ever seen.

The tribe lived in stone buildings with thatched roofs which surrounded a long hall, or elder's building'. There were gutters throughout the village acting as a water supply for bathing and irrigation system. The village was the highest point in the valley, which gave it a military advantage. It was clear that the Quecha existence was static for hundreds of years. This village had not changed since ancient Incan times. No outside technology, a language that had not advanced, and people who lived well beyond their expected longevities. Long life was the norm. Quecha lived into their late 80s and early 90s. Small in stature, dark skin, their native characteristics were almost Asian. It appeared they had not changed since the great migration of humans through the Bering Strait down the Pacific Coast into South America which took place 13,000 years ago.

Upon meeting the tribe their reconnaissance would begin. Pictures were taken of the village, the houses, the main hall, religious altars, the water system, baths, and the topography and layout of the village itself. It was all information Mr. Jones and Ms. Smith would later use to optimally and safely extract DNA. Photos and written descriptions of the Indians living quarters, their clothing, the number of people in each family, and appraisals of the physical fitness of each individual were all necessary information. The healthiest and strongest persons and the most remote would be part of the determination to pick two individuals, a male and a female.

Upon entering the village, the six were greeted as friends. Food, a mix of corn and potatoes and other vegetables, a slaughtered llama, and beer, reminiscent of Kenyan banana beer, were in the great Hall. There were no more than 35 to 40 people in the tribe, and everyone was awaiting their arrival. The chief, his attendants, the community, and the elders were present. The tribe's oral historians who passed on tales of the Quecha's people were seated in a position of prominence. The gang of four plus two would be part of Quecha folklore passed on to future generations. The six outsiders were taken to be colonialists. They were viewed by the tribe like the Spanish in the 1500 and 1600 hundreds. Pictures would be taken. This would be an opportunity for the Quechas to view themselves on the LCD of Hunter's camera. There was an amazement of incomprehensible delight to all the village's women when they saw themselves. They were friendly, open to pictures, they would converse, but it was all from afar. Theirs was a strange mind set. The six outsiders were a form of enjoyment for the Indians. The questions from Ashley and Sabah were answered in a cursory way, not to let the substance of their way of life leave the village. Their wisdom and control of their environment, this small village, was total. Precisely after five hours had lapsed, the outsiders were asked to leave as if they never existed. They would not let the others into their world. They would accept cotton goods and sometimes seed, but the Quecha would never leave God's Heights as they called their valley or let whites into their lives. They would not let anything in or let their true way of life out. Modernity would not permeate their insulated world. This was to change. A little bit of their life would be extracted to save Humankind. This would have been objectionable to the very deepest morrow of their bones if they had known what was to happen to them.

Hunter said, "Imam, what they don't know won't hurt them."

Their simple way of life held the fate of humanity.

Fifty–one

Leaving the village and traveling northeast to Phuypatamarka, and then descending to Machu Picchu, the trail became more heavily traveled. Upon reaching granite stone paths crossing, they were on the southern artery departing from the Quecha village; the northern, more heavily traveled path went directly to Machu Picchu. Jorge pointed out a designated drop-off spot for the reconnaissance. Mr. Jones and Ms. Smith would pick up a black parachute material bag with its contents of pictures and descriptions of the Indians. A GPS locator reminiscent of the old LoJack system was placed in its lining as a redundant precaution for retrieval. The Blackwater operatives were close by, but no contract with the group would take place. The materials reviewed; two people would be violated in the darkness of a moonless night under the eyes of God and the ever brilliant stars. DNA would be extracted.

The group of four plus two and the Blackwater operatives were near each other without having visual or psychic contact. The overgrown trail separated them to such an extent they could have been 20 or 200 feet apart and not known the other's existence. It was as if two ships passed each other in open seas with no recognition or impact. Ashley's, Hunter's, Imam's, Sabah's, Fatma's and Jonathan's involvement in the collection of DNA was completed. They could forge on to Machu Picchu and act the part of tourist.

Their dissent on the Machu Picchu Trail was crowded, 600 to 700 people trekked to this lost city of the Incas by the northern route each month. Their first leg, the six-day adventure to the Quecha village, was on a less traveled spur of the Inca Trail. The rest of the way, the northern trail to Machu Picchu, they would encounter many adventurers with a bent for recreation. They felt estranged, they were people with a cause. Their minds could hardly move from the gravity of their mission. Once an objective was accomplished, its merits were etched in stone. They had to clear their heads and move forward. The proverbial bubble had burst, and a state of acceptance of their place in the defense of humans as they knew them was a harsh reality. For Hunter, Imam, Ashley, and Sabah, the mantle of their youth was shed and a new life lay before them.

At the Quecha village Mr. Jones and Ms. Smith were lying in the brush 500 yards from the long house like military snipers under camouflage late into the night. They were still for almost 4 hours before they approached the big hall. The cycle of day to night in the December Andes limited the hours of darkness. Operation Urubamba was exacting, with no room for error. Their movements were precise and followed that of the highwaymen who terrorized the trail below. Instead of cutting the tent, they quietly entered the stone hall of the elders through a small door. Instead of extracting a backpack, they placed a surgical implement with exact precision deep into the frontal lobe of their victims, and the mechanics of the device did the rest. The probe had been designed to anesthetize the subjects, an elderly priest and a female attendant. They did not feel the pressure of the probe. The total time needed for extraction was less than 20 seconds per subject. Instead of the villagers hearing the bare feet of interlopers entering the rain forest with bounty, they heard nothing. Mr. Jones and Ms. Smith exited as undetected as they entered. The operation was a total success. The two victims would awake with slight headaches. The point of penetration would be so nondescript and so small that any detection of a personal violation was impossible.

Mr. Jones and Ms. Smith arrived in Machu Picchu eight hours after the gang of four plus two. A special collection vile made of titanium that fit inside the housing of Hunter's camera held the DNA at 40°C. Titanium was not a conductor of heat, so even if customs were to check the camera, its temperature would not arouse attention. Peruvian customs did not check outbound travel. The point of entry would be Los Angeles, California, where the Transportation Safety Administration was woefully inadequate. The DNA would be viable for 96 hours because of the vacuum vile and its thermos-like refrigerant. The DNA drop-off would be at Machu Picchu Lodge.

Hunter was taken aback by the size of Machu Picchu. Two large granite pinnacles, one at each end of the ruins, with a central plaza running from end to end encircled by 140 structures. The monolith Waynapicchu lay deep in the back of the Inca complex, with Machu Picchu in the foreground. The ruins were indescribable. Why the place was the great spiritual harbinger of the gods was clear. Its beauty was unmatched. It was like a stairway to the heavens.

Jorge held the group hypnotized by his discussions of the Inca capital and its history. Acting as a tour guide on site he said, Machu Picchu was constructed around 1460 AD. It was abandoned less than 100 years later. The cause of the Incan exodus is hotly debated, but in any event, it was the estate of an Incan emperor. It was aligned with many astronomical events. It was even a prison, a religious site, and a citadel. The classic style of architecture was polished dry-stones of regular shapes. The stones were huge, five tons or more, and were cut to fit exactly. They were cut so perfectly that not even a credit card could fit between them. There are 140 construction sites, almost 100 stone steps, water fountains, irrigation for horticulture, and running water in all the structures. The complex housed the Inihuantana Stone, a sun dial that pointed directly to the sun during the winter solstices. The group walked along the central plaza to the foot of Waynapicchu and climbed to the top for a magnificent view. The photos that Hunter took and the discussion of Machu Picchu made the group temporarily forget about the DNA extraction. Their mission was accomplished. They would be on their way to Los Angeles. The Quecha Indians would be the test case for Operation *those people.*

At the airport in Lima, Ashley said to the group, "That was way too easy. Shoot, this whole thing has been almost tedious and boring from the beginning in terms of success. No one is as good as we are, but we've been way too successful. Everything since we started has been too perfect. We are rich, have incredible parents," looking at Hunter, "unbelievable girlfriends, money and even Fatma has Jonathan," he smiled. "There's something wrong here. I just know it. I feel something is going to fall apart. The DNA extraction was way too easy. Maybe I'm just coming down from an adrenaline rush, I don't know. I don't want to put a hex on us, but everything is too good."

Everyone was silent; they all felt the same way.

Imam said, "I heard my father say, you can't always draw aces every time you get a card. It seems like this whole time it's been aces. I think you're right. I don't know if we have to rethink things. I don't know what we have to be worried about but I think we just have to be very vigilant in what we do. There's so much more that has to be done and needs our attention. We just have to make sure we are in control and brace for something coming down, we don't see right now. I feel the same way."

Fifty–two

Clearing customs at Los Angeles international Airport was just the usual going through the green line for non-declaration of goods and walking down into the bowels of the Thomas Bradley International Terminal to street level. A town car was parked in front of the terminal that took Fatma and Jonathan with the camera and its contents to California State University at Los Angeles. Hunter, Imam, Ashley, and Sabah took another car to the Russell house. The Administrative Justice Department at CSULA had the most sophisticated forensic lab in the country. It was more up-to-date than the FBI lab or any private facility in the United States. David and Diana were contributors to the new facility and had direct influence on its DNA department. The CSI forensic unit at the University was used by local law enforcement, state and federal investigative teams. It was state-of-the-art, and the Russell's' access would give them the results of the DNA tests in less than a week and total secrecy.

It amused the Resells that the television programs CSI and CSI Miami had so much popularity that government and the private sector reacted to it by expansion of Administration Justice programs throughout the educational system. From community colleges to universities, AJ was a major for college students in such demand that it was impacted. More student demand for classes than seats, lead to increased private fund raising and the present size and scope of the program. New monies brought about building expansion and new labs with the latest technology. The CSI phenomenon was television driven, and many people were pleased with the law and order direction of higher education. Diana thought that the O.J. Simpson trial of the 1990s, with its lost blood, DNA analysis, and courtroom drama, was a precipitant for law and order. Barry Sheck, one of Simpson's attorneys, became a technical guidepost for the future of forensic science, hence a push for more AJ. The CSULA lab was the result of public opinion, and the Russell's gift gave them entitlement or entry; this was a consequence of their philanthropy. Their grant of one million dollars was their currency providing the analysis of the virgin DNA.

When Fatma and Jonathan delivered the camera to Professor Stephen Zwelenger, an associate of Jonathan's, *those people* project began in earnest. It was the first of 25 samples of pure or virgin DNA to be tested. The plan for *those people's* DNA would be executed, and a comparison between them and extracted virgin DNA was being made.

Jonathan said, "Well, Steve, this should be a good start. We discussed a system for collection en sutra and cryogenic freezing. Let's hope it works. I want the results as soon as possible because neither of us will sleep until we know something. God, I'm sorry, Steve, this is my associate Fatma Kassar. Fatma, please forgive me. I was so excited I forgot to introduce you. Actually, Steve, she is the reason I'm involved in this project."

Steve said, "Fatma, it's my pleasure, and I understand why Jonathan is involved. We don't meet many women of your stature or beauty in the academic world." He smiled and said, "Do you have a sister? I am partial to beautiful women who are smart. In my communications with Jonathan, your name came up frequently. How smart you are, how organized you are, and how comfortable he was with your decisions. But he never said how attractive you were. He is such a cad. Excuse me, Fatma, Jonathan; I must get to this work immediately. Thanks for the camera. Fatma, it has been my pleasure."

He closed his fist, popped up his knuckles and Jonathan did the same, and they laughed as their knuckles hit. "Boy that was stupid, but I loved it," Steve said. "See you later."

The ride to the Russell house was comfortable. But it took two hours and ten minutes in Los Angeles' worst traffic. They left the campus at 5:30 p.m., in the midst of the rush-hour. First on the San Bernardino Freeway, then to the Golden State Freeway, then on to the Ventura Freeway, and lastly on to the San Diego Freeway; from there over to Mulholland Drive to the house . This was typical for Southern California traffic. The town car traveled 30 miles in just a little over two hours.

Upon their arrival at the Russell house, Hunter, Imam, Ashley, and Sabah wanted to talk to David and Diana.

Ashley said, "The operation was incredible, the whole thing, I really didn't know what to say about the project. It went so smoothly. It was fantastic. We collected all the information for Mr. Jones and Ms. Smith, and they did the rest. We were never in danger. It was so easy, it was scary. Too easy in fact, we always felt that there must be more."

Hunter said, "No problem at all, perfect in every way. Blackwater must be more powerful than I thought. It was perfect."

The girls listened, knowing that if they were at their home in Cairo, they would be talking and the boys would be held in abeyance as a matter of respect.

After a few minutes Diana asked the girls," Imam, Sabah, how was it?"

Their rendition of the trip was exactly the same as the boys'. Imam said, "Maybe it's my feeling only, but I was worried about our intruding on these poor isolated Indians. I even said, 'Hunter we could probably be destroying their balance.' But it was not like the way I thought it would be. I now have the belief that they used us. I could not put my finger on it, but they dismissed us at the end of the trip. I feel better about their DNA extraction because they seemed so contrary to us. I can't put it into words, but they were not so innocent."

David said, "Fatma and Jonathan will be here shortly, so let me ask the four of you something. Do you think we are doing the correct thing? Do you think we're doing this job correctly? We're going to leave a lot of this up to Blackwater. I don't see any alternatives because as far as I'm concerned, this was the first and last extraction for the four of you. We don't want you in the field any longer. Are you comfortable with that?"

"There is a problem," Hunter said. "Blackwater knows everything, and what do we do if they hold this over our heads? What do we keep away from them so we have control? You always said we should control the hand."

David said, "They are a $2 billion operation, so our little $2-$3,000,000 contract won't be allowed to jeopardize their reputation. If this project leaks out its totally illegal, that is how. I also can't imagine how they would publicly stand up to the ridicule and scrutiny if people associated this with them and what they're doing. They couldn't cover it up. So they will be careful; it's in their best interest. Secondly, they feel we are collecting DNA of different groups, but they don't know exactly why. The analysis is totally separate. Jonathan and Dr. Zwelenger are the ones responsible for the DNA analysis. It is totally compartmentalized. I think we're okay on both accounts. They don't want their reputation tarnished, and they don't want full knowledge or access if it could cause them a problem. I don't see a problem."

David continued, "I wanted to talk to you four about something else. I see the organization as having three different layers. The first layer is you guys, your vision and adventurousness. Number two is Fatma and Jonathan, and their technical abilities. Number three involves your mother and me. We are politically connected. We hate to say it, but we are old, God knows we don't look it." He smiled, "but we are. All of our life's work and what we've accomplished and the relationships we have will be directed to this project. We will do everything possible to make it a success. But we will need your help. I know you don't have a say in our world, except that you are our children, but you sometimes see things differently than we do. Your mother and I are sometimes too cautious as we get older, we recognize that. We always do what is expected of us. We've always tried to be just perfect, since Kenya years ago. Our ways might not work so we will defer to your more intuitive ways of looking at things. This is your project, so we count on you. We won't always agree with you, so don't be frustrated, but we will listen. We need to hear the truth from you. Our connections can take us all the way up to the President, if necessary. If we don't know someone personally, we have people who can get to them. But we don't know anyone in the middle, and we don't have a feel for the common guy on the street and what they think.

Hunter interjected, and none of us have a clue about the people at the bottom. We can't relate to them at all.

David said, "Son sometime you just have to do what is best for the people below you. I hope you understand the price of money and power? You have a better connection with the average person than we do and none of us can relate to the poor. We are powerful, but we also know we are really out of touch. So we will need your input on political matters."

You have a better connection with the average person than we do. Sometimes we think we're powerful, but we also know we are really out of touch. So we will need your input on political matters. We can't just push this to the top as usual, the consequences are too great to do business as usual. We have tried to impose our political views on the two for years but we have listened to you even if you don't think so in our many heated conversations. You might have a better pulse on how the average American will deal with *those people* than us. So don't worry, we will be all ears. I think Jonathan and Fatma will be here soon. I will ask them their feelings about the politics of this. Would you like to be with us or have us talk to them separately? It's up to you."

Ashley replied, "That's simple, it's the gang of four plus two. When they get here, we should get their feelings. It's cool you think highly enough to include them. We will get their opinions."

Diana said, "They left the lab at 5:30 p.m. Who knows when they'll arrive? They will call from the car."

Fifty—three

It was almost 8:40 p.m. before Fatma and Jonathan arrived at the house. Jonathan said, "I think the trip from Miami to Los Angeles was faster than from Cal State to Bel Air."

Diana asked if they wanted to clean up.

"No, thank you," Fatma said, "we are excited about discussing our findings. We talked about some facets of the DNA analysis on the way here, and we want to share our thoughts with the six of you, if that's okay."

Diana said, "Can I get you something to drink and we will talk in the living room?"

David said, "We were chatting with Hunter and Imam, Ashley and Sabah."

It struck him that he had referred to them as couples, not as his children or his guests or associates.

"We talked a little bit about Operation Urubamba, and it sounded like a resounding success. Hopefully it can be replicated throughout the world. What is your take? Are you in concurrence? Do you have some insight the kids don't have because of your experience and age? I don't mean that as a slight but we were

talking about the kid's perception because of their age.
"

Jonathan responded, "The four kids were great, and I would like to say, right now, they acted well beyond their years. Even though Blackwater trained us extremely well, the kids were cool, collected, adaptive and innovative on the trail. I have worked with a lot of young people, grad students mostly and administrative assistants, but these four acted hands and heads above people of their own ages. That being said, I would like to use Blackwater strategies and tactics elsewhere in the world. It works. They are thorough and do things other mercenaries can't. Fatma, what do you think?"

"Well, I guess I'm a little like a proud parent when someone talks about their children. I felt they were taking care of me on the trail and they surely took the lead. I agree with Jonathan totally in his assessment of the operation, but I have one request. I want the four of them to oversee all of Blackwater's duties in every single detail, the execution of the operations and the extraction of DNA. They should have final say on where and when and who are targets. They must, I repeat, they must have clear control and oversight of the operations of Blackwater. They must have the final say. We have 24 extractions left, maybe a few more possibly, and I want to make sure all are as successful as Peru. I don't know but everything went so well I don't want to take the chance that someone on their side may become caviler or complacent. All their operatives can't be like Mr. Jones or Ms. Smith so we need the kids for oversight. "

David said, "We are all in sync, and I hope the six of you know how proud we are and how we feel about you. Thanks for being who you are. You did a great job. Fatma, Jonathan, what is your future plans for the project? What do you see after Peru? We know of the pure DNA, what about your plans for *those people* DNA? It doesn't have to be formulated yet, but soon, I hope. I know you just got off the plane and just got here but…"

He was abruptly interrupted by Ashley. "Yeah, isn't it done yet? What's taking so long? We did our part. Well?"

With his trademark jocularity he smiled, "Just kidding."

Jonathan said, "Okay, okay, we actually have a rough draft. Do you have a laptop, or is there enough room for all of us in your office? We can show you if you want."

Diana said, "Why don't you just fill us in verbally and we will see the draft later."

"Fatma put a lot of pressure on Dr. Zwelenger and me to get this done. Her technical background was a great assistance to us. She created a matrix that we can use to analyze the differences in DNA."

He described a matrix much like an input/output table listing 25 subjects and their geographic regions, their ethnicity, their ages, and all other pertinent demographics on one axis, as he called it. And on the other axis, there were different genes and chromosomal links.

"An example, we will look at is the MAOA gene, R2, and look for DNA constancy in all subjects. It will become our baseline. We know it will coincide with the Human Genome Project map and Assembling the Tree of Life Map. It's stable and it won't change for our virgin samples. There is recent evidence that mutations or variances in R2 are a precursor for violence and abnormal behavior, in other words, *those people*. We will collect DNA from *those people* all over the world, and we're sure it will be different. We will show why there are differences and the causations. We will use computer models to extrapolate changes for three generations. *Those people* have short life spans; three generations will be less than 60 years. There should be huge changes in their DNA make-up. This is not at all scientific. We are looking for predetermined outcomes. It does not follow the scientific method, but it will give us quicker results, and we can move from there. There will be criticism form the scientific community, but we need to pass this information to the political powers as soon as possible. This is where you will come in," looking at David and Diana.

"We think the results will be frightening. A true study would take up to twenty years and we don't have that much time. That is not acceptable because of the impending crisis. We're going to use unproven hypotheses not wholly acceptable. Our results will be iron clad but unconventional. No politician can dismiss them if you present them properly. There are always conspiracy theory type people, but the results will be so clear you can get through it. We will begin with the assumption that the changes take place in certain regions of the world and in certain encapsulated environments. Our experts have prompted us in this direction; you were introduced to most of them in New York and here in Los Angeles. A pathogen or bacterium triggered by global warming caused by CO_2 density patterns exacerbates the DNA mutations. We know radiation, heat, infection, and oxidation cause molecular switches to mutate. We think this is the cause of *those people*. Bacteria, infection, toxins, and oxidation, are most likely the causes of *those people*. High levels of certain toxins cause bacterial attacks to the R2 gene and therefore mutations. No evolutionary changes, just chemical changes. This is why *those people* have appeared so rapidly. We will map out CO^2 and other toxic collection points globally and extract DNA in those areas when individuals fit our profile. This is entirely unacceptable in the scientific world, but is the only way we can get an answer in a short period of time. We will find areas of high pollution concentrations, like Cancer Alley, Mississippi. There are people living in unsanitary landfills or near urban areas, and whole regions like the former Eastern European bloc. People will fit our profile, and we will extract their DNA. As of right now, we're working with operatives in Doctors Without Borders, UNICEF, Operation USA, the Red Cross and other NGO's. They can collect the DNA of *those people* coming into their clinics or receiving medical aid. Here in the United States we have people in private hospitals and university hospital emergency rooms. In Europe and Canada, because of socialized medicine, we have people placed in government hospitals and clinics. Our analysis will show all this in detail. We ask for directed assistance from you if and when we need your help for contacting people or setting up operations. Simply put, we collect DNA from pristine sources and analyze it. Then we collect *those people*s DNA and analyze it. And we will show differences on predetermined genes. If all goes well, there will be large explainable differences. We now create a computer simulation of the mutation process, and press it forward and seeing what *those people* will be like in the near and long run. Our research from collection to analysis will be finished in approximately six months. The Blackwater component of *those people* project will take approximately two more months. And we estimate our analysis will be two more months after. Everything is in place. All we need is a mainframe computer at our disposal. This again is where you come in."

Fifty-four

"Jonathan," David said, "we are ahead of the curve. We have a venture capital group called RVC, Russell Venture Capital, which invests in technology and internet-based companies. We are associated with Anton van Leeuwenhoek, a pioneer in microbiology. We are partners in financing a special-purpose supercomputer intended to offer more than a thousand fold increase in performance of complex molecular simulation. The new supercomputer is called Anton. It's a massively parallel supercomputer with 512 specialized processors working simultaneously. It can calculate three-dimensional characteristics of molecules. Hold on, I will get a prospectus. I'll be back in a second."

He handed the prospectus to Jonathan, and continued. "We think the genome or anything that deals with molecular change could lead to new drugs or pharmaceuticals. This is a good place for our money. So that's why we are involved. Very lucky, aren't we? I'm going to stray from our conversation, but I will get back to your requests, and we'll talk about any of your needs. We are one of the largest hedge funds and venture capital companies in the world. We keep a low profile because of our clients. We don't seek outside investors, and we keep away from notoriety. The project about *those people* started in Kenya and was formalized in Egypt when the boys met Imam and Sabah. We were in the process of shedding assets and clients because of the sub prime mortgage crisis in the United States. I brought the boys along to meet some of my old friends and associates, and, of course, spend time with them. I thought just the three of us in Africa would be a perfect trip. Our focus was tourism and time with the boys and a little business. New regulations caused by the housing crisis could force financial transparency and open us up like a can of worms. We had to cut many of our business ties. That was the business reason for going to Kenya. Transparency was unacceptable, but because of *those people* project, we will have to reverse course on some of our assets. We will have to go into the dark again. Now we must proceed undetected. Transparency of this project will kill our credibility and kill off our partners and cause total collapse. We think the project is worth any risk, but we must be doubly vigilant not to be caught. We don't want to lose everything. Diana feels the same way. We are willing to take the risk because the project is so important, but we must be in the shadows. We will get you anything you need. But you will have to be in the light for your own protection. You ask. We deliver. Never ask where things come from or how we get them. You don't want to know. This way will be safer, not only physically, but legally, for you. Jonathan, Fatma, we want to protect you; Kids, the same for you. Imam, Sabah, we have discussed this with your dad. We are involved in a lot of different projects that may be of help, you ask and we deliver. Never, I repeat, never think something is too big. "

Diana whispered to David, "Can I say something to the boys in front of everyone, or should I hold off until we are in private?"

He whispered back, "Jonathan, we will get you Anton. Can Diana say something?" He looked at his wife and said, "Ask them."

She looked at Hunter and Ashley and said, "Boys can I talk in front of everyone? It is important. It's about our past. I feel all of you should know."

The boys said okay. Ashley said, "We were the gang of four plus two. Now it is the gang of four plus two squared."

Then he sang, "we are family...It's fine, Mom."

"I'll make it short, it's a long story, but I'll make it short. When we were in Kenya many long years ago, we were part of the revolution. It was in the early 60's, that's how old we are. We were younger than you. You know what happened; the killings, our arrests, the financial beginning of the Russell Group based on theft, and much more. I want to tell you something very personal and very important. I was tortured, and because of that, I could never have children. In personal terms, it was a very high price to pay for saving a nation. For almost 30 years, there was a hole in my heart. That is why all the charity works and community involvement, but it was not enough. I felt so guilty about all the people who were killed because of me. I felt I deserved to be punished forever. It all changed because of the two of you. When your parents were killed in a car crash in Malibu, your father and I were asked if we could help in some way. Well, you guys brought us a new life. I could not love anyone more than I love you. Even if you came from my womb, I could not love you any more. We have, on many occasions, said we would talk about this. You'd never wanted to bring it up or discuss it. I have to now. We're so much older than you sometimes I feel it's not fair. Ashley, at your graduation from Harvard Westlake, your dad and I were asked how it felt to see our grandchildren graduate. We love you and want you to have more than we do not so much money, but family and principle because maybe we didn't.

I guess this project is our way of supporting you. We are so proud of you. Your dad wasn't always there because of his business, but this, the project and being involved with the two of you, is the most important thing he has ever done. He is with his sons, and I have you by my side."

Hunter said, "We never talked about this because there's no reason to. We see adopted kids who are, don't get mad at me for saying this, but, assholes to their parents. We are the luckiest kids in the world. We don't know much about our birthparents and I really don't want to. Sometimes I feel guilty because I love you so much and I wonder if my life would have been as good if I were brought up by my birthparents. We love you because of the way you treat us. Let's just say we are the lucky ones. I know how much Imam and Sabah love their dad, but it can't be any different than how much we love you. Fatma, Jonathan, when you have kids just remember this night," he laughed.

David said, "You don't know how it feels to get this out in the open. Thanks. Sorry everyone, but we really feel we are all family and we had to bring this up. Let's go out to eat. Enough business and family matters. How about the Cheesecake Factory on San Vicente? Diana and I will talk about our role in *those people* later. I'm hungry."

Fifty-five

Jonathan and Fatma set up their headquarters in one of the Russell's Westside, Century City properties in Los Angeles. A conference room with a world map and a DNA extraction timeline was their working place.

Fatma suggested, "Jonathan, I think we need a couple more extractions based on the CO_2 model. The greenhouse gases concentration patterns are almost exclusively in southern nations."

The areas for extraction covered large swaths of sub-Saharan Africa; almost the whole Indonesian peninsula; the Philippines; Indochina; Vietnam, Cambodia, Thailand, India, and Burma. It included most of South America and parts of Central America as far north as the state of Chiapas in Mexico. Different regions of intense pollution, 12 to 17 parts per billion were in red. Red lining, as it were. Cities with concentrations of particulates above the levels of human safety were identified. São Paulo, Brazil; Mexico City, Mexico; Lagos, Nigeria; Islamabad, Pakistan; Shanghai, China; Bangkok, Thailand; Hamburg, Germany; and Kiev, Ukraine were some of the cities outlined. Extraction along the CO^2 global stream and specifically heavy areas of toxicity were targets for the operation. In the United States, Los Angeles, Chicago, Miami, Detroit, Newark, New Orleans, Pensacola, and Mobile were also tracked. Mining areas in West Virginia, concentrations of oil refineries in Texas, even shipping lanes near the Los Angeles/Long Beach harbor were studied. CO^2 patterns were mostly of southern origin, but heavy pockets in the Northern Hemisphere, primarily United States and North Eastern Europe, were viewed as sites of interest.

The map was 6' x 12' with pattern overlays of pathogenic flows, i.e. avian flu and the Hong Kong flu. It presented a clear and concise story of airborne pathogen's migration that caused the mutation of R2. On the other wall were similar size maps with all the extraction points. Below was a table presenting all salient points for any particular extraction. Number of operatives, cover stories, technology needed, contact points, false papers, airlines, trains, buses, transportation tickets, and customs agents. The operation could be viewed as part of the global pattern for CO^2 pathogenic streams that carried with it the powers to mutate DNA. Places, times, logistics, and even a cost analysis for each extraction were at their fingertips. Fatma, Jonathan, and Zwelenger carefully monitored the results of each extraction.

Four months passed by quickly. Every day they came into the Westside offices looking forward to collecting and comparing the DNA of the two classifications of subjects. The excitement of scientific discovery was more exhilarating than the conjecture of their scientific intuition. They knew *those people* existed;

now they could prove it beyond a shadow of a doubt. It would only be a matter of time. They knew the results. They just had to work the data.

Fifty–six

The Century City office of *those people* project was a beehive of human activity. Hunter and Imam were charged with being custodians of the arriving DNA containers. The process's nature of a 96 hours window from extraction to analysis made expedience and efficiency all the more important. Each transaction and subsequent delivery of the subjects' DNA was not only costly, upwards of $300,000, but a second extraction could jeopardize the project. It could cause alarm or even cause detection. Repeated collections geometrically increased the chances of being caught. One shot at each target was the only acceptable outcome. For *those people* project to work it had to be 100% accurate from planning to extraction to analysis. That was their joss and they knew the importance of it.

Operatives coming into the United States with samples of either virgin targets or *those people* targets were escorted through customs to the forensic labs at Cal State Los Angeles by way of a conduit company, Westgate Labs. The actual chain of custody never left Blackwater's hands. As soon as the Blackwater field agents extracted the DNA, the team was immediately taken to the nearest airport for passage to the United States with Los Angeles as its destination. In some cases private jets were used, but mostly commercial airlines delivered the DNA. It was carried through customs in many forms; housings of cameras, Mount Blanc pens, Tiffany necklaces, and other receptacles engineered to deliver the DNA at 40°C. Outside the terminals, cars waited to whisk the DNA away to Westgate couriers. who delivered it to Cal State LA.

A system was developed by Western Overseas, a customs broker and freight forwarder based in southern California. It tracked each operation from beginning to end. The tracking procedures were similar to FedEx's, allowing the product to be followed in real time anywhere in the world. Hunter and Imam were responsible for every one of the more than 50 deliveries and passages to Cal State LA. Ashley and Sabah were charged with the responsibility of tracking the DNA results at the forensic lab. They followed and monitored the DNA once it reached the labs at Cal State LA. They made sure the results were accurate per entry. Tracking systems were developed. The DNA was followed in the lab from one station to another so no cross contamination took place or mix up of results occurred. Each analytical procedure was signed off at every change of custody. Every activity was logged in by the responsible party. The trail for each DNA sample was a map showing where it had been and what analysis had taken place. A detailed tally of volume and weight of DNA used for each examination was carefully logged. An accounting of every milligram and every millimeter of DNA was made. Ashley and Sabah followed and documented all samples and compiled a database of each sample individually and all the samples collectively. A program was developed allowing numerous comparisons of every subject's DNA. The exactitude of the work was taken very seriously by Ashley and Sabah. The gang of four collectively were responsible for monitoring the extraction of the DNA, its whereabouts at any moment in time, its analysis at every stage of testing, and the compiling of all data.

Fifty-seven

Jonathan and Fatma were recipients of the four months work and would mine the forensic data for DNA mutations. This provided the actual evidence of *those people*. Their collaboration with Steve Zwelenger created comparison standards for the two DNA sample groups. It was simple, clear science, making replicated comparisons. They used a derivation of the double-blind method used in testing pharmaceuticals. The baseline of virgin DNA would be compared to that of *those people*; very simple, but ironclad.

It didn't take much time or energy for this part of their scientific responsibilities. Their major efforts created a program for Anton to simulate trillions and trillions of cell divisions and nano-incremental changes showed a chemical change in *those people*s DNA. To show mutations was one thing, but to create a simulation would extrapolate the mutations and forecast what *those people* would look like in two, three or four generations was another. The logic and sophisticated mathematics were mind-boggling. They would seek help from the Bill and Melinda Gates Foundation's Mosquito Genome Project that was trying to affect a cure for malaria. It had properties showing how the mutations of certain genes lead to a different subspecies of mosquito. The same model of projecting changes in mathematical formulations was used by Anton for *those people*.

Dr. Zwelenger entered the office and Jonathan welcomed him. "You are here early this morning, Steve."

"Yes I am, Jonathan. Is Fatma here? I want to discuss some things with the two of you. We should put our collective minds together."

Jonathan said, "I'll go get her."

Fatma came in the room and said hello.

Steve proceeded, "Experimental work with superconductors to model molecular interactions has been going on for decades. Simulation of folding proteins into three-dimensional structures and their interaction with drug molecules has been a slow process, but has led to many new drugs. Genetic engineering, as it's called, has been a godsend. Amgen, for example, and Genetech for another, have used the process. With Anton, the process will be thousands of times faster and results will be more exacting than previous technologies. The principal advantage of Anton is it will save thousands of lab hours. We will simulate the R2 gene and others in the cerebral cortex and see a three-dimensional high resolution image. The old IBM Blue Gene/L. superconductor and the Stanford Folding superconductors are much slower and simulate a very narrow set of biological processes. They simulate in short bursts or durations, tiny intervals of a femtosecond or one billionth of one billionth of a second. Anton, because of its computer power, will expand that time frame a thousand times longer, and a real picture of proteins and any changes will come into play. It will give us the ability to see genes actually change before our eyes. We will have the power to see them mutate. It's virtual but accurate. We will be seeing a new biological process never seen before. We will be able to do our simulations thousands of times longer and thousands of times faster. The protein or DNA changes will come into play. My preliminary findings are positive. When we get our DNA results, we can amend them for the Anton input protocol. We will be able to begin our project almost immediately. It should be a fast turnaround from importation of data to actually seeing a simulation of *those people* DNA and how it mutates. We will compare this with pure or virgin DNA and its stability in the same timeframe. We better be ready for the results."

"Steve," Jonathan said, "I think we are ready as soon as the DNA has been processed. This might not take the two months we had discussed for analysis."

Fatma interjected, "There is more. Before we begin running our simulation, we must develop a simulation for a business model of the Russell group as a cover. I have put a lot of thought into this. I'll explain. Essentially, we need to use Anton twice. Once for the Russell Group traceable if needed. Once for our DNA analysis which must be wiped off the computer's memory; every detail, without the ability of ever recovering a single fragment of its existence. We have to develop a way of deleting its existence from the most ardent forensic scientist or IS or IT people. We will leave traces of the Russell calculations that can be brought up if someone ever investigates. It will only be a financial history summation of the Resells' dealings with the Al Nassars. It will show some kind of derivatives, but won't be clear.   Again, we must be careful not to leave any trail of *those people*."

Fatma continued with the game theory and outcome strategies for equity investments the Russell group would need for its time on Anton. The cover up had to be realistic.   She used models for developing new sets of financial derivatives for newly issued cover bonds that would collateralize mortgage backed securities held by banks on their balance sheets; a very sophisticated analysis would never be seen in the light of day under usual circumstances.   It was so sophisticated it could have been used by hedge funds or central banks.   If ever investigated, it would be the perfect cover-up.

Fifty–eight

"We are all together for what is quite anti-climactic," Jonathan said. "We all know there is a difference between the DNA of normal people and *those people*. Little surprise, but, well, I'm not a person of hyperbole or one who exaggerates, but our findings are extraordinarily bleak."

The room was quiet with anticipation. Hunter, Imam, Ashley, Sabah, David, and Diana were looking at Jonathan flanked by Fatma and Zwelenger as authoritarian panelists ready to render a verdict.

"Stephen, the floor is yours," Jonathan said.

Stephen began, "The whole time Anton was creating a simulation, we knew of its findings. The clarity and resolution and its sheer definitiveness is hard to explain. We use words like 'ironclad,' phrases like, 'no other explanation,' but this is a lot more. We have actual images showing a composite of the cerebral cortex and other brain parts of *those people* and how much it deviates from ours. People may think or sometimes will say or euphemistically express human beings being superior to other animals.

We would say our DNA is 99.7% similar to that of chimpanzees, but that three-tenths of one percent is the human trait of reason, advanced language, and even sometimes we discuss our dexterity and nimbleness as reasons for superiority. It's that three-tenths of one percent which makes us human, different or superior. Here's where we have a real problem. The images of *those people* three generations out show they are at least 3% percent different, and the divergence is gets larger in an exponential way on each successive generation we simulate. The DNA is mutating at a faster rate than anyone would have ventured. We created a new way of looking at them. The imaging and simulating we used to create CT scans and MRI's of their brains for comparison with ours show quantum differences."

He put the scans and MRI's on a light board to show what *those people* look like next to MRI's and scans of normal sample people. There was no need for explanation. The differences were extremely divergent. The CT scans and MRI's spoke volumes. The cerebral cortex of *those people* from generation one to generation three shrank by over 30% and there was compensation in other parts of the brain that did not bode well for humankind and its existence.

"One area of the brain shrinks and another part expands," Zwelenger continued. "I will discuss my analysis in two different parts. One: the cerebral cortex, its diminution and forecasted consequences. Two: the parietal lobe, temporal lobe, and occipital lobes; and their augmentation, growth and forecasted consequences. Let's start off with the cerebral cortex."

He continued discussing the scans and MRIs of *those people.* "An over 30% constriction or shrinkage of the cerebral cortex without any increase in its density, volume or other mitigating circumstances means humans will have diminished capacities for core human functions. *Those people* will have less ability to sequence complex multipurpose step-tasks, and the flexibility of their thinking will diminish, to a point that all their activities will be rote for everyday functions. Simple learning will take place but give way to intellectual stagnation and rote activities. There will be great personality changes. They will have no problem solving abilities beyond a ten or twelve-year-old, and their language skills will be primitive. A smaller cerebral cortex will affect their standing as humans."

"Their intellect will be that of pre-teenagers but with anger and inflexibility exacerbates their frustrations. The diminished language skills will impede socialization, and their frustration will be expressed in violence. They will have limited problem solving skills even for the most elementary tasks. Simply put, they will be angry, inarticulate, violent, and have no socialization or judgment. Not a good picture."

Stephen continued, "The second portion of the analysis, the augmentation or enlargement of the temporal lobe, parietal lobe, and the occipital lobe is again extraordinary. Their sizes increase 25 to 30% to make up for shrinkage of the cerebral cortex. The overall brain size and weight will be that of a normal human being, but the distribution of brain areas will be different. The cerebral cortex will be smaller and its DNA will be altered appreciably. The lobes will be much larger but have huge variations making them almost unrecognizable. First: the parietal lobe. It's clear *those people's* abilities to visually focus and be attentive will be greatly impaired. *Those people's* attention spans will be considerably less than ours, and any detailed analysis of outside stimuli will be virtually impossible. The temporal lobe's mutation and size increase will affect language skills in a very negative way. Adding to their cerebral cortex deficit, spoken skills will be extremely limited. But the worst manifestation or change will be aggression. They will be aggressive and violent. They will be like people on steroids; road rage to the nth degree. Finally: the occipital lobe. Hallucinations, delusions of grandeur, and the inability to read and write are the major characteristics. Putting it in a nutshell, they will be aggressive, inarticulate, illiterate, and very violent. They will have an attention span of a flea and the meanness and aggression of a cape buffalo. Their aggression and the violence will be unmatched by anything in humankind."

Fatma got up and said, "I guess I have the worst news of all. We took *those people*'s projected CT scans and MRI's to groups of psychiatrists and psychologists: some to UCLA, some to Stanford, some to the American Psychological Association, and some to the CDC that's the Center for Disease Control and Prevention. We just gave them the scans and the MRI's without content. We said we did not want to taint their findings or readings of the situation. So we offered no collateral materials or psychological or psychiatric makeup of the subjects. We said we thought the scans showed birth defects or abnormalities and wanted a map of where to go from there. We asked for clinical evaluation of what they saw. We asked for a psychological makeup of how these people might function with the pretense of setting up a case for treatment. We acted surprised by the scans and MRI's and we were seeking their opinions because we were not familiar with anything like this. We had never seen it before nor had we read anything about it in the literature. We used the Los Angeles County General Hospital in Harbor City as our home institution and had cover as staff members."

"The results were sent to us and the findings could only be seen by us. We had total control of the information flow within the hospital's neuropsychiatry department, and it could not be traced. Our information technology people wiped out all e-mails and instant messaging from any of the research institutions we had correspondence with by way of a 'cookie'. No trace."

"The research agencies and institutions were disparate and their research staffs were known to us. We feel there is no chance of being discovered by an outside audit or investigation. Let me sum up our findings. All the responding institutions said *those people* were prone to violence. They were psychopaths with such diminished intellectual capacities they could not function in a technological world, and were delusional."

Fatma continued, "The reviewers recommended institutional domicile or social mayhem as the only alternatives. Either be locked up, or they would create havoc in the community. Over and over the referrals came back with the same answers, they cannot live in a structured civilized world. They don't have the intellectual capacity or psychological makeup to assimilate. The only rules society could apply to them was institutionalize, or if left at large, they would be nihilist, seeking total destruction of any social norms. Their potential for violence and their forecasted way of life could not be addressed by custom or tradition or even laws because they were amoral and could not control their aggression. All the findings were similar. Each one had an anecdotal conclusion. Get them institutionalized as soon as possible, was the consensus. A UCLA analyst compared them to an extra Y-chromosome person. A person prone to excessive violence, but he stressed he wanted to make it clear this was much more dire, and its consequences, if not attended to, could be horrendous."

"One colleague said, 'Send them into Afghanistan, send them to the tribal territories and let them kill everybody. When they get back, kill them. Or better yet, kill them there.' He said they were not really human."

The room was filled with murmurs and sighs. No one knew what to say.

David finally broke the silence. "You all did your jobs beyond any expectations. I said the project was in three different parts. One: you kids found them, uncovered them, and brought them into the light. Two: Fatma, Jonathan, and Steve, you analyzed them and proved their existence. Three: I said awhile back that Diana and I would discuss our role, and we will. It will be our job to figure out how to bring this to the public's attention. You did your jobs admirably. Let's hope Diana and I can combine our seventy years of political and financial experiences bringing about some positive political action. We will have a brief for you next week. Your input and collaboration are imperative. I don't know what else to say except, my father said something, a long time ago, 'You expect it, but it can be so overwhelming, it can be unexpected.' I knew this was coming, I looked forward to it, but I can't tell you how much more powerful it is than I ever thought."

"How in blue blazes," David exclaimed, "how are we ever going to disseminate this information without being taken as a crazy lunatic or a racist agenda evoker?"

David dropped his head and said, "Well, this is our job, and we'll do it no matter what it costs or what the consequences may be. It's like telling someone they're going to have kids who will have cancer later in life so they should kill them now."

Fifty—nine

After that meeting, David was at a loss. He and Diana asked the kids, Fatma, Jonathan, and Steve if they wanted to go out to dinner. They were turned down.

Driving home, Diana said, "You don't bring up your father very often unless you are stretching or reaching for something. I know you're not okay, so how can I help? We will find a way to deal with this. We always do."

David said, "Since we were kids, I feel I have been a problem solver, and you bring a human side to everything we do. You are intuitive and kind, but you know, we have talked about it, you are impetuous, and that's what I love about you. Also, I am sometimes stagnant in my thinking. We really need to think this out and come up with a plan. We can't be hasty. I don't know if we have a way of dealing with it. How can we formulate an approach? How do *those people* get out in the open? We need to bring about some action from the community, whoever that is. We talked about it before, if we don't bring this up correctly, we'll be viewed as Nazis, or racists, or just crazies. We'll be viewed as rich pieces of garbage. We'll lose all our political and social capital. That's what worries me, not so much we will lose everything, but not being able to get to the right people."

Diana grabbed his hand as he stared at the road ahead of him. He was driving in rote much like *those people*. He could navigate his way, but couldn't see anything in front of him. He was preoccupied by an unsolvable task. His frustration and his anger were building.

Diana said, "Listen, darling, you always draw on your father in hard times. It's funny but the older we get, we find a wealth of knowledge and answers in what we did when we were young. You're lucky you have had two fathers in your life; your dad, of course, William. He is your conscience your moral compass. We will seek his advice and counsel."

David said, "Diana, I was thinking about that. He will have a different feeling for what to do in a general sense. He doesn't know our political landscape and how things actually work here in the United States, but his insights are always right, he's a clear thinker. There's something else. He will have to deal with this on his own front at some point in time. We need to be on the same page. You're right, I should call. Maybe we should also talk to Omar? I am sure he knows the findings by now. Imam and Sabah probably called him from the car. I wouldn't be surprised if Fatma hasn't already called. We should send both of them a packet of our findings. E-mail it, and in the meantime we should call. They will both have different views than we do on this. It can't be the same as ours; they have different cultures and a different environment. Thanks, sweetheart. You're always there for me. I feel a little better.   Before we go home, do you want to go anywhere or just eat when we get back?"

Diana said, "I don't care.   I am not particularly hungry.   You should call Omar and William, either form the car or from home.   Just call now.   We'll both feel better."

"Diana, it's about 11:30 pm in Nairobi and pretty close to the same time in Cairo.   Maybe I should call in the morning their time?"

"David," Diana said, "Call both of them now, it's important enough.   It will make them feel needed if they know the urgency of your request."

David picked up the phone.   "William, it's David, old friend.   I know it's late, am I interrupting?"

William said, "David, my son, you can never intrude, my attention is always yours.   It must be important if you call at this hour.   I am with Martin. He heard your name and says hello.   What can I do for you?"

"You will receive an extremely important e-mail.   It is encrypted, you know the key.   The PDF file is very long, you should receive it in the morning.   I want you to read it carefully.   It's not about our financial dealings. It's more important than money.   Information has come into my hands, and I'm at a loss.   I need your thinking on what to do. I know I am talking and not saying much, but the file is too long and complicated to discuss it with you without you having seen it.   After you read it, you will see its importance as I do.   I await your call.   I've been speaking in general because of my concerns for privacy."

"David, this phone is clear and safe.   Your file can't be detected, so you have no worries.   I will call as soon as I receive it and pass the materials on to Martin.

As I said, he is sitting right here. We will call. Which phone should I use?"

David said, "Call my cell. You have the number."

David immediately placed a call to Omar. "Omar, its David..."

Before he could finish the sentence, Omar said, "I just talked to my lovely daughters and within three minutes, Fatma called. I am aware of the project's findings. I was waiting to call you later, but it is nice to hear your voice now. We must discuss this in detail and figure out what to do about it. I want to come to Los Angeles. I can have my office charter a jet, or I have use of my brother-in-law's. With no questions asked. I think I need to be with Imam and Sabah. I will not be in their way. I know they confide in Hunter and Ashley, and rightfully so, but they sounded a little desperate. I will bring their mother. She is better at giving comfort than I am. I think you and Diana will like her."

David thought, the girls and Omar, had never even mentioned her name. He wondered what she was like. "Diana and I want you and your wife to stay at our house. You can't say no. We insist. But I'm a little embarrassed; I do not know your wife's first name."

Omar said, "It's Doha. You will like her," he said again. "We will be arriving in Los Angeles in 15 to 18 hours. I'll email you our flight plans."

Sixty

"David", William said, "we have discussed your correspondence, and we have concerns, but we feel you will be disappointed in our response. We have felt this in our hearts all along. Our feelings have been more primal than fact. We tried for many years since the revolution to be democratic and forward thinking, but always knew other tribes were inferior. It was one tribe trying to be more powerful than the other; this was our form of superiority. Some of us are more westernized because of our proximity to the British when we were under their control. They preached equality for all whites, so we felt there might be equality for blacks as well. We were schooled and filled with their racist ideas, but we molded them into our own form of equality for all Africans. I look at you, I think I have tried to be white or act white because of our relationship. You have always made me a better person, my brother. I always felt that white was superior. We Africans are all the same. We seem inferior. I have overcompensated in my feelings of equality, but I always told people that we are equal. Our African history with laws and customs are rock solid. They can't be broken. We are tribal and we will always be that way. I have thought this for so long, and so has my brother, Martin. This paper puts a wedge in my heart. I feel this just proves it. We are not equal with each other. I have lived a lie. My sadness is matched by my awareness that this problem of *those people* must be addressed."

This was the last thing that David and Diana expected. Disappointment was not a strong enough word to express their emotions.

David said, "I know this is sudden, but do you really believe your life's work was based on a British lie? Do you feel all whites are equal, but blacks in Africa are not? Some Africans are inferior and some are superior, and you are not inferior to whites? I do not understand, my brother. Is there so much difference that some people should be killed? I am not judging you, but I seek your help in what Diana and I must do in America. We have a different set of customs, Judeo-Christian, but they are customs. Customs don't make you unequal; they only limit opportunity. I truly believe we are all the same; except for *those people*, they are not human."

"David and Diana," Martin said, "may I share a few thoughts? I think we are closer to the truth in Africa than you are in America. Our simple lives are based on survival, and yours are based on excess. We let nature educate us, and you let other people educate you. We are seen as tribal because our actions are predicated on survival. We know in our hearts other tribes are different. It is not learned, it is nature's way. We have killed each other since the beginning of time. We have eaten each other as a gesture of total contempt. We fear each other not because we are similar but because the others are animals. They are dogs. European ways have kept us apart because we fought the whites, not ourselves. We had not fought each other for fifty years until the whites lost all power. Look at us in Kenya. It is tribalism once more. We do evil things to each other because others are less human and they are dangerous to our simple way of life. Your paper only proves that. We have spent a life long quest for equality; I think you scientific findings only prove it has been a folly. I cannot sustain this thinking any longer. But, we will do what you want, my brother. This feeling of hate is raw. It is at the very core of our hearts. I hope we are wrong, but I don't see that to be the case. This paper brings back old truths and old memories. We pray you can dispel our beliefs. We are talking today about forming a unity government with the other lower tribes, and after receiving your report we see no reason. Martin and I feel the same way. What do you propose my brother? I am asking you for advice."

William said, "David, Diana, we are closer to this than you. I hope we are wrong, but we know *those people* exist today. They are inferior people. It is simple. Our tribal ways will allow us to bring about their destruction. We as people are born with a notion of distrusts. We sense they are different. Over the years we have cleansed our villages and our lands of enemies. We have poisoned their food and their water. We have killed their women and children. We have even raped them to plant our seeds to make them as we are. It has been our way before the colonial whites came, and it will be our way now that they have effectively left. It has taken only fifty years for our ways to resurface. David, my friend, you were at our political gathering a short time ago. You heard what we preached. I can't forever pursue the unattainable. I still can push for democracy and equality if you wish. Just say the word and these papers will be destroyed and never mentioned or recognized again. We will disavow the message if you wish. Never to be spoken in our lifetimes, if that is your desire. If this is your wish, it will be our command. I know in my heart even today *those people* are different. They're not just another tribe. They are like dogs, attacking all that surrounds them. They can't be part of our unity government because they are not intelligent enough to participate. We can play political games and seek recognition as equals and bring them into our parliament. We can set them up in a position of power, but they will fail. We can even get them to vote to liquidate themselves. That's how inferior they are. If we can do that today when there is a little difference, it will be easy, my brother, to do more later when *those people* are truly inhuman. Look all over Africa and you see the same thing. Your Western values are such that you can't get involved to stop the cleansing or killings. You have every reason of logic not to stop people from doing things wrong for society. Your protection of the minority at the expense of the majority will always prohibit you from acting. Our simple primitive lives based on survival tell us ways of solving problems, no matter the consequences. Yes, we can kill them. Your laws don't let you accomplish what is best for society because of your British or white feelings of equality. If you protect the minority, they will kill you. Look at terrorism and how you hope to counter it. U.S. is failing at every turn. Even here in Africa, you did not act in Rwanda or Darfur where 1,000s of people were killed before your very eyes. I'm afraid you will not act in the United States or Europe for the same reasons of indecisiveness based on your learned ways of equality."

David listened. He was speechless.

Diana said, "William, you have solutions at your disposal. I don't agree that today's people are different. I think that today we are all alike, but there is no doubt about tomorrow. You make it sound hopeless today, but for sure, in the next three generations, things will be impossible. We are not asking you to be democratic and continue to follow our ways. We have always felt you and Martin are our brothers. We are like you in all ways. Only the experiences of your life and the sallow color of your skin make us different. We are all humans, we are family, but *those people* are not."

David said, "William, I called you for council, but it's your honestly that rings clear in my ears. I don't know what I will do, but we must stop *those people*. They must be separated from us. If it is my lack of closeness to nature or my diminished senses because of my wealth or excess or if it is my culture that is lying to me; it does not matter. I must realize *those people* will destroy our world. You think that they have always been here? I see them coming in a short period of time. There is little difference. I accept your recognition as being dissimilar; I accept the recognition of lowly tribal people and I also recognize you have gone against the wind and suggested democracy for your people. You pledged your soul and suppressed your feelings for something not entirely in your heart. You have honor, my brother. Do what you think is best for your people. Having knowledge of *those people*, I know you will do what is right. Diana and I must find the correct path here, and it will be a difficult path. You are insightful.

Diana and I might not be equipped for this, but we must live up to the realities presented by the existence of *those people*. I trust we will talk soon. We all have much to consider and to reflect upon."

Diana said, "Goodbye, William. Goodbye, Martin. I hope our future conversations will be of our children and our families as opposed to harsh realities of humankind discussions."

David said, "Diana, these are two of the most progressive people in Africa. They have the stature of Nelson Mandela and Desmond Tutu. I hope they didn't do their life's work for us. They must have believed in equality and democracy for them to have sacrificed as much as they have over the years. I am sure they believed Kenyans had the capacity for self-governance and equal rights. We were there. They didn't just lie to themselves all these years. They just didn't lie to us to make us feel better. This is new. Martin was having great reservations and outward expression of contempt for *those people* when I was there with the boys. He felt they were an inferior people, and in some cases, actually a subspecies of humans. It could be that William did not want to see it or he suppressed it. It is very clear to him now. He sees huge change. His allegiance to his dream of democracy is deep down in his soul. He wants the colonial British to be correct and their ideas to be expanded by Africans as well. He feels there should be equity for all blacks. He is torn. What he has seen doesn't fit what he wants; but everything has changed because of *those people*. I don't know what I expected, but I'm glad we heard what they had to say no matter how contrary it is to my belief system. I don't know what my father would say but I have a good idea, too bad I don't cuss like he did

I'd feel a lot better. We will call William again when Omar and his wife, Doha, get here."

Sixty-one

The Al Nassars landed at LAX 3:30 p.m. Customs agents were waiting on the tarmac. The flight crew of six, four hostesses, the pilot, and the copilot, were the only people accompanying Doha Bishara and her husband, Omar AL Nassar. They came on her brother in law's Boeing 727. It would wait for them as long as need be. Doha looked to be in her mid-forties. She had highlights of red in her dark brown hair, she had large olive black eyes, she was an unusually tall Egyptian woman of 5 feet, 9 inches, and she had a smile that was disarming. Her voice was loud. It commanded attention. It was her custom to carry a Louis Vuitton shoulder bag filled with pockets of tip money, as she called it. Ten dollar bills for the US, five pound notes in London for her family flat on Belgravia Road in Knightsbridge, and five euro notes for her frequent visits to the family's seven bedroom flat off the Champs in Paris.

The Russell's in their Queen Mary-like Chevy Suburban laughed when Doha exited the plane. Her first words were, "My darlings, it was nice of you to come for us by yourselves, but we need another car for my entire luggage. I guess Omar did not say much about my eccentric ways."

The copilot proceeded to bring out 12 Louis Vuitton bags. Doha's were real. She said they were limited editions and laughed.

"You will get used to me. Most people do."

Omar just stood there.

"People don't know what Omar does with me, but I am wiser than you might guess. Where are my daughters?"

Diana introduced herself and said, "They are at our house waiting for you."

Omar and David followed them to the Suburban. Doha had the Russells in the palm of her hand telling stories and laughing while she held court for the 25 minutes ride home. They were all bystanders to her show.

Inside the gates of the Russell house, Imam and Sabah were standing together holding hands. Their eyes lit up as they both yelled, "Mommy!"

It was clear that Doha was the parent of choice. Omar said to David and Diana, "They love their mother. She is very special. She is one of the most powerful people in Egypt. She has family money, and her connections can open up any doors in the Middle East. I am more of a businessman. Doha is more connected to the political powers. She is the Egyptian ambassador to Macedonia, it's ceremonial, and it costs a couple million dollars a year to help subsidize our Greek compatriots. She was asked by the Mubarak family and could not say no."

Doha was introduced to Hunter and Ashley. She smiled and said, "My daughters need your fullest attention. I know you're good to them, for they tell me everything," and she laughed. "Diana, is it too late to go to Beverly Hills shopping? This is my recreation. Everyone knows me there. I have an enjoyable time with the store owners; I spend lots of money and make them laugh. We should go and let Omar and David talk to each other. You and I must speak. Our children are in a serious business, and I need to know from you that they are alright. You drive, let's take the girls. Hunter, Ashley, do you want to come along?"

The six left in a hurry. It was Doha's way; not a minute without entertainment or decision to be made.

David said, "Omar, I didn't know what to expect. Is she always so take charge?"

Omar said, "David, your family will come to love her. She is my greatest ally and confidant. We met at the University of the Americas in Beirut more than 25 years ago. We've grown up together, but we have separate lives in business and politics. Our family is our common life, and my daughters and I are the lucky ones to have her. She knows about *those people* and has some strong opinions that I share. She is more political and worldly than I am. So she will speak for the two of us. She is wise. You should listen to her, my friend. I am not sure if Sharif has discussed her, but most likely he talked about her family. She can open many doors. Her business dealings cut through the underbelly of the Third World, and her family has political ties throughout the Middle East."

It was 9: 30 p.m. when David got a call from Diana. She said, "Why don't you and Omar meet us for dinner at Maestros? David, I can't tell you how much fun we're having. She shops for recreation. She knows everyone here in Beverly Hills. It's crazy."

It was the Egyptian way to eat late and eat well. David and Diana soon found how easy it was to fall into a different lifestyle.

Sixty-two

The next morning Diana prepared breakfast for the Bishara/Nassar family, the kids, Fatma, Jonathan, and Steve. Doha would hold a different kind of court. Her blunt, accurate description of the Middle East and how it would react to *those people* was pointed and powerful.

She started by saying, "I've read your summary from Anton's analysis and find nothing surprising. We have followed the progress of your research from the beginning. It is clear *those people* cannot be allowed to live. The question is: how do we kill them and under what pretext? We also need to show my equals how we lower the pollution levels and not affect Middle East oil. Just killing them won't be enough if they continue to be created by the effects of pollution. We need numbers, we need locations, we need assets and logistics to be used if I am to carry this to every capital in the Middle East. Sharif and my dear Omar will tell you I have access and I am persuasive. We have to present this as a completed unquestionable action without any dissent. It is a moral imperative for us to kill them and eliminate the cause of their existence. It must be presented as cold facts with no alternatives. The capitals of our world must have irrefutable information. They will follow this as if it comes down from the heavens. Our culture is autocratic, it's dictatorial, and our people, as well as our leaders, function when they see unblemished truths, and if there are no other points of view. Clarity is the mainstay of action. The simple truth is *those people* are a threat to our way of life making the decision of eradication easy to sell. In the Middle East, we have a few families who have large fiefdoms and total control. It is the traditional simple rule. A Khalifa, a grand rasuli, a king, a pharaoh or a dictator, these are people we believe, and they demand respect through ruthless exercise of power. People are followers; no matter what the price, they accept the rule of law because they will enter the kingdom of heaven and reside in the house of God forever and ever. To rebel is blasphemous. The Jews, the Christens and we Muslims have the same God, the same apostles, the same disciples and we speak of the same history. We are humble servants enduring the failings of men to rest in heaven. We don't want democracy. It is easier to listen, be directed and have no voice than it to oppose the words of the prophet or the words of God. If we speak of *those people* as a threat to our simple ways, a Jihad of unimaginable acceptance will set upon them. They will be killed, each and every one of them, to the last drop of their blood. The same people who kill them will be honored and have the status of jihadists. They will be taken to the house of the Lord or God or Ali, no matter what your religion is. This is how we all believe. I feel many Christians believe the same way, look at how much hatred they have to gays and nonbelievers. If the Islamic world, most notably the Wahhabis, have brought such wrath to Americans for a simple intrusion upon our religious and cultural ways, imagine their righteousness and their hatred for *those people*. Imagine what their feelings would be for *those people*. If they hate you, death to the Americans, just imagine if we expose them in the right way. Our simple people would give their lives to eradicate them as a threat to Islam."

Everyone in the room knew Doha was more than she appeared to be. Shopping wasn't her only activity of privilege. She was tough minded, brilliant, and complex.

Omar was right, David thought, he did not have to say one word. David, Diana, Hunter, Ashley, Jonathan, and Steve just listened. Omar, Imam, Sabah, and Fatma knew her persuasive powers and her ability to formulate a point of view. She could hold off any form of opposition. She was outstanding, she was extraordinary, she was a leader. She commanded respect and Middle East leaders would listen.

After breakfast and a second shopping outing, it was clear to all this was recreation, Doha's way of relaxing. She purchased twelve pieces of luggage just to make room to take some gifts back home for family and friends. They ate lunch at the Montana Café a small Santa Monica bistro where she orchestrated the chief to prepare a 15 course meal fit for a queen. It lasted almost 2 hours before they went to the Santa Monica Third Street Promenade. David finally felt he had come up for air as he and Diana walked together behind the shopping party on the promenade. This was the third shopping venue for the day.

David said, "She is unbelievable, our friends would never believe this in a million years. I love her. We have money but nothing like this. It's like she's some kid in a candy store, but she is also a very complex powerful woman. What she said this morning is irrefutable. It's almost exactly what William and Martin said. It is so clear for all of them. It is so simple for them. Just do it. It's not even debatable. But how in the hell are we going to sell it here? If we can't sell it with all our contacts and the rest of the world can, then our political reluctance will be responsible for the destruction of mankind. Our conservative outlook will be out of step just like our global warming position at the U.N. Diana what the he'll are we going to do? Now I really sound like my dad. Every day we wait or fail to get the message to the right people, it will get worse. Some day we won't be able to pull it back, there is a tipping point when Those People will take over making life changes in everyday activities if we don't act even if the rest of the world does. It is clear the US holds the key to eliminating *those people* and I can't see how we can do it. Can you imagine the ACLU? Maybe William was right, our desire for democracy and equality may be our undoing. It's so easy for them. I just don't know how we are going to do this."

Sixty—three

The five days went by quickly. Doha and Omar were ready for their drive to LAX and their trip home by way of Marballa, Spain. Even though it would be Mediterranean cold in Puerto Banos and not the tourist season, they felt comfortable, as Doha would say, because all the Arabs would be gone.

Diana leaning over the island in the kitchen, preparing a small breakfast for everyone, looked up to see David, Doha, and Omar approaching from the guest side of the house.

Diana said, "I can't tell you how much it has meant to me to have you as guest in our house, not only for *those people* but for the ability to get to know you. I, no we, feel like we have known you forever. You are from a different world," she laughed. "I truly mean it, it's been lovely. I know there's a more serious side to all this, and we are indebted to have your involvement. You are remarkable, and your advice is well taken but it is your friendship that will be cherished."

Omar spoke up. "We feel the same, if Doha will let me speak for us. It has been wonderful. I will talk to our mid-east friends when we return to Cairo. You have to give us all the information Doha seeks, but believe me when I say it will be in good hands. I think you agree."

Doha said, "Omar usually does not speak for me so I will say he and I hold your friendship scared."

Doha was ever vigilant when it came to business and matters of state. She said, "I am going to Hong Kong in March for some meetings about my fishing company. It is called Aquamarine."

She had many businesses that were separate from Omar's. Her business ventures and partnerships with her family were numerous. "I will be able to discuss this with my Asian partners and friends. We are in the midst of purchasing a cannery for our catch off the coast of the Horn of Africa and the Red Sea. We have a fleet of thirty ships. We quick freeze the fish right on our boats. Then we have them transported. They can be in China's southern economic zone, Fushan, in eight days. If everything goes well, we will be delivering 100,000 tons of crustaceans and 200,000 tons of fish, that's smelt and anchovies, per week. We are a large provider of food stuffs in Southern China and that gives us political leverage. I will bring in my South Korean and Filipino partners. We find all Asians take bribes to do business. We are big enough our bribes go all the way up to the very top of the political chain. They will listen to our call. I think you'll find their reception to our problem of *those people* and their attitude quite similar to mine."

In Doha's usual manner, the subject changed quickly. "I want to thank both of you again. Before I came here, Omar had spoken of you often. He wanted to place our children under your supervision here in the United States. It was something with which I was uncomfortable and unacquainted. We have never left our children in anyone's care. Omar was steadfast in his approval of you and the conditions of your family keeping an eye on Imam and Sabah. He was right. This is why I love him. He's always right when it comes to the girls. I thank you a thousand times. It is unusual for us to take anything from others; especially something so personal. Thank you again."

She put her hand on Omar's shoulder and said something in Arabic, and he smiled.

David said, "We should call the kids, and the eight of us will take the Suburban. By the way, Omar," he laughed, "I have a van that will take your luggage to the airport. No one will believe this so I am taking pictures. I've never seen so much luggage in my life. I must be serious for a moment before we go to the airport. I know you can bring *those people* to the attention of the powers that be in the Middle East and Asia. I know that you can get something done. We will have problems here in the United States. I suspect the same in Canada and Europe, but we will get it done. Then we will coordinate a worldwide effort to eradicate *those people*. We also will come up with a viable plan to eliminate environmental hazards and the causes of *those people*. No more of this. We will miss you. We will miss the both of you dearly. Let's go, your plane is waiting."

Omar said, "They can wait. Let's go shopping." Everyone laughed.

Coming back from LAX on the 405 freeway to Bel Air, David's and Diana's thoughts were scattered. They were apprehensive about their ability to deliver on *those people* project. They were joyful for the boys and especially happy about Imam and Sabah's family. They were at a loss of words about Doha, but knew she was something unique. They now had to formulate a plan for their part of *those people* project. The task was prioritized as urgent, and everything else would be secondary.

Sixty-four

"Diana, do you have plans for later today?" asked David.

She said, "No."

David said, "I'm going to call Bill Love. We will meet Bill at Dale's 50's Diner and discuss this with him. I'm sure he's playing tennis right now, but he'll see to it. He can meet us there for a late lunch or an early dinner."

William Cecil Love was the most prominent black American in Long Beach, California. He was chairman of the board of directors of Community Hospital in Long Beach, the 29th largest hospital in the United States. He was on the police commission, he was a past head of the boys club, but of greater importance, he was the president of the NAACP. Bill was a moderate and he was cautious in politicizing racial issues. He was a consummate politician. His fingers were on the pulse of the black community. He was a conduit between the streets or 'hood,' as it was called, and the police department, the business community, and the city populace at large. He was a consensus builder, and his reputation was untarnished from the streets to the burgeoning upper-middle class of African Americans in Long Beach. His political arms reached to Sacramento, the state's capital, and beyond. He was a man above reproach and was considered to be brilliant.

Love would be the first of many trusted people David and Diana engaged while creating a plan to bring *those people* into the light and doing something meaningful about their eradication. This was not the Middle East or Asia. The art of politics was needed. William was their man in the African American community. David and Diana, over the years, had donated large sums of money for political influence, some for social causes, and some for business. Bill was astute and could read the political tide better than anyone they knew, so they relied on him. He knew the political landscape. Long Beach was a perfect model for *those people* project. It was typical in the 200 mile continuance of cities from north of Los Angeles to San Diego. It was about 30 miles from David and Diana's house.

Eighty-five percent of Californians live within 10 miles of the Pacific Ocean. The density of population from Los Angeles to San Diego was that of a mega-city. Southern California, as it was called, extended from north to south over 100 miles. The western boundary of the Pacific Ocean to the eastern boundary of mountains and deserts was as wide as 30 miles and as narrow as 5 miles. It was one large city, and Long Beach was in the midst of it. Long Beach's population was almost 550,000. It was representative of Southern California, its demographics were transient, which was the case for most of California. One in five people living in Long Beach had lived there five years or less. For every one Caucasian leaving Long Beach, he or she was replaced with another Caucasian within a year. This was called attrition and replacement. For every black, replacement was 4 to 1 within a year. For every Asian, replacement was 6 to 1 within a year. For every Hispanic, replacement over a year was 11 to 1. Replacement could be because of birth or migration, legally or illegally. The numbers were almost identical throughout Southern California.

The increase in population was mostly driven by economics. The wealthier people, Caucasians, had fewer replacements. The poor people, minorities, had greater numbers of replacements. White wealthy people who tended to be older had a stagnant rate of population and none, or no measurable increase, in *those people*. Poor people or minorities had a burgeoning population, and because of socioeconomic living conditions, had greater increases in numbers of *those people*. The demographics of Long Beach were similar to the rest of Southern California. It would be a good testing ground or greenhouse for studying the politics of *those people*. This is where William Love would come in.

David and Diana pulled up to Dale's. It had not changed in thirty years. It still looked like a 50's cafe with 'blue plate specials'.

Bill was waiting at a booth. He stood, kissed Diana and shook David's hand and said, "Are you slumming it today?" He smiled. "It's great to see you. How are Hunter and Ashley?"

David and Diana filled him in on major points of *those people* project. Diana had concerns about bringing this up to the African-American community.

Bill said, "I can bring this up to the black community, but you have to find someone for the

Hispanic community and the other minority communities. And you have to find someone for the white community. As for the black community, I have three names at the top of my head that we should discuss. It's not what you would like to hear, but you have to hear me out before you say anything. We should begin with Willie Brown, the former Speaker of the California Legislature and the past mayor of San Francisco. We should discuss this with Maxine Waters, a member of the United States House of Representatives. And we should meet with Mark Ridley-Thomas, a Los Angeles City Councilman."

David's and Diana's eyes rolled.

"You have picked the three worst people in the world," David said. "They all hate white people, and you can't trust them. You know our history."

Bill said "That's why I picked them. If you can win them over, then you can go far with this."

"No," Diana said. "Remember when you called us and told us we should contribute some money or actually we should just give money to Willie Brown? I know it was legal, but the money was for a Harriet somebody, I forgot her last name. She was supposed to be appointed to the State Department of Education. She was very liberal and met our litmus test. He took over $200,000, and in committee, we were assured he had this in his pocket. Remember she got turned down by a 7 to 2 vote in committee? Then he had the gall to tell you he needed our money, and had orchestrated the whole thing. And after the summer recess of the legislature he finally got her appointed. By then the school year started. She was not effective. And you want us to talk to him. You're crazy."

David said, "Before you defend yourself, I have to say something about my friend Maxine Waters. Wasn't she the woman who said publicly at the Lemiert Park rally that she would never vote for a white man for the Presidency of the United States because she couldn't trust any of them? She still maintains that AIDS was a white conspiracy developed by the government to kill all black men. You think for *those people* project, we should go to her? Diana is right, Bill, you have lost your mind. I can't help it, remember she said the Contras had the United States government's approval to sell cocaine and crack in south-central to finance the Nicaragua war? I can't believe you would put us in the same room and ask her for help. And then there's Mark Ridley-Thomas, he has never met a white person he liked. He hates white people. Is there a chance we could talk to any of them?"

Bill shook his head and said, "I don't know if you two have noticed in the last thirty years, but I am black. I will talk to them."

Sixty–five

Bill said, "You guys, I know I drive you crazy. But more to the point, I am thinking about using a hospital as a veneer to ask our distinguished friends for help. I will tell them, one-on-one, that we have been seeing case after case of *those people* at the hospital. I'll explain it in very simplistic terms and ask them what they think I should do. I'll just feel them out. I'll convince them it's kind of like autism, but it's worse because it's so prevalent. We have a police lock-up at Community, and I'll say a lot of juvenile offenders pass through and they stick out, not kids with the problem of a chip on their shoulder, but people with the problem of being different and uncontrollable. Not a mental defect, probably worse. I'll get to them, by saying they're not people we can help, Jim Brown couldn't even help them. I'll tell them they're unsalvageable. These are the shooters and assassins for the gangs, their foot soldiers, and what makes them so bad is they have no guilt. I'll even mention their eyes. It will be like a heads-up for them."

David inquired, "What do you think their reaction will be?

William replied, "Well, David, I can just surmise. You know they're typical politicians and they'll give me typical bullshit. But at some point, I know all of them will think it over and get back to me, if for no other reason than they know they owe me. Even if all three agree there is a problem, and they put forward some kind of plan to get rid of them, they will give me a program so simple and nondescript they won't be tied to it. They are politicians and I think they will realize how dangerous this is. Another problem is they don't speak for all the African-American community. We are not a melting pot. We're not a group of homogeneous thoughts or actions. We're a polyglot of diverse interests, sometimes I think only self-interest. I do have an advantage in speaking with them. Not only my long political relationship with all three; but my color. We have spoken over the years of how much discrimination there is in the black community over the color of one's skin. I am considered really dark, which has its advantages. I am pure, and people listen to me. They will listen to me. You know sometimes my color has been a disadvantage. Do you remember the Elks Club, when Bob Kerrey was served? He is so light he wasn't offensive. You and Diana and I went up to the bar and you ordered three drinks.

The bartender made two and said, 'We don't serve no niggers here.'

You wanted to kill him and I had to defuse the situation. I pointed to Kerry, you remember, and said, "What in the hell do you think he is?"

"He don't look like a nigger to me" was the retort.

All we could do was shake our heads. It was evident we couldn't change him or punish him. He would never figure it out. You sat me down as if I needed to be cooled off and he gave me that speech. I was the one who cooled down, but you gave me the speech."

David interrupted, "William, what are you getting at?"

Diana said, "I remember. It was a pep talk. It wasn't appropriate for what happened, but I remember it was kind of powerful."

William resumed, "You told me in certain circumstances, my color would be of great advantage. You said in the correct situation I had the advantage. When I came into a room filled with white people, it made them uncomfortable. Their expectations would be so low I would sound profound, if not extremely intelligent, if I were articulate and concise. If I dress better than them, if I talk better than them, and am a man of few words, you said that was very powerful. You said I was always smarter than most people, so I had to figure out a way to use my color, and I would be powerful. That's what you're going to do after I talk with Willie, Maxine and Mark. I will get them to give me a way of developing a consensus in the black community, and you will talk to them. We can get to Jesse Jackson. That's easy. Everyone in Chicago who was forced to give him money owes us. The alderman, the mayor, and even members of the house, if they are from the Chicago area, they were politically extorted to give money to the Rainbow Coalition. We know them all. I'll call Reverend Sharpton. He's close to Louis Farrakhan. And ultimately, we will get to Cornell West and Julian Bond. Bond is on the board of the NAACP and he will listen. So here's my plan. I will meet with our three friends. They will give me a way to proceed. You, as a white guy, will have the advantage you talked about so many years ago; you will talk to the heavy hitters in the black community. I will script it out, and Diana will dress you"

David just smiled. He knew he and Diana had come to the right place. William Cecil Love was the best. His friendship and his insight was the rock that David and Diana clung to so many times in their lives. He was their harbor on so many occasions. William felt the same way about his two lifelong friends. It was truly a heartwarming sight; three old friends were still chasing windmills and chopping down the biggest tree. They all knew this project was the right thing to do.

"Maxine, its William Love. How are you doing?"

"William, this must be important because we are always calling you for help and money. This is the other way around. Well, what can I do for you?" she asked cordially.

"We have to talk. It's something I have to discuss with you in private. Can you meet me today? Clear your calendar and see me this afternoon. It's that important."

"I will come over to the Crenshaw district; maybe, Leimert Park."

Maxine Waters was the heart and soul of South Central Los Angeles. Not since Kenny Hawn, the County Supervisor, had anyone championed the needs of the African American community as she had. She was ironfisted, tested politician of many decades in the US House of Representatives, and leader of the Black Caucus, and a person of will. William had known her and had worked with her for over twenty years.

Maxine's anti-white message, as David had called it, was more for political consumption in South Los Angeles; she was a reasonable person, but her views on race were radical, and she lived by them for political survival in the heart of black Los Angeles. She was always flanked by her political lieutenants, but today she would meet Bill by herself in the infamous Crenshaw district that television highlighted in the 1965 and 1992 riots, which had taken scores of African American lives.

The Crenshaw district, with Leimert Park at its epicenter, was considered the home of the African American renaissance in the United States. Once gang infested, this community now supported coffee shops, playhouses, a shopping center and fine eateries and now had political clout. It stood east of Baldwin Hills and Windsor Hills areas of *Essence* and *Ebony* magazines' fame. So much fame the magazines just called them 'Baldwin Hills' or 'Windsor Hills; never even mentioning the city or state. The African American community recognized the area as it's wealthiest in the United States. Magic Johnson opened his first cinema there and brought gentrification to the area. His wife, Cookie, opened a boutique in the Crenshaw Center. Crenshaw symbolized the rebuilding of the African American community and the growth of a new middle class. It was everything good about America.

William pulled up at Magic Johnson Center in Ladera Heights, a little west of Crenshaw. He met Maxine Waters at 3:30 p.m.

"Maxine, please excuse me, but we will get to the pleasantries later. Do you want some coffee?" he asked as he pulled up two chairs to a small table on the patio of Starbucks. This was one of 100 or more Starbucks Magic Johnson had franchised in inner cities throughout the US. It was a social gathering for upper-middle class African Americans in the west end of South Central Los Angeles. It was a predominately minority area, but whites were taken in and treated well. No racial tensions at all. This was the integration that everyone wished diversity would bring to the nation as a whole.

William said, "We have a problem at Community. I need your help." He discussed *those people* and expressed his fears. He plainly stated that the hospital thought they could be a human subspecies, not an inner city cultural product phenomenon. He showed her some pictures of *those people* given him by David and Diana. Their haunting eyes and William's description of them as violent and antisocial made it abundantly clear to Maxine Waters the truth in what he was saying.

"Maxine, I don't know what to do. This is just an informal discussion between two old friends." He knew she would not divulge this material in any public arena.

"This can not be managed. If the presence of *those people* gets out, I can't imagine the consequences." Maxine said, and they both knew.

"Well, I need your help," he said again. He presented a hypothesis of competition: us and *those people*, with *those people* winning out.

"Well, William, I'm at a loss for words," she said. "This explains a lot. The violence, the inability of parents to control their kids, the inability of these kids to be educated; I just don't know what to do. What do you want me to do with this? Is it just our kids, or is it more pervasive?"

He proceeded to tell her its scope, and that it was not predicated on race or ethnicity, but the vagaries of the pollutants spreading their evil.

"You are the first person I relayed this to," he said, not lying, but pushing the truth. "We have to map out a strategy for our community. Then, I have to take this to the rest of the world. My God, it's a problem superseding all else."

He reflected for a second and then said, "Do you think you can call a black leadership conference of trusted people so we can pick their brains? It must be a select few, to minimize the chance of this getting out. If it gets out, I don't know how we could stop a social catastrophe. It's happening all over, regardless of color or background. I don't want people to perceive this as the black plague. If they hate us now, imagine how we would be treated if this is framed as a black issue only. But the truth is it affects whites, blacks, Asians, and Hispanics. We are all facing the same thing. That should make it somewhat easier to sell. *Those people* are a threat to everyone's way of life."

"William," Maxine said, "I like your idea of a leadership conference. That's a good way to be under the radar. I will bring it up at the Black Caucus. I'll make up something. You have to help me out. You have to set the agenda. You have to bring in people who can give authenticity to this. Let me know who you want as participants, and we will go from there."

Sixty–six

Maxine placed a call to Mark Ridley-Thomas as soon as William Love's car left the Starbucks parking lot. "Mark, this is Maxine Waters. How are you?"

"It's a privilege, my sister, it is my honor to hear your voice," he replied. "How can I be of service?"

She recanted her conversation with William Love about *those people*.

"He is too white," said Ridley-Thomas. "There must be more to it. We must investigate this. It did not come from the hospital. There has to be pharmaceutical money behind this. We have to follow the money if Love is involved. I think there's something missing in all this. It has to be a government plot to eliminate black people, gone awry. Just like the Tuskegee experiment, just like AIDS. We have to address this problem, my sister."

Maxine then said, "Do you really feel in this day and age the government is still doing those things? This is conspiracy theory. It will play well in the hood, but hard to sell to educated black people."

Mark Ridley-Thomas said, "My first intuition is we have to get reliable scientists who are familiar with the history of our struggle to look at this stuff and get their opinion. Tell Love you need to see more evidence because you are concerned and don't want to rush to judgment. It will give us time to figure out what to do. We don't want to dry up his support, my sister. We can take his white money and not let him feel betrayed if this gets locked up by someone else."

"Mark," Maxine said, "you are right. He said he would call you, so be prepared to be supportive to his face. Don't question the science. Tell him it will be hard to convince people. I told him I would bring this up to the Black Caucus. He suggested a leadership conference as a guise for us to consider looking into *those people*. He also said it was not just affecting African-Americans, but it cut across all lines. People of color, and white as well. I think he wanted to make it bigger and deeper than it is to get my support."

Ridley-Thomas said, "Love is always where the money is. This smells white to me. Maxine, I will talk to Love, but I will misdirect him. He knows I need his money to run for mayor. He thinks I will Uncle Tom for him. I'll make it sound good. Who else did he say he was going to approach?"

Maxine said, "Initially, you, me, and Willie Brown. I don't think he's talked to Willie yet; we should get to him first. You want to get hold of him, or should I?"

"Even though I know him better, you call him, and I'll follow-up," Ridley-Thomas said. "I don't know as much as you do about *those people* and Love's reputed truths, so I could misrepresent things. You call. Let me know when you're going to call, and I will follow-up. Willie will feel our show of power if the two of us talk to him. He reads things well and he will represent our view. Between you and me, Willie will follow us, my sister. Even if there is some truth in this, we can't act on it. It would be political suicide. There's no way, even if all of it is true; we can't just go out and kill people."

"We've got to get to the science so we can find an alternative," Maxine said. "Mark, Love says it's too late to do anything about it. There may be no way to stop it. He says there's nothing we can do. No alternatives. I know it's just a ploy to strip us of power and his lackey's way of passing along a white man's message. I am not sure what the truth is about *those people*, but *those black people* cannot be exterminated. They don't exist, but even if they did, the white man created them, so it's his problem. I'll call Willie right now."

Ridley-Thomas said, "Call him and get me on the line."

"Mark, I just thought about it. I can't do it right now, I'm at Starbucks in Ladera Heights. I will call when I get home. It will take about 20 minutes max. Should I call you on this number, or do you want me to call you on your cell?"

Ridley-Thomas said, "I'm still in my office. I don't care, just call him now."

Willie Brown answered immediately. "Maxine, Mark, I feel your pain," said Willie Brown. "Don't think it's simple to take advantage of my friend, Mr. Love. He never shows all his cards. He isn't wealthy and well-connected because he is a stupid old Uncle Tom. William has been at your back for years because he benefits from you, period. He knows you will betray him. He knows your agendas. We have to ask ourselves why he confided in you. He will call me, and for good reason. He knows I can find out where all the bodies are and pass information along to all the right people. I think, from all you've told me, William feels *those people* do exist. Black and white and brown and whatever, and he thinks they are a threat. I don't think there are any circumstances that will allow us to kill them. I don't know what Love wants but I will listen. My feelings are with you, my brother and my sister. I am with you unless Love has a way of changing my mind. I know that would disappoint you, but this issue is far too big for me to show allegiance before I know everything about it. I once was at a meeting with Vice President Hubert Humphrey, and he said civil rights were so vast he would defer to the people on the ground. That's when he sought out Martin Luther King for help. He knew King knew best, I don't know who knows best. I'm listening, but this is too vast a question for us to make it a racial issue. Remember, don't underestimate William Love or overestimate yourselves. When I started my law practice, I went after the Police Department. I represented pimps in San Francisco. Everybody knows they were not just pimps, they were businessmen. They were smart. William is not just a little pimp working for the whites. You're outclassed by him, Mark; if you think you can take advantage of him, you are wrong. If you want to be mayor, you need his help. Figure out what he wants. It's not always race. He's from Long Beach but his influence reaches further than you might want to know. Be careful, my brother. Maxine, have William organize that leadership conference. Let William set up his agenda and invite all the people he requests. I will do my best to find out as much as I can. Worst case is a truth will surface. We can always react to it. We want him to put his cards on the table."

Sixty–seven

"David, Diana, we have a meeting set up with the Black Caucus leadership group. All Caucus members will be present. They are inviting Jesse Jackson, Cornell West, and Andrew Young. Al Sharpton will be hooked up by satellite. All the heavyweights of the black community will be there. I think you should address them bluntly. You should start off with a scientific model from Anton. Then your abbreviated environmental model to show how to slow down *those people* mutations and eliminate what caused them. Make sure it's implemented in a global strategy. It's a lot for them to digest. Don't talk down to them but make it educational. I think your goal should be to ask one of them to represent the interests of the African-American community in some kind of presidential or global summit. We can figure that out later. Keep in mind how resentful they will be because you're white. I think Jesse Jackson will try to fight with you," William said.

"William," said Diana, "I have put a lot of thought into this, about Jesse Jackson and Cornell West and how they will try to knock David off the mark. I think he should attack Jackson on personal level; personal grounds. He would never expect that. You know, that love child, and of course, calling Obama a nigger and accusing him of betraying the black community and being out of step with the needs of African-Americans. He is a bully, and he won't take it well if David goes after him. Like all bullies, he's a coward. He will wilt. William, what do you think?"

"It will work if his son isn't there. He is extremely protective of his dad, and he is formidable. I'll make sure he is not invited. David, present everything as fact about Jackson. Don't hold back anything. No one will back him if you intimate that you have stuff on them, too. No one wants the closet opened up. Make it uncomfortable for them all, but tell them you've taken part in indiscretions, even if you have to lie. Make sure you don't sound pious. Color will evaporate if you come off flawed, but don't tolerate any of Jackson's sanctimony. Cut him off at the knees. As for West, he is all talk. He likes to hear himself a lot. He does not make sense. Every time he laughs that condescending laugh, it's because he's full of crap. Attack his premises. His conclusions are not consistent. He covers up his lack of intellectual rigor by using clichés and anecdotes. He does not make sense. He is arrogant and fancies himself as a word merchant. You know Andrew Young; he respects you and your views. Point your discussion to him. He has no color and sees the larger picture when necessary. He is the conscience of the NAACP."

David said, "William, I want to bring along the kids and Imam and Sabah. Fatma and Jonathan will deliver their separate scientific presentations. Her look should completely put to rest any color discrimination.

This is their baby. They should be there. What are your thoughts?"

"Well, I don't think it's such a good idea, but if it's important to you, then bring them. Sounds like you have already put thoughts into the planning." William continued, "If the kids are necessary, have them only work on questions and answers. They better be prepared. It will surprise the Caucus if everything goes well. Ashley and Hunter should be policy wanks. Have them discuss environmental issues, present a plan. Discuss the pollution damage by using existing treaties and laws. Don't let the girls do anything; just make sure they are there. You know what kind of sexists black men can be. The Caucus is weak on particulars and anything that is policy related. They will accept it because it's too much work for them and their staffers to read actual legislation and position papers. They don't use think tanks. It's all verbal, mostly flash, no substance for them. They are a word-of-mouth, so make sure Hunter and Ashley are specific. They will be impressive because the Caucus and their staffers are not masters of hard work and due diligence."

"Okay, William, is there anything else?" David asked.

William thought for a second and said, "David, you have the upper hand. You know they will try to throw you off script. Don't get trapped and you'll be okay. The boys will be fine. And as I said, Imam and Sabah should only be there. David, when it's over, talk to Young and ask him to represent you. He may say no. So ask him to choose a spokesperson."

Sixty-eight

David, Hunter, Ashley, Imam, Sabah, and William left the conference room. There was total silence. They walked down the corridor to the elevators going up to the suite where Diana was waiting with Fatma and Jonathan who had left earlier after making their presentations.

Diana's first words were, "Well, how did it go?"

William said, "Diana, you can be proud. We left a room where a pin dropped on the floor would have been deafening."

"David was masterful and followed the game plan perfectly and you two gave such a succinct informational presentation. You know your business. David may have had a little problem not overstating his contempt for Jessie Jackson. They saw how much he truly hated the man and did not know how to deal with David's personal aggression."

William put his arms around the shoulders of Hunter and Ashley and said, "They could not have been better. They were men among men. Let David tell you the rest."

David said, "I came in right at the beginning and I walked right up to the podium. You were right; changing the conference to the Four Seasons Hotel gave us a total advantage. You should have seen them, they were impressed with the hotels, but some of them, as soon as they saw me, were just pissed; that rich white stuff. What is he doing here? How did they get invited? You should have seen some of their faces. I did exactly what we scripted. I held off starting my presentation. I stood at the podium for about 30 seconds. It seemed like an eternity. Then I told them we paid for the research. That it was not the hospital. And we contacted William to have Maxine Waters under false pretenses set up the conference; we would be totally open and transparent. Fatma and Jonathan gave them the science and I said, 'Have your people review it.' Just like William said, Jesse Jackson tried to take over and attack me. I cut him off immediately. I said he had lost all credibility. He was an old horse was so disloyal to the cause he was running home to the wrong barn. Not everything was about him or color. He started to interrupt again, and I told him I would personally cut off his money train. I would use all my resources, if need be, to make sure we would never receive another penny. I told him if he continued to interrupt me, he could leave. The room was abuzz. That pompous Cornell West got up as if he could intimidate me and started to pontificate, you know, that brother stuff. I listened; then I tore him apart. That being said, I now had total control and discussed the need for action. The boys followed. They gave a great presentation of the causality of *those people*, with a few twists. They said that there was a correlation between the amount of pollution and the number of *those people*, but they went a little further. Guys, tell mom what you did."

Ashley said he presented it, but Hunter, Imam, and Sabah developed the science. "Basically, I told them that every American contributes about 6 pounds of hydrocarbons a day into the atmosphere. I discussed the prevailing wind patterns and the chemistry of pollution. The two elements together cause 1,340,000 of *those people* per month. I discussed where they would be distributed. I stated worldwide, there are 120,000,000 births per year and *those people* constitute approximately 15%. The rates of proliferation of *those people* and the math behind accelerated growth for three generations would have them take over the human race. Hunter, Imam, and Sabah were there for questions and answers. Dad then Fatma and Jonathan had already presented *those people*'s profile. It all came together. It was amazing. We asked for questions; there were none, the room was quiet. We got up and left, all of us together. The five of us just walked out of the room and came up to the suite."

Williams said, "They will get back to us. They always do."

Hunter said, "Mom, we were good."

It took 30 minutes for the first call to come in. Andrew Young was calling from the lounge. "David," he said, "you got my attention and my complete support. I know it's not racial. That is really important. What can I do? I will take this any place you want, but I'm afraid many people feel I'm too old and not Washington-based. That doesn't play well in the inner city. I can reach almost anyone who was here at the conference and we can use them as surrogates. By the way, that Jackson and West thing was handled perfectly.

They are pompous asses and they are embarrassing. I want to thank you. You got everyone's attention; now we have to get their loyalty. That may not be easy."

Calls continued coming in for the next hour and a half. The meeting had been successful. It was a prideful father and mother who watched and listened as their two sons were called and queried about their part of the presentation.

William said, "It has been a good day."

David replied, "Well, I think we've done the easy part first. We have to create a plan to take this to the white community and the Hispanic community. May the truth be known, I don't feel as comfortable or good about that as I do about what we have done today. After we discuss this with the white and the brown communities, we go to Hong Kong and see your parents," as he looked at Imam and Sabah.

"They were setting up a conference to discuss *those people* with their Mid-eastern and Asian connections. From there, we go to see Obama. Let's get out of here. Let's get something to eat or go for a walk. It's been a long day, I need to be outside." David opened the door to usher everyone out, but the phone rang.

Andrew Young was calling and said, "David, our person is Carolyn Cheeks Kilpatrick. She will represent us. She's a member of the House of Representatives for the 13th District, Detroit, Michigan." He hung up the phone.

Sixty-nine

Back in Los Angeles, David did not have time to savor the group's accomplishments in Washington. He called William Love.

"William," David said, "I just want to thank you again. You are a trusted good friend, and without you, we could not have pulled this off."

"David, there has to be more to this call. I will sit down," was William's response.

"William, you read me well. Am I that predictable? We need your input on how to get to the white community. You know Diana and I both have trouble with the white moral majority and the mindsets of whites in general. We might be too critical to objectively deal with them. Diana always says she can't stand how racist and myopic they are. Their homophobia, their fundamentalist positions on prayer in school and abortion, and their righteous preaching almost makes us feel guilty to be white. We feel liberal white values on the East Coast and in California and maybe Oregon have been endangered by the last eight years of the Bush administration. Look, I know we must seek them out, we need the religious right, we know that, but it hurts to even talk to them."

"Diana, are you on there?" asked William.

She chimed in and the three were on the call. "Yes, William, I'm here, and of course, thank you again. We do have a problem."

William said, "We can use their convoluted thinking to our advantage. We can set up our science tells us *those people* will be bisexual and their promiscuity will accelerate their proliferation, and, of course, Armageddon. There's only a short window, and something will have to be done. They have no problems with manipulating science, so this should be easy for them, cheating to advance their agenda. After they hear what you have to say, their new agenda will be *those people*. We can call on them under the pretense of using their scientists and religious thinkers to develop 'intelligent design' helping us sell our ideas. They have started coming over to our ideology on environmental issues, so we can easily move them on the idea of greenhouse gas legislation as a way to forestall this impending horde of heathens. You can talk up the Scriptures and that homosexuality is not God's chosen way. Talk up *those people* must be exterminated. They will buy it. We know how politically powerful the evangelicals are." William smiled on his end of the phone and said, "Not bad for just off the top of my head, is it? You get the idea. Have the boys give them the right kind of numbers. This will be on TV in about five minutes if we're not careful. They hate gays. They flat-out hate them. Be sure to tell them to hold this until we get other political allies lined up. That's important; don't let this leak out. I've a couple of things to do today, so why don't you bring the brain trust over for dinner and we will talk. Vergie has my ears on all this, and as a UCLA grad she understands anything you can throw-out."

David cut him off, "William, you guys met in college. That was many, many years ago," he laughed.

William said, "Okay, but Vergie would like to voice some thoughts on this, and she is the consummate hostess. She would like to meet the girls. Also, bring along Fatma and Jonathan and Steve if you wish; the more brain power, the better. Goodbye, see you at 7:30 tonight."

Dinner was a specialty of Virginia Love. She was white-haired, with high cheekbones, and an olive complexion giving her a stoic look. It was apparent Virginia Love was a beautiful woman and time had been good to her. Her manners were genteel and proper and her eyes flashed with passion and depth. William showed his small town parochialism on a few occasions. He expressed the pleasure extolling Vergie's attractiveness when he talked about what a "looker" she was.

After a dinner of fine food, talk of Hunter and Ashley's fortune of finding Imam and Sabah, intimation of romance between Fatma and Jonathan, the serious *those people* topic and the white strata of American society was on the table.

William said, "After such a wonderful dinner and all her work, Vergie gets the floor."

David said, "We should eat like this more often. We not only get to hear Vergie we get fed like this."

She said, "Okay, David, let's get down to business. I want to put the moral majority and the poor white trash and white Middle America all into one group. I have a different view of them than you do because of all the institutional and historical discrimination perpetrated on blacks in general, and me, in particular. I have felt it personally. They are not evil like I thought when I was young, but they are dumb; really dumb. I must put that into proper context; intellectually and culturally dumb, but obviously smart when it comes to the control of money and politics. They are the majority political force in America. We can't dismiss them. They have more power than us. William is correct; the homophobic, religious stuff can work against them. We have to broaden our base when we talk about whites. Besides the evangelical stalwart types like Falwell and Pat Robertson and the new real powerful guy, Richard Viguetre, we have to reach down to the Aryan brotherhood in San Quentin, the Hell's Angels, the Nazi low riders, the Ku Klux Klan, the Barbours in the south, the skinheads, the creativity movement types, and others. I can go on and on, but we have to reach into the asshole of the beast." Vergie's passions were building up. She said, "Their hate for gays and poor blacks, their stereotypes of fags and niggers are targets we can point out to them. We can say quietly eliminate them. They will love it. The whites will be easy to control. David, your intuition on the middle to low life whites is correct. You are right, they are repugnant, but as you said, we have to deal with them. They will be easy. We need a summit or white leadership conference of some type. We need Southern and Mid-Western politicians, we need the religious right, we need representatives of the Aryan gangs, and skinheads, and of course, the KKK, and the Nazis. David, you guys have the presentation down already. All we need to do is pick the right time and place, and of course, the right participants for our wonderful white gathering; same rules and same protocol as the black conference you called.

Imam and Sabah felt a kinship with Vergie. She reminded them of their mom. They were happy to have been invited into the Love house. It was interesting to Imam and Sabah that the inner circle of *those people* project was growing, but its common purpose never changed. All alpha types, young and old, and they meshed as one. The synergism of brain power in the room gave them a clear vision. They were ever closer to the meeting with the President of the United States. They were consolidating their alliances and expanding their base.

Seventy

The success of the white leadership conference led to another representative for the President's meeting. Senator Thad Cochran of the state of Mississippi asked for and was granted the responsibility of articulating the white community's position. The template was set.

David made a call to Los Angeles Mayor, Antonio Villaraigosa's office. He had worked with Villaraigosa on many civic organizations, especially the mayor's quest to take over the Los Angeles Unified School Board. Los Angeles was notorious for its poor public education and the entrenchment of the United Teachers of Los Angeles Union and its profound ineptness. In the mayor's opinion, the only thing worse than the union was the district's administration. David and Villaraigosa lobbied Sacramento, the state capital, to have the district report to the mayor like in New York City. They felt total control was central to problem solving. David knew Villaraigosa would want to be involved in *those people* project. His ego would mandate his participation. He was very pro-law and order. His constituency was East Los Angeles, the second largest population of Mexicans outside Mexico

City. His political views were traditional values of the Mexican-American community; the values of family, hard work and religion were central to his ascendancy to mayor. Gang violence of second-generation Mexican Americans coupled with illegal migration of Central American gangs to East Los Angeles made it one of the most violent cities in United States. Villaraigosa would be open to help from David. He needed support on many fronts, but gang violence was a priority. He always appreciated when David called.

"Antonio, its David Russell. Can we meet for lunch? Something has come up. It is very important. How about the Palms today, if you have time? I need your help."

Villaraigosa assessed the importance of Russell's request and said, "David, I can't make it for lunch, but I'll meet you in the afternoon. If we go to the Palms, it has to be early because the Lakers are playing the Celtics and you know it's going to be a sellout. Also at the Nokia, there is a Stevie Wonder concert. Do you want to go someplace less crowded and more private?"

"No, Antonio, if we are seen in public, it is a social dinner, nothing of importance. Do not bring your entourage; just you and me. See you then."

Antonio Villaraigosa, a very popular mayor, was a person who never met a reporter or TV camera he didn't like, except for a highly publicized extra marital affair quieted down in three weeks. His political capital was so great an affair with a TV anchorwoman was of no consequence politically. He did cause himself and his family considerable personal pain bringing about a divorce, but as he said that was personal and out of political bounds.

At a booth in the center of Palms restaurant, David discussed *those people* and their impact on civilization. It seemed odd the restaurant's walls were festooned with cartoon characters of Hollywood's finest and signatures of Los Angeles' political and social dignitaries. The thought of *those people* and their dead eyes juxtaposed to the lightness of the restaurant's decor was ironic.

David laid out the science and its implications to the mayor and handed him a folder with attendant materials. "Antonio," he said, "we need the backing of the Latino community. We have already allied ourselves with the African-American community," and he discussed the leadership conference.

He said that Carolyn Cheeks Kilpatrick would represent their position in a summit with President Obama. He knew Villaraigosa well enough to discuss the white community and his troubles dealing with them. Its racism hit him to the core and the mayor was aware of it.

"We will have Thad Cochran of Mississippi represent the white community. Antonio, I hope you will help us consolidate the Latino community and be its spokesperson." He discussed the presidential summit.

"David," Antonio said, "I am on board, just from what you have said. I have felt something I could not put my finger on, the streets are killing streets in East Los Angeles, and of course, South-Central. Between you and me, I always thought these people were animals; but not this type of animal. This really makes me think. I never truly thought all the gangsters could be recultured into good citizens. I always thought many of them were bad seeds. This shows what we have been up against. You know I have pushed for a

10,000 strong police force." The Los Angeles Police Department at 9,200 has the smallest per capita police department of any metropolitan area in the United States.

"We need to get to the Latino community," Antonio said. "We are not as sophisticated as other communities, but we can pull together. On the streets are a network of gang counselors reaching all the way up to the 18th St. Gang in the Pico Union District." The 18th St. gang was reputedly the largest gang in the United States with an estimated 18,000 to 22,000 members.

"We have to get to the Mexican Mafia; we have access to them at Pelican bay." Pelican Bay was the most secure prison in California a prison for the most incorrigible in the state system the most dangerous of the dangerous.

"We need to get to the Nation of Aztlan. They are very radical. They espouse a separate Mexican state in the United States. They are anti Semitic, antisocial, and fiercely homophobic. If we can control them, they could be the foot soldiers in any type of killing of *those people* because of their homophobia. There are, of course, the college kids, Mecha and the Chicano Student Movement. We need United Farm Workers of America. We need a Hispanic Caucus in the House of Representatives. It's doable, I can get a meeting set up with all these groups, and you go from there. David, between you and me, there's a lot of gay resentment in the Latino community. Most Latinos are tired of gang violence and they will be open to doing something. I am on board. I know this has to be done. The logistics will have to be coordinated at the national level, but that's why Obama is there. It's kind of strange; I don't talk to you or see you for a while, and then you called me, and my stomach tells me something is wrong. I think it's the schools, I think it's the budget, I think it's the police department or immigration, or something. This is a hell of a thing to drop in my lap. David, you have always been there for me. We have fought a lot of wars together. This is personal because if we don't act, I can't imagine what will happen. I can get to Richardson in New Mexico. He is really heady and can deal with Obama. He commands great respect."

On the way home, David called Diana. "You're right, he is a very proactive and hands-on. I have always liked him. He is your man, and I know why. We can count on him. Call the kids and tell them to get hold of Imam and Sabah. We have a Latino leadership conference to set up. We only have a couple of weeks, before we are off to Hong Kong and where we meet with Omar and Doha and their people. We need to prepare."

Seventy-one

Diana had the boys and Imam and Sabah over for a working breakfast the morning after the Latino Community Leadership Conference.

"Hello, gang," she said. "From here on it's up to you. We talked to Omar and Doha, and they feel you two should present our findings for what they are now calling the Hong Kong Compact," as she looked directly at the girls.

"In a nutshell, you are only going to get respect in the Arab world if you are the spokespersons for the project. It's the four of you, and the girls must be the moderators if they are to get any future credibility in the Middle East. Women have many burdens in the Middle East and Asian nations. This has been broken to some extent by your mom, Queen Nora of Jordan and Ms. Sadat of Egypt. You will be empowered to advance the cause of women's equality, and this conference is the vehicle. Doha said you would understand. You are her girls. Omar is 100% behind this. Hunter and Ashley will help; they will field questions and, if necessary, discuss the science. Imam and Sabah, you will speak for us all. You will take the lead. We have two weeks to prep you. It should be easy, you developed most of our materials, you helped oversee the research and you have been an integral part of the team all along. You have access to everything. It should not be too difficult; a lot of hard work, but nothing beyond your knowledge. We will be speaking to your mom and dad today. They are on their way to Agami. From there, they will meet us in Hong Kong in about two weeks."

Imam started to tell Hunter about Agami. "Hunter, you would love it. Mom and Dad have a villa; a small one, seven bedrooms, on the water, just west of Alexandria. It's all white sand beaches on the Mediterranean. The place is just beautiful. Mom is famous for barbecuing. We always have family come with us. We go there every spring instead of the farm because it's so beautiful. It's more of a retreat. Mom and Dad do a lot of the work there. It is secluded and really quiet. I'm sure Mom and Dad will have you come and stay with us. I miss Agami."

The two weeks leading up to Hong Kong Compact were total preparation for the gang of four. It was agreed Hunter and Ashley present their findings to the President of the United States. Imam and Sabah had a secondary role. Just the opposite in Hong Kong; Imam and Sabah present, and Hunter and Ashley would be responsible for questions and answers. As the day progressed, they were in constant contact with Omar and Doha. Fatma and Jonathan acted as mentors and coaches. It was absolutely clear the gang of four was up to the challenge. They honed their speeches by repetition, adding additional materials to the final product each day. It was ready in ten days. A mock conference room was set up at the Russell House to act as a stage for their presentation. Each day it became easier and their presentation more professional. Their confidence level increased to the point of readiness.

Their flight to Hong Kong from LAX was eleven hours. The first-class cabins gave them solitude and they could make any necessary adjustments to their speeches. It also gave David a chance to talk to his boys on the plane. He waited for an appropriate time to speak to Hunter and Ashley.

"You guys, there is something I need to tell you both," he said. "It is really evident and pathetic that I did not spend enough time with you when you were young. I decided I should spend some time with you in Africa to start making up for my mistakes. Your mom and I talked about all this, but there is much more to it. When we got there, I was embarrassed by the two of you. I was ashamed of your thoughts and your callousness and your arrogance. I feel very guilty. Your intuition about *those people* was right, and mine about you was disgusting and shortsighted. Our journey from Kenya to Egypt, and then you guys went off to New York, and came home, and then Washington, and now Hong Kong, has been the journey of my life. Your mom and I did a lot when we were young in Kenya, and we made tons of money, but that was by opportunity: right place, right time. You guys are different. You did this all on your own. I admire you for the courage of your convictions on *those people* and the hard work and planning that led us here. We were lucky, your mom and I. You are directed and disciplined, and as a parent, I cannot tell you how much that means to me. I have learned so much from you guys. It's your courage, not our family's money that got us here. I am so proud of you. Whatever happens from here on out, I can only say thanks."

Ashley kicked the bulkhead and said, "Augh, Dad."

Hunter looked him straight in the eye and said, "Thanks, Dad."

They landed in Hong Kong on Lantu Island, a $37 billion project completed in 1997 when the Chinese took over Hong Kong from the British. It was updated for the 2008 Olympics; making Hong Kong the gateway to Asia.

A car waited for them. The thirty minute journey to the Buddhist monastery which houses the world's largest Buddha statue. Doha and Omar were waiting with lunch prepared and a guide for their hike to the Buddha. The Compact would be in three days, and a hike in the bright sunlight after a long transpacific flight would hold off the effects of jet lag. Diana and David had not been to Hong Kong since 1996 and marveled at the new airport.

Diana said, "Kids, you won't believe this, but at the old airport on the Kowloon side of Hong Kong, the planes came in so close to the high-rise buildings when you landed, it seemed like you could lose the left side of the plane because you thought you were going to hit something. I am not a fidgety person, but I thought I was going to die the first time I came to Hong Kong. When we get to Kowloon you will love it. Lantu is remote and beautiful, but it is nothing like Hong Kong."

After lunch, David said, "What a great first day."

Doha said, "This is just the beginning; we will drive to the hotel."

Omar said, "Kids, Hong Kong is a lot like New York, but much more congested. It's urban, beautiful, and after the Compact, we will spend a few days touring while your mother shops." They all rolled their eyes and laughed.

They drove 40 miles to the Kowloon side of Hong Kong. The city of Hong Kong, or the "autonomous territories," as it was called, was divided into three parts; the actual Hong Kong Island, the Kowloon side on the mainland, and the new territories which led up to the Chinese border. They were staying at the Intercontinental Hotel, previously the Regency Hotel. Six suites were booked; one for David and Diana, one for Omar and Doha, one for Hunter and Ashley, and one for Imam and Sabah, and one each for Fatma and Jonathan. Even though both families were progressive and aware of the realities of youthful love, tradition won out and the four were segregated for the sake of parental comfort. The Intercontinental Hotel was at the end of Nathan Road. Its magnificent view of Hong Kong and its harbor was legendary. They checked in and dropped off their luggage.

They walked four blocks to the famous Peninsula Hotel for high tea. Arrangements had been made. Admiral Raffles of the British Navy started the tradition of afternoon tea, and the Peninsula Hotel was the upper crust. Its view of the harbor and the hotel's elegant Louis XIV decor made it special. Doha and Omar had been in Hong Kong three days before the gang of four plus two arrived. They planned a full day of sunlight activities to hold off jet lag and the accompanying nerves before the presentation to the Hong Kong Compact. Tea lasted from 4 p.m. to 6 p.m. After leaving the hotel, they crossed the harbor by way of the Star Ferry and then took a van to the Stanley Market down the slopes of Victoria Peak. Everything was planned to maximize big sunlight and to acclimate to the time difference between Los Angeles and Hong Kong. Shopping at the market was cheap tourist merchandise, but that did not stop Doha from bargaining and laughing and brightening up the already bright afternoon.

The drive back to the hotel was court for Doha and her legendary shopping stories. She said, "Today nothing could have been better than this setting. I am with the Russells, my husband, and my daughters, and of course, Fatma and Jonathan. This afternoon has been amusing, nothing but tourism and shopping, but tomorrow will be all business. So, when we get back to hotel, before you all drop, let's clean up and go up to the restaurant on the top floor for dinner."

The view from the Intercontinental Hotel Restaurant had no rivals in Asia. The light show of Hong Kong Harbor and its skyline were breathtaking. To Omar, the only skyline view matching the beauty of the Intercontinental Hotel's was the Grand Britannia Hotel in Athens and its view of the Acropolis. After a wonderful meal filled with lighthearted talk and laughter, they all went down to their own suites.

They would meet for breakfast on the lower floor of the hotel at water's edge. They had to start working to gain the simple degree of excellence needed for their *those people* presentation to the Hong Kong Compact.

Seventy–two

During breakfast, Omar and Doha brought the group up to speed.

"In one day, we will have the meeting here at the hotel," said Doha. "There have been some major changes. The Chinese are sure the projections are wrong. They are too low by a factor of three. New computer projections are predicted on the spread of SARS and show a greater infection or mutation rate than the Hong Kong flu or the avian flu. Our estimate of *those people* proliferation is more than 10,000 a day; but it could be much more by their models. Thirty thousand is at the low end of their projections. They are hopeful a blood test can be developed to detect mutated people and separate them from those that are not. This blood test will be a national priority in China. The Chinese act instantaneously to any perceived threat. After the earthquake disaster of 2008 they mobilize at a drop of a pin. *Those people* numbers are increasing so rapidly the Chinese are making their detection and elimination the number one national priority. With a blood test, hospitals can kill them at birth. Or perhaps chemically neuter them if need be. They could surgically neuter them. This can be an alternative to just killing them. The Chinese are willing to deal with third world nations who have no medical sophistication. These nations don't have the resources to identify or track *those people*. They don't have the facilities to blood test them or to kill them. The Chinese are willing to expend $100 billion for that purpose, with money spent as a deposit for natural resources. They will trade policing for resources. They will guarantee the elimination of *those people* for resources and also guarantee jobs to third world nations. It is so important that Xi Jinping, the vice chairman of the Chinese Communist Party and heir apparent to Hu Jintao, the chairman of the Communist Party, will attend the Compact. South Korea will send President Lee Myung-Bak. Indonesia will send Vice President Dr. Mohammed Hatta. The Philippines will send President Gloria Arroyo. The Arab world will be representative by satellite hookup. We have assurances from Jordan, Saudi Arabia, Syria, and the United Arab Emirates, Iran, and Kuwait. They will act in concert with the Asian elimination of *those people*. In the Middle East and Asia, there is no political process. A threat to our societies will be reacted to immediately. Everyone from the farmer, to the beggar in the slum, to the holiest of men, to the government bureaucrat, to the very rich, will accept the elimination of *those people* without any question. They will accept our solutions. We can solve this problem. There is a solution if we kill *those people* now and eliminate future causes of their creation. Tomorrow Imam and Sabah will shine like the stars of the desert. We have assembled the leadership, they will all be here. All you have to do, my daughters, is affirm their beliefs of impending doom."

The meeting took place at 1:30 p.m. It exceeded any expectations of the participants. Imam and Sabah were the closers. Their articulation of the problem and its solutions were brilliant.

Vice Chairman Xi closed the meeting by saying, "Ms. Al Nassars, Mr. Russells, we applaud you for your courage to pursue *those people* and oversee the scientific truth of their existence. Imam and Sabah, your presentation makes our decision an easy one. We have to act, and we have to act now. We have to solve the problem of *those people* before they overtake mankind. We would be privileged if you would take part in our planning for their identification and tracking and extermination of *those people*. Your courage and commitment will not be forgotten by the people of China. Thank you."

In the next two days while waiting for responses from conference members every fashion house, every electronic store, every jewelry store, and every watch house was frequented by the Russells and the Al Nassars, as Fatma and Jonathan tagged along. Finally Xi Jinping of China called and gave a timetable for the gang of four to meet with President Obama and coordination with the Hong Kong compact. Two days later, David received a call.

"Mr. Russell. David, if you don't mind, I will call you David," said Xi. "We are summarizing our meeting's notes, and I will send you a copy, plus our specific plan of attack on *those people*. Thank you and your children. President Obama will receive the same package of materials through proper diplomatic channels. As soon as he signs off on them as received, we will instruct you to set up your appointment with him. He will receive the Hong Kong Compact briefing, and three to five days later; we want you to set up your summit. We do not know much about Obama, but our relationship with the United States is at its best since Chairman Mao. We say, 'Strike when the embers are white, for the fire will mold a scrap of steel into a sword for the true warrior.' Once Obama and his colleges receive the communiqué, we will contact you. Set up the meeting, present the facts, which, by the way, are irrefutable, and we will follow. A united front of East and West will preserve the world for our children."

Seventy–three

While eating at the Hong Kong racetrack, overlooking the city Cemetery after an exhausting day of shopping in the Causeway Bay district, David received a call from Xi Jinping. "David, we sent the communiqué, and the President responded personally. He said he read the briefing with great interest and thanked us. Obama said he would fast track this and get back to us as soon as possible. We have set up everything on our side."

David announced to the group that Xi called, and he said they would go directly to Washington, DC. He suggested Doha and Omar accompany them. He placed calls to Kilpatrick, Cochran, and Villaraigosa, and said when he knew the scheduled time with the President, he would call to set up transportation and lodgings for them. The black, brown, and white delegates stayed at Four Seasons Hotel in Washington, DC. David and the group flew over the cap to Washington, DC on a chartered 747. Doha suggested she summon her brother's plane, but David said arrangements had already been made.

On the plane, Hunter asked David and Diana how they set up a meeting with President Obama.

Diana said, "We can get to anyone. We know Obama to be approachable. His M.O. is not as open and receptive to new ideas as he is made out to be. But we are bulletproof on our analysis and with our money. $1,500,000 is how we got to him. We had to give money to the DNC, the Democratic National Committee, we set up a PAC, political action committee, and we are funding a nonprofit charity. He will listen. He will set aside two hours and 15 minutes for us and our community representatives, as we called them. G. O. F. E. M. has done well. It will finance a large portion of the cost of all this. We will incur the rest. Dad calls it your living inheritance. It's ultimately your money. We are just spending some of it now."

Diana smiled. "The whole bill will be about $3,500,000 for the president, Kilpatrick, Cochran, and Villaraigosa. It's always money, guys, it's always money. At the meeting, Obama will bring the Surgeon General, someone from the CDC will be there, and the Secretaries of State and Defense. We asked the Chief of Staff not be there. He's too political. Hunter, this is not all it costs. Our political capital had to be used to set up this meeting. Calls were made on our behalf to the President's office. We had to donate money. We had to endorse particular judges for this. We set up soft-money accounts. The worst thing was we actually had to pay lobbyists to get to talk to a member of the House of Representatives. Can you believe that? But we did it. All Obama knows is that this meeting is important. He has seen some of the particulars from the Hong Kong Compact. Hunter you are going to lead. You are the oldest. You and Ashley will have 45 minutes to address the President and his support staff. Kilpatrick, Cochran, and Villaraigosa have 15 minutes each. The President will have 45 minutes or any part thereof for his remarks; it will be a one, two, three. No deviating from the script. The agenda is structured, there will be no changes. You make it easy for him like Imam and Sabah did for the Hong Kong Compact. Just lay out the facts. Kilpatrick, Cochran, and Villaraigosa, our community representatives, will express their concerns and discuss what should be done. Finally the Hong Kong Compact will express their views. Obama will see the political concerns at home and globally. It should be a slam dunk. Hunter, Ashley, this is our part of the project. After this, it is out of our hands; the end of the road for us. Obama will deliver. He has to. It's so clear."

David interjected, "Your mom and I are proud of you. We passed the Russell baton to you and you have run with it."

Ashley asked, "What do you mean 'the end of the road?'"

Diana replied, "This is not like Asia or the Middle East, where political considerations are made by guns, and authority is unquestioned. Your dad and I have done everything humanly possible by going all the way up to the President of the United States of America. If this doesn't work, we're at a loss. Doha and Omar have already delivered. This is our job; to get to the President and have him act. This is all we can do. I don't want to sound pessimistic, but in business, you must always be aware of the downside. You have heard that from your father since you were little kids. There is always the possibility of failure. I think it is remote, but you still have to consider it."

The contingency arrived at the Four Seasons Hotel one day before the scheduled meeting. It was clear how the presentation was going. Kilpatrick, Cochran, and Villaraigosa were all given talking points. Hunter and Ashley had trained and rehearsed with Imam and Sabah, and they were ready. The meeting was scheduled for 10 a.m. Hunter and Ashley had hoped it would be earlier. It would be the longest morning of their lives. They arrived, by presidential transportation, at the White House and were taken directly to the Oval Office. It was strange to Hunter and Ashley that upon meeting Obama he did not come off as personable. He seemed distant. His chief of staff, after a perfunctory introduction, took them to a conference room on the White House East Wing. Nothing was said between the President and the gang of four. The three minute passing between rooms was uncomfortable at best.

The meeting started exactly at 10 a.m. Hunter and Ashley shared their allotted 45 minutes and did so with the precision of synchronized Blue Angels flying overhead. They presented a history, the scientific facts, and a plan of action for *those people*. It was masterful. Every element came into place. Not one word was misspoken, not a flaw in articulation. Totally on point.

Kilpatrick spoke passionately about *those people* and the need for action, but she deviated from the script and softened her stance on how to deal with them in the political arena. Cochrane, almost verbatim, discussed *those people*s existence. He discussed their danger in ominous terms, but again, softened his position on a plan of action, stating that the coordination of the political differences of the white community would be tricky. It could be a big political problem. He made it sound like he wanted a bone for his effort to present a united front for all the diverse elements of the white political landscape. Antonio Villaraigosa was the most ardent on what had to be done, but he was not sure in his heart if there was a political solution for the extraction of *those people*. He said they had to be killed, but he could not offer a way to do it. He said it was up to Washington.

One hour and thirty minutes had transpired. Hunter was uneasy with President Obama's responses to the presentation. It was as if he was preoccupied or non-attentive. It seemed as though he did not grasp the gravity of the situation. Hunter felt the urgency of pressing the President, even though it would break the convention of not cutting into someone's time. Before Obama could speak, Hunter felt compelled to say something. The world was at risk.

Hunter said, "Mr. President, I think you see we are a united front on *those people*; couple this with the Hong Kong Compact that you received three days ago, and it is evident we must act now."

You could see the irritation on the president's face. He held back his staff with a simple wave of his hand and said, "Mr. Russell, I will consult with my staff shortly, but let me address the issues. I did not receive a document or communication from this group you called the Hong Kong Compact. So you are grossly mistaken or ill-informed. As for *those people*, your science seems indisputable, but we need to have further study." This was an old tactic of the Bush administration to slow down scientific truth.

"We can't be brash with the fate of the world in our hands. I stressed change and a new politics in my administration, but we can't have either without consensus. I listened to your science, and it is only intriguing. It is problematic until we corroborate it with further study. I listened to Kilpatrick, Cochrane, and Villaraigosa. I hear no solutions. I hear no unanimity on how to solve this problem. All of your representatives feel the same way. There is no political solution to *those people*. My white grandmother used to say, 'If there is no solution, there is no problem.'"

He hesitated for a long moment and said, "I thank you for your interest in this matter. We'll get back to you, time permitting. Gentlemen and ladies, I have other responsibilities today. This meeting is adjourned."

Hunter leapt from his seat and said, "Mr. President, are you saying that you have no further comment and you are not willing to do anything?"

Obama said, "That is exactly what I am saying." He stood up, turned his back, and walked out.

EPILOGUE

"Cruel end for an L.A. homeless man"

By John Engels and Rita Gray, Los Angeles Times Staff Writers

October 11

He had called the multi-ethnic Mid-Wilshire neighborhood home for more than a decade. Sitting outside a shuttered dental office near Berendo and 3rd streets, the homeless man with the Buddha-like frame rarely asked for money. But he got it anyway.

Regulars at the California Donut shop bought him coffee and doughnuts in the mornings, a couple of Asian men took him for showers and a haircut, and poor Central American and Mexican immigrants would give him spare change or food.

"His priorities were cigarettes, Dr. Pepper, hot Cheetos and, once a week, he would buy C batteries" for his radio, said Asit Bhowmick, the Bangladeshi owner of the Bengal Liquor store.

The homeless man, who many in the neighborhood knew simply as "John," never bothered anybody, said Jorge Garcia, owner of La Morenita Oaxaquena restaurant.

About 9:30 p.m. Thursday, Garcia said he was at work when a woman ran inside the restaurant, screaming for a fire extinguisher. He ran outside to find the man lying on his back in a nearby parking lot, his body still ablaze.

The man's clothes had been burned off, his face blackened and swollen, the tips of his clenched fingers sloughed off. The smell of gasoline hung in the air.

"There's no name for what they did to him," Garcia said.

Los Angeles police said someone splashed gasoline on the man and set him on fire. No arrests have been made, and investigators are still puzzling over a motive for the grisly attack.

"This is one of the cruelest crimes you can imagine," said Deputy Chief Sergio Diaz, who oversees the LAPD's Central Bureau. "As an officer who had responded to many murders over the years, this is amongst the most horrific."

One resident, who did not want to be identified out of fear for his safety, said he spoke to someone who reportedly saw the crime. He said several young men got out of a Honda Civic, doused the man with a flammable liquid and set him on fire. Police could not confirm this account. The witness said the young men looked strange, ominous. There was something scary about their eyes.

Russell C. Arslan, retired University economics professor with entrepreneurial portfolio describes himself as an internationalist bent on geopolitical and environmental issues. Just as importantly, he is a storyteller who will entertain you and stretch your awareness. Having traveled extensively in Asia, Central and South America and Africa for more than five decades, he brings his knowledge and experiences into his writing. Political and scientific themes, may they be as contentious as global warming, nuclear proliferation or as threatening as terrorism.